The Misadventures
of
Carson and C.J. Crenshaw

Dylan,

Enjoy Your

Misadventures!

Davy K Kyn

The Misadventures

of

Carson and C.J. Crenshaw

In Search of the Book of Life

Danny K. Koger

Art by Mishele Beaman

iUniverse, Inc.
New York Lincoln Shanghai

The Misadventures of Carson and C.J. Crenshaw
In Search of the Book of Life

iUniverse books may be ordered through booksellers or by contacting:

iUniverse
2021 Pine Lake Road, Suite 100
Lincoln, NE 68512
www.iuniverse.com
1-800-Authors (1-800-288-4677)

This is a work of fiction. All of the characters, names, incidents, organizations, and dialogue in this novel are either the products of the author's imagination or are used fictitiously.

ISBN: 978-0-595-42365-1 (pbk)
ISBN: 978-0-595-86701-1 (ebk)

Printed in the United States of America

Contents

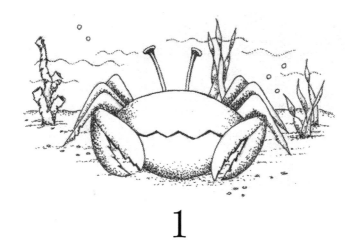

1

The Mother Crab

As dusk fell on Barracuda Bay, the beaches came to life, in more ways than one. A fierce storm was building off the coast and was ever so slowly moving in. The winds and surf steadily increased. Still, small groups of children with nets and flashlights searched for sand crabs crawling about for their nightly stroll. Parents lazily tagged along behind their children before corralling them back to their beach house for bed. Not so for one single parent named Thomas Crenshaw. He darted along the beach and netted crabs before his two energetic children, Carson and C.J., could even see them.

"Hey kids! Look at this one!" Mr. Crenshaw stood his tall, thin frame straight up, whisked his black hair out of his eyes, and held out the net for his children to see. They stood and tapped their feet in the sand, looking extremely cross with their father.

"Oh, right. You want to catch some too." He spoke sheepishly as he discarded his catch, wiped the sweat from his forehead with his bandanna, and retied it around his neck. He shone his flashlight along the edge of the surf and spotted two small creatures with eyestalks, headed for dry land.

"Crabs! Crabs!" yelled Mr. Crenshaw.

"I've got the one on the right!" Carson charged after her first potential captive, which scurried sideways across the sand. Carson was thirteen years old going on thirty and loved being anywhere near the water, which accounted for her bronze tan from socializing at the local pool back home, even though it wasn't even summer yet. She was average height for a seventh grader and had long hair, blond like her mother's had been, that she kept in a ponytail pulled so tight she gave herself a facelift every morning when she tied it back. Carson was an excellent sand-crab catcher, and she captured her prey with one strong sweep of her net.

"I think I got him, Dad!" she boasted, rushing back to her father.

"Shake him down and let's see," said Mr. Crenshaw. "I'll bet he's in there. He couldn't outrun the fastest girl in her class."

Carson shook the handle forward and back, her brown eyes eager as the sand sifted through the tail of the net until legs and then body began to surface.

"I told you I got him, Dad—I told you!" Carson looked up to see how her younger brother C.J. was doing.

C.J. might have been short for a sixth grader, but he was the hardest to catch in freeze tag during Phys Ed. He could change directions on a dime; he just couldn't do it so well on sand. C.J. wasn't having the same luck that Carson was. He repeatedly hit the sand with his net, making it appear that dozens of crabs surrounded him, when in fact only one was scrambling for its life. With each slam of the net, a loud, angry "Got you!" was heard, usually followed by an "Oh, no, you don't!" or a "Come back here!" The crab made a run for the surf. C.J. continued to slam the sand inches behind it the whole way.

Near the water's edge, three boys walked toward C.J. One stopped the other two to point and laugh. "Hey, check out the goofball chasing that little crab. I mean, how hard can it be to catch an itty-bitty crab? What a loser!"

Carson stopped, turned to the bullies, and began, "Why don't you—"

At that instant, the fleeing crab attempted to escape into the surf, so C.J. dove one last time with outstretched arms to try and catch the pesky crustacean. He landed face first in the sand and got blasted by a crashing wave that knocked the baseball cap off his short, sandy blond hair. He immediately jumped to his feet, covered from head to toe with wet drippy sand. Being careful not to let any sand escape from his net, he commenced the shaking down of the sand with determination, thinking that perhaps he had snagged his prey. Little by little, the wet sand sifted through the net, and little by little, tiny wiggling legs surfaced. Eventually what looked like a miniature biscuit surrounded by eight legs stared up at C.J. from the tail of his net.

"Yes!" C.J. dashed back to his father to show his prize, ignoring the fact that his shorts were now full of wet sand. With each step he took, his trousers fell toward his ankles and exposed his underwear.

The boys howled with laughter and pointed at C.J. Carson was furious. She purposely released her crab in the sand, knowing it would dash straight for the surf, which just happened to be where the boys stood.

"Watch out! A crab!" she shouted and pointed as it raced sideways toward the boys' bare feet.

They reacted in a rush, running from the oncoming crab, and were crashed by a wave that knocked them down and left them all lying flat on their backs in the wet surf.

"Talk about your goofballs." Carson ran back to her father and C.J.

Mr. Crenshaw peered down into his son's net. "I see you got your man, C.J. When you make up your mind to do something, you do it." He looked down the beach, and then winked to Carson. "And I see that you got your men."

"Mine's small, but I'll bet he was the fastest crab on this beach," declared C.J., unaware of his appearance.

"It's probably a male," said Mr. Crenshaw. "Sand crabs are a bit like black widow spiders. You see—"

"Oh, sweet," chimed in C.J., sticking out his chest and his net a little bit farther.

"You mean we've been chasing these things and they're poisonous?" interrupted Carson. She turned, shining her flashlight back down the shoreline at the three boys, who were slapping sand from one another's backsides. They blamed each other for their sad state of affairs, which soon resulted in a shoving match that threw them right back into the water, where they were immediately doused by an incoming wave. The waves picked up in intensity and frequency, and the boys were being toppled almost as soon as they could stand.

"No, no," said Mr. Crenshaw, always ready to teach. "They aren't poisonous. It appears to me that you two have corralled a couple of males, because the females have a wider tail flap, making them slighter bigger. Female black widow spiders are bigger than the males also, although much bigger." A smile of bittersweet relief grew across Carson's face.

"Girls rule, boys drool!" declared Carson.

"Once a dame, always lame," C.J. retorted. "Do you think there might be mother crabs out tonight, Dad?" He tugged up his sand-soaked shorts just before they reached plumber level. He flipped his net and released his captive, which dashed to the surf and was engulfed by a breaking wave.

"Ah, mother crabs ... the biggest of them all. I'm sure they're out on a night such as this, but judging by the rate at which those young fellows are wrestling with the waves, the storm appears to be coming in sooner than forecasted. I think it best that we make our way back to the beach house and call it a night. It looks like most of the other crab seekers are doing the same." Mr. Crenshaw pointed to other small groups of bouncing light beams as they left the beach in various directions. "There will be plenty more nights to try and catch the big ones. With the two of you on their trail, the mother crabs won't stand a chance."

This was followed by numerous *Please pleases* and *Aw-come-on-Dad-just-a-little-longers*, all of which fell on deaf ears. "We'll try again some other time," he said. "Besides, the first day of camp is tomorrow morning. Are you excited?"

"I can't wait," said C.J.

"Me neither," chimed in Carson.

Mr. Crenshaw was an archaeologist who was employed as a professor at a major university. After a couple of years of listening to them beg, he had finally agreed to let the children come along with him on one of his expeditions. In the past, he had enrolled them in science-based camps ranging from two weeks of roughing it in the Arizona desert to diving with ocean life in the Gulf of Mexico.

In the desert, C.J. attempted to pick up a beetle, only to find out after it stung him that the beetle was no beetle at all but rather a scorpion. He spent the next two days reading *Dangerous Animal and Plant Life of the Western United States* in the local hospital while he recovered. At ocean life camp, C.J. found a conch shell in the reeds, and when he put it up to his ear to see if he could hear the ocean, the shell's inhabitant, a rather angry blue crab, locked onto his earlobe. He wasn't allowed to go back into the water for the rest of his time at camp for fear the eight stitches would get wet and the wound would become infected.

While the children were at camp, Mr. Crenshaw traveled to one historical place or another to verify the existence of some unique artifact or to find out if it existed only in the minds of the citizens who heard of it from someone who heard of it from someone else. In these cases, no one knew who heard of it first.

This year was different. Mr. Crenshaw searched the Web for this summer's camp and happened upon a site that excited him even more than it did the children. Camp Remnant let children explore and excavate ancient ruins on Crater Island, located off the southwestern coast of Mexico. Coincidentally, a report had surfaced in the latest issue of *Ancient Artifacts Quarterly* regarding strange occurrences on the island, and Mr. Crenshaw persuaded the university to allow him to visit the island to gather information from the locals about the odd happenings. The article described events possibly linked with an artifact rumored to be found there. He was there for work; the kids were there for camp. It was the perfect plan.

"Yeah," said C.J. "I can't wait to see what the camp looks like."

"Just don't get bitten," said Carson. "Or get stung, or fall down, or put anything up to your ear, or—"

"OK already!" C.J. kicked sand at his sister.

As they climbed up the dunes to their beach house, Mr. Crenshaw couldn't help but notice the rumbling of thunder, now loud enough to be heard over the sound of the surf. The storm lurked off the southern shore and was on the move, headed directly toward Barracuda Bay. He turned and saw flashes of brilliant lightning that lit up the Pacific sky. It looked like the storm was going to be a mean one. The children paid no attention; they attempted to negotiate ice cream before having to turn in for the night. They successfully did so and were almost back to the house when C.J. spotted a large sand crab twenty yards away. It emerged from its hole in the sand and scooted off at a quick pace down the beach, away from the Crenshaws. Without hesitation, C.J. was off.

"It's the mother of all crabs!" he shrieked, with his crab net reared back. He did his best to keep the light on it while he ran full speed over the sand. "We'll see if girls rule!"

"I'll give you five more minutes and that's all!" Mr. Crenshaw could smell the rain as the thunder and lightning intensified. "This storm is coming in fast."

It didn't take long for C.J. to close the distance between himself and the crab. Again he pounded the sand with his net every few seconds, and the crab narrowly escaped each attempt as it darted first this way, then that way.

"I thought the big ones were supposed to be slower." Carson chuckled as she watched her brother chase the crab farther and farther until he disappeared around a large outcropping of rock that almost reached the water.

"I'll go get him, Dad."

She took only two steps before she heard her brother yell something that she couldn't quite make out but that sounded like swear words you won't find in the dictionary. C.J. ran back toward them faster than she had ever seen him run, carrying only his flashlight.

Carson shaped her hands like a megaphone. "Where's your net?"

"I threw it at them!" C.J. yelled at the top of his voice.

"Threw it at—" was all she said before she saw what "them" were.

"It's the mother," C.J. screamed from halfway back. "And father, and sisters and brothers, and they've got lots of friends. Don't just stand there ... run!"

"Holy crab!" shouted Mr. Crenshaw.

From around the rock wall emerged a sea of sand crabs. They advanced fast on C.J., who never looked back. Mr. Crenshaw and Carson held out their hands, encouraging him to run faster. It sounded like hundreds of people rapidly beating keyboard keys, and it got louder and louder. They were right on C.J.'s heels. He didn't pause by his sister or his father as he passed them on his way up the dune that bordered their beach house. Carson turned and stayed with him stride for stride as they bounded up the stairs of the cottage. C.J. slammed into the door and then grabbed the handle.

"The door's locked! Hurry, Dad, and bring the keys! Come on! We need ..." C.J. lowered his voice after he and Carson turned to look at their father.

Mr. Crenshaw stood atop the dune and watched, at his best estimate, millions of stampeding crabs. They moved down the shoreline as if on a mission of organized frenzy, yet they appeared to have no intention of harming anyone or anything at all. Almost as suddenly as they appeared, they raced on down the beach, out of sight. With their departure, the rain from the storm arrived. The first drops sent Mr. Crenshaw up to the porch to join his children.

"Well, you don't see that every day," he said. "Everyone OK here?" He smiled, put an arm around each of them, and then looked back up at the lightning.

"Dad, I don't think I ever want to go crab hunting again," declared Carson.

"I'm not scared," boasted C.J. "I'm ready. Bring 'em on."

"You know, those were the exact words I heard come out of your mouth a moment ago, when you were running for your life," said Carson with her arms folded. "As a matter of fact, Colonel Courage, now's a good time for you to go and get your net. We'll wait right here."

"Listen, you two," said their father. "I have a hunch that might explain what we just saw. Let's get on inside. You guys go upstairs and get ready for bed. I'll fix three bowls of ice cream and fill you in when you come down. Let's hope your next two weeks at Camp Remnant are as exciting—just not as scary."

2

Barracuda Bay

The power went off and on with each flash of lightning, but C.J. and Carson still managed to get themselves bathed, pajama'd, and focused on their strawberry cheesecake ice cream. The spring nights brought temperatures down into the forties, so Mr. Crenshaw started a fire with the few pieces of wood left over in the fireplace, but he absentmindedly waited too late to bring in more firewood before the torrential rains fell. The howling winds made the house moan warnings of the storm's strength as it bore down on the roof. Lightning was so close that for split seconds daylight seemed to come and go. Oddly enough, none of the Crenshaws appeared to be frightened by the conditions outside. Instead, it was just the opposite.

"I love storms," said Carson.

"This little island seems to attract them." Mr. Crenshaw wiped his sooty hands with his bandanna. "Lots of airplanes have disappeared off the radar screens while flying over or near this island. Bad weather has almost always been to blame. One plane called the Doldrum Diver, flown by a historian named Baron von Nickleburg, went down around here about twelve years ago. More small planes have disappeared since. With the way that storm outside blew up so fast, I can understand why."

"But it's not dangerous for us, is it? I mean ... in here ... we're safe. Right, Dad?" Carson looked for reassurance.

"I met Baron once at a university lecture," her father continued, still in his own world. "I said, 'Right, Dad?'" she asked again, emphatically.

"Sure, Pumpkin. We're ..." A second before he spoke the word "fine," the power went out again, leaving the fire as their only source of light. The wind burst open the back door and whistled its way down the rear hall, bringing in palm leaves and other items as it continued around the corner to the den. Mr. Crenshaw and Carson sprang up to close the door. The fire cast their long shadows on the wall. Thunder shook the house. C.J. let out a low-pitched scream. Carson and her father turned and ran back to find him moaning on the floor with both hands clasped to his temples.

"Oh my gosh! What happened?" Carson held her hands up to her face. Mr. Crenshaw sat him upright. "What is it, son? What's the matter?"

"Brain freeze," C.J. replied and pointed to the empty ice cream bowl.

"As soon as that knucklehead of yours thaws out, I'm gonna give you something to scream about!"

Carson placed a hand over her chest to keep her heart from beating out of her torso. Her other hand was balled in a fist.

Mr. Crenshaw went to close the back door.

"Well, would you look at that?" He announced from around the corner. Both kids sprang up to look down the hall. Sitting just outside was a sopping wet dog. "He must have gotten separated from his owner in the storm. Let's get him in and dry him off."

C.J. made a gesture for the trembling dog to come in. It gingerly stepped one front paw over the threshold, then the other. "It's OK, boy ... come on." The dog shyly put his head down, barely glancing up at the Crenshaws. Carson found a towel, gently approached the dog, and dried it off, with C.J.'s help. Clearly shaken and disoriented from the storm, the dog began to come around, and it wasn't long before he started to check out his surroundings.

"Dad, what kind of dog is it?" asked C.J.

"I believe that's an Australian Shepherd." Mr. Crenshaw poured a bowl of milk. "Let's get him something to eat and he can stay with us for the night." He set the bowl down, and the dog immediately lapped it up as if he hadn't eaten in days.

Just then the power popped back on. "Hopefully we'll have lights long enough for me to tell you a story that might have something to do with the crabs." Carson and C.J. tuned in with anticipation, for they had never heard their dad tell the same story twice.

"My theory on the crabs has a lot to do with why we came here in the first place. It also has a lot to do with how Barracuda Bay got its name.

"Many centuries ago, this island was the perfect location for a tribe known as the Wagapi, who wished for a place they could live and thrive. Crater Island has a moderate climate, seclusion, underground water sources, trees in abundance for building, fruit, and even fertile soil to plant crops.

"The problem was that the tribe, made up of about fifty members, had an appetite for fish and wildlife that, strangely enough, aren't found on this island. The chieftain of the tribe asked the spirits for a blessing in the hope of satisfying his people's taste for meat and fish. They held chant dances by their campfires and offered handmade treasures of gold and gemstones to the gods.

"One morning the chieftain felt moved to go to a cave on the north side of the island. Inside the cave, on rocks that resembled a stone altar, he found a leather-bound book with a cavity inside, as if the pages had been stuck together and a hollow space carved out of them. The leather was decorated with imprints of animals and fish, and bound tightly with a strap that appeared to be made from the skin of a reptile. Nearby were parts of animals, such as bird feathers, wild animals' teeth, and fish scales.

"He placed a white feather in the book and closed it. Light beams burst from the book, illuminating the cave. The chieftain began to hear a sound, and when he went outside, he saw that the sky was full of white geese. The tribe thought their prayers had been answered by the sudden appearance of the birds, animals, and fish that appeared from then on, never knowing of the book that their leader kept secret. He realized from the moment it was in his possession that this book came with great responsibility, and he saw the trouble it could cause if it fell into the wrong hands. As long as the chief kept the book safe, everything the Wagapi needed and wanted was right here on this island, their paradise.

"For many generations, the book was passed down in secrecy from one chief to the next. Hundreds of years later, a chieftain carelessly left it on the stone altar the temple, where his two sons discovered it. The chief had no choice but to explain the book to his sons, thinking them to be trustworthy. The older son respected his father's wisdom, but the younger son became jealous of the power held by the keeper of the book. Being a younger son and only the second heir, he knew the book would never belong to him, but to his brother. Thus the younger son devised a plot to kill his older sibling."

Suddenly a flash of lightning, followed immediately by quaking thunder, made Mr. Crenshaw and the children duck their heads instinctively. Then, after the thunder subsided, they looked around to make sure the building wasn't going to crumble around them. The dog leapt up and nudged his way under a blanket, quivering. The electricity went off again and left them by a dying fire with no more firewood. Mr. Crenshaw continued his story as he searched for, and found, several candles in a cabinet.

"The story goes that one day the older brother was sent out on a boat to the shallow reefs to catch fish. Weeks before, the younger brother found a dead barracuda on the beach, and he took a tooth from it. On the day his brother fished, he crept into his father's quarters, located the book, and replaced the fish scale inside it with the tooth from the barracuda. His father awakened and started to speak, but the younger son fled with the book. All that ever washed up on the shore were splintered wood fragments from the boat and ripped clothing belonging to his older brother, stained with blood. Without the book, there were no animals, no birds, and no fish. Eventually the tribe left the island in search of a new paradise. As I said before, when the Baron crashed his plane twelve years ago, his notoriety sparked interest in Crater Island. That's how they found the ruins that you will explore."

"Is that why they call this part of the island Barracuda Bay?" asked C.J., sitting on the edge of his seat.

"That's right," said Mr. Crenshaw.

"So you're down here trying to find the book?" asked Carson.

"The story I just told you could be true or could be a myth," said Mr. Crenshaw. "The Book of Life, as it's called today, may or may not exist. That's what the university sent me down here to find out."

"Dad, that sounds dangerous. The book is obviously here; think of all those crabs."

"Don't worry. Killer will protect you, Dad." C.J. pointed to the dog, trembling under a blanket.

"We're not naming him Killer." Carson rolled her eyes at her brother. "Dad, what if ..."

"Carson, there's no need to be concerned," said Mr. Crenshaw, comforting his daughter. "I'm just down here to check things out. If I get strong indications that the Book of Life does exist, then I'll go home and form a team, and we'll return and locate it later."

"Yeah, and you can bring ol' Sherlock here with you," smiled C.J. "He's got a great sniffer for finding stuff like that." C.J. pulled the dog's paws away from its eyes. Lightning flashed and the dog covered his eyes again.

"We're not naming him Sherlock either!" Carson shook her head with a sigh. "So, Dad, while we attend our camp, you'll be touring the island asking questions, right? Are we safe here? I mean, the crabs, and the story of the barracudas, and ..."

"I wouldn't let you go if I thought you were in danger," interrupted Mr. Crenshaw. "The crabs were not after us. They seemed to be on a predetermined path. You two will be fine, and so will I."

"OK, boy!" C.J. spoke to the dog. "It looks like your new name is He-Who-Will-Not-Be-Named."

Carson tried her hardest not to laugh but found it too funny to keep her mirth inside.

"Just act like you don't know me at camp, OK?" Carson pleaded, laughing.

Suddenly He-Who-Will-Not-Be-Named lifted his ears and looked in the direction of the sliding glass doors that led to the patio at the side of the house. He started to bark, then whimpered and darted back under the blanket. C.J. glanced up to see what had caught the dog's attention. The glass doors were mirrors because of the dark outside, and C.J.'s face was reflected back at him, glowing weirdly in the flickering light of the candles Mr. Crenshaw had placed around the room. Then a flash of lightning lit up the patio.

"There's someone out there!" C.J. screamed. He sprang to his feet and pointed at the glass doors that reflected his frightened face. "On the patio! I just saw him! A man in a dark cape with his face all bandaged up."

Mr. Crenshaw stood and turned toward the patio. The glass stubbornly reflected the inside light, and it was impossible to see anything on the other side. Thunder exploded, shaking everything. Carson was right behind her father, holding onto his shirttail as she peered around his waist. Mr. Crenshaw reached for the patio light switch and flipped it up and down, forgetting that the power was still off. He grabbed the door handles and slowly slid the glass panels apart. He squinted into the night as the wind blew the rain furiously under the patio ceiling. Lightning flashed, and Mr. Crenshaw jumped backwards, yelling "Whoa!" and tripping over Carson, who screamed and ran with C.J. to hide around the corner of the hallway. The blanket on the floor shook frantically, and a long howl issued from underneath it. Mr. Crenshaw got to his feet, breathing a little harder than usual from the excitement, and shut the doors firmly, locking the storm outside.

"It's OK, guys. It's not a person. Come on out."

"I saw him, Dad. I saw him right there." C.J. pointed as he moved closer to his father.

"What was it, then?" asked Carson.

"It's a beach blanket that blew up here with the wind. It's hanging on the umbrella stand outside. Some of the blanket is torn and shredded ... that's probably the bandages you saw."

Lightning flashed, and they all saw the blanket whipping in the wind at the top of the umbrella stand. C.J. made himself see the image of the man, then the blanket, over and over, until his mind was convinced that it had been just a blanket after all.

"It's just your mind playing tricks on you," said Mr. Crenshaw. "I just told you a kind-of-scary story, and with the lightning and all, it made you see things that aren't really there. I'm sorry about the story, son."

"I'm not scared, Dad." C.J. smiled. "Tell us another story."

"No more tonight. Bedtime," said their father. C.J. and Carson kissed him and headed for the stairs.

"Dad," said C.J. "Can we leave the lights on upstairs? Oh yeah. The electricity is off."

"Dad," said Carson. "Can't we stay up with you until the power comes back on?"

"I'll tell you what," said Mr. Crenshaw. "Take this candle into my bedroom and you guys can sleep with me tonight. I'll come to bed in a few minutes."

"Yes," they both responded.

Mr. Crenshaw looked toward the patio every time lightning flashed as he straightened up the den before retiring to his bedroom.

The storm continued for another hour, until it calmed and passed off the island. It took at least that long for the children to fall asleep. The dog didn't sleep. He hardly even blinked, and he never took his eyes off the glass doors.

3

Camp Remnant

The drive to the camp the next morning turned out to be an obstacle course. The Crenshaws took the island bus service, which did not use a bus at all, but a four-wheel drive SUV that veered off the road frequently. The roads around the outside of the island were paved, but the one that led up to the camp in the middle of the island was more like a dirt trail. Given the amount of rain Crater Island received, it was no small feat even for a four-wheel drive to make the climb. It bounced and spun its wheels often as it maneuvered through mud and around fallen limbs.

At the top of the hill, the road leveled off. Although the children had attended many camps, they had never seen anything like this. The great stone entrance was made up of two serpents coiled individually around each column, meeting at the top to form an arch where their necks wound together. Hanging from the center was a dragon's head carved of wood with evil eyes, one with a C in the pupil, the other with an R.

"There's the camp logo, just like on the letters we got in the mail. Oh, man, this is going to be sweet!" exclaimed C.J.

Scaredy-Pie, the last name that C.J. had given the dog, whined and hid under the front seat. After failed attempts to identify Scaredy-Pie's owner, Mr. Crenshaw called the camp to see if pets were allowed. They weren't.

"It's all right, boy. It looks like you're with me. You can be my bodyguard."

Past the entrance, the muddy, rocky road was lined with flaming torches on poles. The palm trees were so dense that the only open spaces in the woods were manmade. Every so often there were huge carved boulders that looked as if they were part of a structure that no longer existed. The thick vegetation made it clear how the ruins remained undiscovered for so many years. After a few more bends in the road, the Crenshaws arrived at the campsite.

Thatched huts that served as barracks were located on a large flat clearing, along with two pavilions, one a meeting hall, the other a dining area.

The campers would be divided into teams named for animals indigenous to the island, so each barracks was emblazoned with that team's animal symbol. The larger pavilion was being used to register incoming campers, and it was quite busy at the moment. Two wide trails ventured off in different directions away from the camp and disappeared into the jungle. The SUV came to an abrupt halt in a gravel parking lot near the pavilion. The Crenshaws and their new four-legged friend emerged. They looked around for a moment, then grabbed their luggage and made their way to the registration table.

"Hello! Welcome to Camp Remnant!" A young lady with long black hair smiled at them. "I'm Kamia, and we're excited to have you with us this week."

"We're the Crenshaws," said Mr. Crenshaw. "This is Carson and C.J. This looks like a great camp."

"So you're Mr. Crenshaw, the archaeologist. I've heard a lot about you. It's a pleasure to meet you."

"Dad, we didn't know anyone knew who you were," said Carson.

"I didn't either," he answered. "But I'm flattered. It's a pleasure to meet you too." Kamia shook hands with Mr. Crenshaw.

"I have you two listed on the Stingray team," Kamia said to Carson and C.J. "That's my favorite team. Of course, I am a bit biased, because I'm the counselor for the Stingrays."

Carson chuckled, but she was slightly disappointed to be on the same team with C.J. He beamed.

"We've made some great discoveries here in the past few weeks, and you'll take part in making new ones, including some that may have been locked away for centuries. Let's check you in so you can get squared away and be ready for your adventure. I'm afraid we don't allow dogs at the camp," said Kamia, looking at Scaredy-Pie.

"Oh no, Carson, you'll have to stay with Dad." C.J.'s laughter was briefer than the pain he felt in his left shoulder after Carson frogged him. The dog didn't take this news lightly. He growled and stared at Kamia. Mr. Crenshaw picked him up and put him back into the SUV. He continued to growl and never took his eyes off Kamia.

"Sorry about that," Mr. Crenshaw said. "I guess he really wanted to come to the camp."

After they signed in and filled out In-Case-of-Death forms, the children said good-bye to their father and headed toward their barracks.

"I'll talk to you in two weeks," said Mr. Crenshaw. "No phones are allowed at camp—a lot of camps do that these days. You two take care of yourselves and have a great time." Mr. Crenshaw climbed into the SUV. He looked back and waved as the SUV disappeared around a bend in the road.

"I can't believe it—we're in the same group. How lucky is that? We're both Stingrays." C.J. glanced at his sister.

"Lucky. That's right … that's just the word I was thinking of. You can't be any luckier than that," she replied.

Two scurvy-looking boys made their way down from the barracks toward Carson and C.J. Both had uncombed hair, saggy jeans, and black t-shirts. Carson recognized them instantly.

"Well, look who's here, Bane." One of the boys tapped the other on the chest.

"I don't believe it, Ven," replied the first boy, obviously named Bane.

Two of the three boys who had ridiculed them the previous night stood directly in Carson and C.J.'s path. "We meet again," said Bane. "Just when I was thinking this trip was going to be boring. Now I know I'm going to have plenty to laugh about with Junior Crabslapper here at camp." Bane high-fived his friend with his fist.

"I don't think we've met," said Carson. "My name is Carson, and this is my brother C.J. I'm assuming your names are Curly, Larry, and … where's Moe?"

"Very funny," said Ven sliding his hands back and forth against each other. "Actually, this is going to be fun."

C.J. bent over to tie his shoe. While he focused on his laces, Bane winked at Ven and motioned toward C.J.'s luggage. Ven winked back and talked to Carson, to keep her attention.

"Moe, I mean Daegel, is up at our barracks. We're Hermits, the best group—you know, the one that's going to win the Challenge here at camp. What group are you in?"

"Stingrays." Carson wished she had something to sting them with.

She fumed as she listened to Ven's insults. C.J. continued to tie his shoe. Behind Carson, Bane leaned over and unlatched both fasteners on C.J.'s luggage. He coughed each time to make sure no one heard the snap.

"We're going to bury the Dolphins, the Scorpions, the Dragons ... but especially you wimps—the Stinkrays." Ven bragged, grinning like a hyena. "None of you stand a chance. The Hermits have won the Adventure Challenge two years running now. Seeing as how this camp has only been around for two years, we're the only team that's ever won."

"Boy, you are bright," said Carson. "Did you figure that out all on your own?"

"Watch your mouth, Stinkray," said Bane. "The people who run this camp know who the athletes are, because they put them all on our team. They put all the puny ones on the other teams like the Stingrays. Go on up and meet your loser teammates. We're out of here." He chuckled and gave his buddy another high fist five. They walked intentionally between C.J. and Carson and bumped them out of the way. Still, the boys kept glancing back every few seconds.

"Boy, I'll bet you're glad to be a Stingray and not a Hermit, huh?" C.J. let his sister know that he got her sarcasm earlier.

"You got that right," she replied.

C.J. reached down, grabbed the handle of his suitcase, and lifted straight up. The entire contents fell out the side, which set off a roar of laughter from Ven and Bane.

"Those creeps! Here, let me help." Carson bent down and pushed her brother's belongings back into his suitcase.

They made their way to the barracks. Each hut was made of simple cane poles with palm leaves used for walls and a thatched roof, all held together by vines. Over the porch was an angry orange stingray set in front of the word *Rays* in dark blue. The thatched hut seemed much bigger inside than it appeared on the outside. The front entrance opened to a large meeting room decorated with the team's colors and filled with furniture made from carved wood. Off to each side were separate boys' and girls' sleeping quarters. The other Stingrays were already chatting in the meeting room when C.J. and Carson entered. Two of the boys in the group approached them. The two could not have been more opposite: they were the same height, but one was thin with curly red hair and glasses, and the other was round with short brown hair. The round one held a dripping thick sandwich in one hand and a soda in the other. A slingshot was sticking out of his back pocket.

"Welcome. And if my hypothesis is accurate, you must be C.J. and Carson," said the lanky one. "We've been coming here for the last two years, and you don't look familiar."

"It's our first time here. I'm Carson and this is my brother C.J."

"It really looks tight," said C.J.

"It rocks," said the round one as tiny food missiles flew from his mouth.

"My name is Ollie Patrolli." The thin one reached out to shake hands as he pushed his thick, large-framed glasses back up on his nose. The glasses made his eyes appear almost as large as his ears. Then he gestured to his friend. "And this is Tank McLemore."

"Ollie—that's a cool name," said Carson.

"This is my third time coming," said Ollie. "I'll probably move up to the senior level next year. I've been a Stingray every time"

"Stingrays rock," said Tank. C.J. and Carson ducked to avoid mustard missiles.

"We've never won the Adventure Challenge, though," continued Ollie. "I've devised some ways to improve our chances this year."

"The Adventure Challenge rocks," said Tank, as Carson and C.J. ducked again, a little quicker this time.

"I've read a little on this Adventure Challenge," said Carson. "Tell me more about it." C.J. kept one eye on Tank in case he opened his mouth again.

"This camp is incredible," started Ollie. "Besides digging and exploring, there's an Adventure Challenge with events that relate to customs of ancient tribes. There's target shooting with spears and things, and trapping animals in the jungle. We have to make a fire using ancient methods, and we have to concoct a medicine that actually cures something. At the end we get to blow a huge horn that's supposed to have been used in ancient tribal ceremonies to send spirits back to the afterlife."

Carson and C.J. examined the other group of kids. One with sandy straight hair frequently stuck his index finger up his nose and pulled it out to survey his fingertip. Another with short brown hair looked like he hadn't bathed in weeks and scratched his body in funny places. A slim girl with long black hair sat at a table, resting her head on her folded arms. She appeared to be sleeping.

"This is our team?" C.J. asked, his tone conceding the Challenge.

"Don't worry, we may not be athletes, but we make up for our lack of muscle with skill and intelligence. I've spent the last eleven months dedicating my time and effort toward winning this year's Adventure Challenge. I acquired a list of campers and then sent in a request to have all of us placed on the same team. You see, each one of us is on this team for a reason. We all have something to offer. For instance, Tank is deadly accurate with his slingshot. For the past couple of years, we've finished dead last in the Challenge. Tank managed to win the Target Shoot, though."

Tank pulled out his slingshot faster than John Wayne could draw a pistol and pretended to shoot everything in sight. Each time, food fired from his mouth along with his *Bang* and *Pow* special effects.

"The sandy-haired boy with the dark complexion is Cosmo Jeffries. His father is a pharmaceutical advisor. His grandfather was a medicine man for one of the largest Indian tribes in the early 1920s."

"That doesn't look like medicine stuck on the end of his finger," said C.J with a disgusted look. Carson punched C.J. in the arm, but she wore an *eew, gross* expression on her face.

"The girl is named Sebastian Rodriguez. She may be small, but she's fast as lightning. She's tired because she ran a marathon in Rio last week. Her parents are runners also; they travel the world running in marathons. The last one, over there, is Dusty Pickles." Ollie pointed to the boy who looked like he needed a bath.

"He's an excellent surfer and snorkeler. He was here last night as an early arrival when the storm hit, and he helped put things away during the heavy rains. That's why he looks the way he does—our showers aren't up and running yet due to the storm. There was damage to the water tower on the island, but I hear it should be fixed soon. Adding you two, that makes our team of seven. Trust me, with this group, as oddball as we may seem, we stand to have our best shot ever at the title."

Ollie walked Carson and C.J. over to meet the team. After everyone introduced themselves, Carson and C.J. took their backpacks and luggage to their quarters. When they came back out, the group was ready to leave.

"Let's go, guys," directed Ollie. "It's time to get this party started. Everyone is to meet at the central pavilion for rules and stuff."

"Let's rock!" said Tank, as he exited the barracks. Cosmo, in front of him, scratched the back of his head as if something had hit him.

"Ollie, we have three main goals here this week," declared C.J. "One, have a great time exploring and digging. Two, win the Challenge. Three, teach Tank some words other than *rocks.* "

Carson exited last. She had an eerie feeling that she was being watched. She turned toward the thick jungle brush behind the barracks, squinting as she tried to focus on a silhouette in the foliage. She couldn't tell whether it was a shadow from the trees or something watching her. Heavy breathing sounds came from the area. She walked closer to investigate. She stood in front of the brush and reached out both hands to separate the leaves.

"Carson!" Ollie walked back to her and motioned to come on. "We have to go. The meeting's about to start."

Carson jumped back and turned to face Ollie.

"You scared the jelly beans out of me." Carson placed her hand over her heart. "I'm coming. I'll be right there."

When she turned back toward the jungle, everything looked different. No shadows. The only heavy breathing she could hear was her own. She reached out and pulled apart the leaves. There was nothing there.

"Get a grip." Carson whispered to herself. "Your mind is playing tricks on you. Silly girl. No, check that. Silly beautiful intelligent girl. Ha, ha, ha."

Carson convinced herself that her mind was playing tricks on her, and she explained away everything she saw as shadows and everything she heard as the wind. She forgot all about it the moment she arrived at the pavilion. But she shouldn't have.

4

The New Captain

"Welcome, everyone, welcome," said a tall, thin, narrow-faced man with a long gray ponytail who looked as if he was in need of a bath and a shave. "My name is Blake Dawson, and I'm the camp director. Staying with our theme here at Camp Remnant, call me Chief. I see everyone managed to make it here on time today even after the storm last night. It was a doozy, as they say, and word is that your water should be back on by the time we get finished here." Everyone turned and glanced at Dusty. Tank, who was sitting beside him, let out a loud "What are you looking at?" that made everyone turn back around, although you couldn't tell if they were afraid of him or if they were afraid of getting struck by flying food bits.

"As I was watching you arrive, I noticed that most of you have already introduced yourselves to your teammates. Teamwork is something that we stress heavily at Camp Remnant. Many of the tasks before you will require a strong commitment to your teammates."

"One of the first things we need to do is to get all of you to take a quick twenty-five-question quiz. The scores will be tallied immediately, and whoever has the highest score will be your team leader. I would like to meet with all the leaders after lunch to give you some extra information, such as guidelines for excavation, to help you make your team as successful as possible. Team leaders also will be chaperones in your barracks. Even though they're on your team, they will be expected to inform me of any misbehavior on your part."

Ollie wore an expression of confidence, knowing he had just assembled the greatest Camp Remnant team of all time. "Now for some rules. First, stay with your group at all times. There will be occasions when you will leave the campsite and follow trails through the jungle. Stay on the trails and stay together, not because we anticipate dangers, but rather to help us keep up with everyone. You will be given a schedule of activities for the next two weeks. This schedule will include times at the ruins, meals, breaks, meetings, and of course the events that make up the Adventure Challenge. You must follow your schedule at all times. Anyone not where they're supposed to be, as listed on the schedule, is subject to serious consequences.

"Now, about the ruins. Direct your attention to the space in the middle of the three metal poles wired with lasers here to my left." He pressed a button on a remote, and a multicolored image appeared beside him, spinning in midair. A chorus of "Wows" and "Awesomes" came from the campers. Tank gave his usual "That rocks!"

The glowing light was an image of the ruins where the campers would be spending much of their time for the next two weeks. The stone entrance opened onto a long stairway leading down to a small square room that connected to a much larger rectangular room to the right. The larger room connected to two smaller rooms through doorways at the other end. A large green horseshoe shaped structure surrounded the rooms at the same level as the entrance. It looked like a toilet seat, and that did not go unnoticed by most of the campers, who giggled at the sight of it.

"I'll bet we might find a lot of crap in there," laughed Tank as he elbowed Dusty to make sure he got the joke. Then he stopped laughing and wiped dirt off his elbow.

The director continued. "The tribe that built these ruins is called the Wagapi, and we're getting more and more clues linking them to several other groups who lived on islands nearby at about the same time. We're still not sure if they're from the same tribe or if they're a different group of people with different beliefs and rituals. All the rooms you see here are underground."

More "Tights" and one "That rocks" resounded. Tank was starting to get glances that said "how obnoxious."

"The green areas are those we have not yet explored. The blue are chambers that have been opened, but exploration and excavation is not complete, and the red are rooms that we have finished exploring. The rooms have been identified as to their purpose. For example, this red one was the meal chamber. Foods were prepared and served here. We found ancient bowls and crude utensils used for cleaning and eating wild game. There may be more rooms than we have depicted on the image, but these are the chambers we have identified so far.

"The series of large green mounds surrounding the site is called the Horseshoe. We have surmised that since the site is underground, this is where they piled the dirt as they continued to build below. We believe they built below the ground for a certain reason. As you saw last night, this island is often hit by powerful storms, and building underground provides safety. They probably built above ground several times and lost their villages to storms. You may have noticed many large stones lining the road on your way here this morning. Those stones are more than likely from their first houses. We're not exactly sure how far the site extends underground, but judging by ..."

Blake's words became faint to the campers as they saw the colors of the holographic image becoming brighter, almost radiant, as the sky darkened. Cosmo leaned over to Carson and C.J. and whispered, "Look." He pointed outside, at a counselor who was staring up at the sky above the canopy, but the children couldn't see what she was looking at. By now almost all the other campers had noticed either the glowing image, the counselor, or the fact that it was getting very dark outside on what had been a bright sunny day only moments ago.

The counselor slowly lifted a finger and pointed upward. She mumbled "Ba ... ba ..." over and over. From where C.J. was sitting, he could see only clear blue skies. A handsome brown-haired boy named Levi Tucker, a Scorpion, stood up and walked over to the edge of the pavilion. He stepped outside, looked up, and took on the same frightened look as the counselor. He managed a few words like "What the ..." and "Is that what I think it ..." A female camper followed him and let out an ear-piercing scream. Everyone rushed outside, and the scene turned to chaos.

"Bats," Ollie said calmly. Up in the sky, eclipsing the sun, a large, black, rolling cloud grew bigger and darker every second.

"Are you sure?" asked someone loudly, sounding frightened.

"Where are they coming from?" asked a camper from the Dragons, pushing the words through chattering teeth. "Because the group seems to be getting bigger, but I don't see any extra bats flying in!"

"There aren't any more bats flying in!" yelled Ollie. "They're getting bigger because they're coming closer. They're flying straight at us!"

What started with only a few yells and loud shouts turned into a jumble of piercing screams. The bats closed in on them, and by now you could see that they weren't just bats, but bats with their mouths open, showing large white fangs. Their wingspans reached almost five feet. Everyone raced back under the canopy and gathered tightly in the center. Most covered their heads, not knowing quite what the bat drill rules were, but catching on quickly. As the bats rained down, Ollie remained outside. All the children heard the flapping of long wings.

"Pteropus vampyrus," yelled Ollie. Everyone got quiet. "The kalang is its common name, but we call it a fruit bat. It's harmless to humans—at least I hope so!" Ollie knew the creatures were harmless, but he couldn't resist the opportunity to appear brave by standing out in the open. The rest of the Stingrays joined him as the bats continued to dive. Then they swept off in a great burst of wind over the pavilion and disappeared into the jungle, leaving the day as bright as it had been before the bats eclipsed the sun.

"Oh, you were so brave," said a freckle-faced Scorpion girl as she looked at Ollie with goo-goo eyes.

Ollie threw out what little chest he had and rolled out his bottom lip like a confident know-it-all.

Tank, who had whimpered like a puppy moments before, shouted, "I knew there was nothing to worry about." The campers gave him "Whatever" looks.

"There's just one thing." Ollie placed a hand to his chin.

"What's that?" asked Carson.

"The kalang doesn't live in this part of the world," said Ollie.

"What are they doing here?" asked Tank.

"Dad says there have been a lot of strange things happening on this island lately," said Carson. She winked at C.J. without letting anyone else see her.

"Well he can add that to the list," said Ollie. "Nothing to worry about though."

Among the campers in the middle of the pavilion, as pale as a ghost, was a burly boy with bandages on at least half his body. Carson nudged C.J. and said under her breath, "Look familiar?"

The boy stood and dusted himself off. It was the bully from the beach, the one named Daegel. He was bigger than any of the other campers, and his curly hair was thick and messy.

"It's a good thing they flew off," he boasted. "I was just about to grab one of them and beat the rest to death with it."

"Yeah, us too," Ven declared, and looked at Bane.

"Can you believe those guys?" said Carson. "We'd have had more help fending off fruit bats if they'd thrown oranges at them." Everyone chuckled, and a few were heard to say "Losers" and "Weenies."

"I wonder what happened to him," asked Sebastian.

"Looks like he went crabbing without a net," said C.J.

"You said it, bro." Carson gave C.J. a high five.

"OK! OK! Let's all settle down. Return to your seats," the director shouted. It took a while, but order was eventually restored.

"I am sorry for the scare. We haven't seen bats around here in some time, especially in the daylight hours. Harmless, but curious to say the least." He continued to give instructions and information, but it was clear the bats had derailed his train of thought.

"Let's go ahead and take the quiz. After that it will be time for lunch. Before you leave the dining area, we'll tell you the scores and name your team leaders. As the counselors hand out the tests, I want to remind you that you'll be given team outfits to wear this week. We supplied everything you need with the exception of boots, which you were supposed to bring with you. Good luck on the exam, and enjoy your meal. It's all-you-can-eat."

Carson received her test and glanced at C.J. He was already putting down answers without reading the questions.

"What a moron," she sighed. "And he's my brother on top of that."

The test was made up entirely of true and false questions. There were questions on tribal names, rituals, even how to make medicines. *I'll bet Cosmo knows number one,* she thought to herself. *How would I know if the ground leaves of a Fermango mushroom can be used to offset the poisons from the sting of a Talavera Hornet? I say True ... number two ...*

C.J. stood up and handed in his paper.

"I must say," said Blake with a look of disbelief on his face, "That must be the fastest anyone has ever completed one of our tests."

"Nothing to it, Chief," bragged C.J. "It was cake."

Twenty minutes later the majority of the campers had turned in their papers, but much to Carson's surprise, Ollie was not one of them. He was the last to turn in his test, and as he did so, he heard a chatter that grew to a loud rumble of conversation as everyone asked one another about the test questions.

"How did you finish so quickly?" Cosmo asked C.J., followed by several "Yeahs" from the other Stingrays at the table. They all ducked from Tank's "Yeah," but they were so focused on finding out how C.J. finished so quickly that they didn't notice that Tank could say "Yeah" and insert a meatball sub into his mouth at the same time.

"True and false tests are all the same," boasted C.J. "Once you know one answer for sure, you can use the pattern to get the rest of the answers."

"What?" asked Sebastian. "What do you mean?"

"True false tests are patterned like this: True, False, False, True, True, True, False, True, True, False, False, False. All you have to know is one question and then you can figure out the rest."

"Look at me," Carson said to C.J. She held her fingers in the shape of an L on her forehead. "Instead of putting down Ts and Fs, you should have put down Ls for Loser."

"Carson, that's no way to treat your new leader," he said back to her with a smirk.

"The only team you'll be leading is the dork team," she replied, with a giggle that faded quickly as she looked at her teammates and realized she was on a dork team.

Within minutes all the papers were graded and handed back.

"Well, what did you all get?" Cosmo displayed his 20 out of 25 so that all the Stingrays could see.

"Eighteen," said Sebastian.

"Eighteen also," said Dusty.

"Sixteen," spewed Tank.

"Twenty-three." Carson rose up from under her table where she had sought cover from the word *sixteen.* C.J. didn't look at his paper but held it up for the rest to see. "Say hello to your new leader ... me."

The team laughed.

C.J. looked at his answer sheet. The only way it could have had more marks on it was if it had been dipped in a bucket of red paint. A large red zero was at the top.

"I'll give you this much," said Ollie, "You may have something there with that pattern theory of yours."

"The only thing I can figure is, I missed my sure bet question. I falsed when I should have trued and trued when I should have falsed." C.J. tried to cling to what little dignity he had left.

"Well?" Carson motioned to Ollie. "Let's see it, Einstein."

"Twenty-five. I got them all again this year!" said Ollie.

"Congratulations!" said Cosmo to Ollie, and the others offered their compliments also.

Sebastian held her hands to her lips like a megaphone. "Speech!"

"Well, I'd like to thank all the little people who made this possible," said Ollie. "Seriously, I'm only interested in one thing. We will win the Challenge this time. Let's put our hands together … on the count of three … one … two … three! STINGRAYS!"

On the walk back to the barracks, C.J. said, "I wonder why everyone laughed when we yelled *Stingrays*."

"Probably because they all know we're going to lose. We don't stand a chance in the Challenge," said Carson. "I like all of them, but let's face it, we aren't exactly a bunch of superheroes, now are we?"

Carson stopped and cocked her head as she caught a glimpse of something out of the corner of her eye. "Hey! What's that?"

This time she was certain she saw a shadow move in the brush at the rear of their barracks. "Did you see that?" she asked, squinting.

"I didn't see any dark, shadowy figure go into the jungle," answered C.J.

"Then you saw it too!" she exclaimed. "Could you tell what it was?"

"No. It just looked dark, and then I saw the brush moving where it went in." C.J. pointed.

Near the back of the barracks they saw a shiny object on the ground. Beside it was a piece of paper with writing on it.

"I think that's …" said Carson.

"It looks a lot like …" said C.J.

"Dad's pocket watch!" they both yelled together.

Carson leapt to pick it up. The kids had given their father a pocket watch last Christmas with their names inscribed on the back. She turned it over while C.J. looked over her shoulder. On the back, etched in tiny letters, it read "#1 Dad! Love, Carson and C.J." C.J. snatched up the paper and held one side while Carson held the other. The paper trembled as Carson read out loud:

Carson, C.J.,

I need you to find the three stones.

Tell no one.

Dad

"I don't think that's Dad's handwriting," announced Carson, "but this is Dad's watch."

"Maybe he wrote it in a hurry," reasoned C.J.

"Stones." Said Carson. "Hmmm. If Dad did write it, he probably means gemstones. You know, jewels, like emeralds and sapphires, the ones that were in his story about the island."

C.J. bounded toward the jungle where the shadowy figure had vanished. Carson grabbed his arm and swung him around.

"You can't go in there," she said. "You heard what the Chief said about not leaving your group and staying on clear paths and stuff. Besides, how do we know that was Dad?"

"What if Dad is in trouble?" asked C.J. in a frightened, angry tone. "We can't just sit here and do nothing. The note says we can't tell anyone." C.J. looked around in his confusion and saw Ollie returning from the pavilion.

"There's Ollie," he said in almost a whisper. Carson concealed the watch in her hand. C.J. folded the paper behind his back and put it in his pocket. Ollie spotted them.

"Hey guys! We only have a few minutes before we meet at the trail to go to the ruins. It's too cool. We need to get changed."

"Be right there, Ollie." said Carson.

Carson motioned to C.J. to walk with her. C.J. wanted to do something, but he had no idea what it might be. He just stared at his sister and waited for some signal, some sign, some direction.

"We've got two weeks." Carson placed a hand on his shoulder. "Let's just go through our schedule today."

"What if Dad's in trouble?"

"Don't worry. I don't know what kind of situation Dad has gotten into, but you know from all those stories he's told us that he can take pretty good care of himself. We're always begging to go on his artifact hunts. Maybe he's giving us our shot."

"Hey, yeah!" said C.J. His expression changed; Carson was right. "The note says he wants us to find three jewels. Maybe they're important diamonds or rubies."

"We can't tell anyone about this," said Carson. "We'll talk about it later. Remember, act like nothing has happened, and don't tell anyone."

Carson managed to calm her brother, but she didn't quite convince herself of her own words. Perhaps her father was in danger. She knew the note wasn't in her father's handwriting. She turned back and glanced at the thick brush where the shadowy figure had disappeared. In the coming days, she wouldn't be able to take her eyes off that spot.

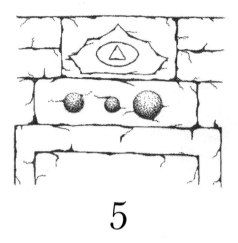

5

The Sealed Doorway

Although the group wore their team outfits when they emerged from their quarters and gathered in the meeting room, it wasn't hard to pick out who was who. The waist of Ollie's navy blue shorts was pulled up to the bottom of his chest. Part of Tank's belly tested the button strength of his orange shirt. Sebastian's outfit looked crumpled instead of simply wrinkled, like a discarded piece of paper. Cosmo's clothes were inside out. Dusty's clothes needed to be laundered, even though he had just put them on.

"How did you …? Never mind." Carson looked at Dusty and shook her head. With the exception of C.J.'s navy blue cap on backwards, Carson and C.J. were the only ones who wore the team outfit normally.

"I'll bet Dad wished he had clothes with this many pockets when he was a kid." C.J. turned out all the pockets on his shirt and pants to count them.

"My uniform doesn't have any pockets," said Cosmo.

"Your clothes are inside out," said Sebastian. "Is camp over? Can I leave now?"

Tank shoved snacks into every pocket he could find.

"Why do we need so many pockets anyway, if we have team backpacks?" asked Dusty. They were all given backpacks with the Camp Remnant logo and Stingray name tags.

Ollie got their attention. "Is everybody ready to go? I've posted our schedules on the board." He pointed at the bulletin board on the wall of the meeting room. Ollie had separated the master schedule into three parts: a schedule for the whole two weeks, a daily schedule, and a list of the dates and times for the individual competitions of the Adventure Challenge. "First up, let's go meet Kamia. She'll take us to the main site."

"I can't get these boots on." Cosmo grunted and puffed as he tugged on his left boot. "Can someone give me a hand over here?"

Tank tried to push from the bottom, but Cosmo toppled over backwards.

"Oh, for Pete's sake," grumbled Sebastian. She began to help Tank, but to no avail.

Cosmo sat up on the couch, and Ollie joined in to help Tank and Sebastian. C.J. picked up the other boot. Carson and Dusty helped him attempt to push it on Ollie's foot.

"They must be too small!" said Sebastian.

"Everybody, on three!" directed Ollie between huffs and grunts. "One ... two ... three!" Everyone pushed at once. Instantly the couch flipped over and they all fell forward in a pile. Cosmo stood up and looked down.

"Uh-oh." He looked troubled. "They're on the wrong feet." Everyone took hold of the boots while Cosmo held on to a support pole. His body was totally off the ground, and he was the center of a tug-of-war between the pole and five Stingrays. Both boots flew off simultaneously, sending the kids barreling across the room.

"OK, let's get them back on," instructed Ollie. His teammates took their places, and on Ollie's signal, they gave a combined push that once again sent them somersaulting over each other.

Cosmo stood up and looked down at his boots. "These aren't my boots."

"You've got to be kidding!" yelled Carson. "I can't believe you!"

"Well ..." But before Cosmo could finish his sentence, the group knocked him back on his rumpelstiltskin and tugged at the boots with all their might, which resulted in a tumbling of all across the floor as the boots popped off.

"Where are your boots?" asked Dusty, barely able to catch his breath.

"I don't have any myself," said Cosmo. "That's why I brought my brother's." He pointed at the boots they had just pulled off.

"Oh for the love of ..." screamed Sebastian. "You get them on yourself."

The rest of the team sprang into position and pushed with all the energy they had left. The boots went on with as much twisting and turning as Cosmo's feet would allow. After the mission was accomplished, everyone caught their breath, tucked in their shirts, and put themselves back together.

"OK, I think we need to go now or we're going to be late," Ollie said, short of breath. "Everyone check to make sure you've got your backpacks with all your stuff. Oh, and don't forget your work gloves."

"Where are your gloves, Cosmo?" asked C.J. with a grin. "Your gloves aren't as hard to put on as your boots, are they?"

Cosmo had an Oh-dear-Lord-please-no look on his face. He looked up reluctantly and said, "They're in my boots."

The team made up their lost time, due to the incredible speed they achieved as they chased Cosmo to the head of the western trail.

Kamia was waiting there. The Stingrays thundered to a halt and almost ran into her.

"My, it's good to see a team so eager to get started," said Kamia.

All the Stingrays looked sternly at Cosmo.

"And it appears that you all remembered to bring your backpacks. Awesome. Those backpacks are stocked with items you'll need. I'm your counselor for the next two weeks. I'll take you everywhere you need to go and help you as much as I can. The Wagapi Ceremonial Chamber is full of golden relics, jewelry, and artifacts. That's where we're going to start today."

"Where are all the other campers?" asked Sebastian.

"They have their own schedules," explained Kamia. "We do some things together, but most of the time our activities don't match up with the other groups."

This was bad news to Sebastian. She realized that she would be spending most of her time over the next two weeks with her fellow Stingrays. She had met a nice, handsome boy on the Dolphins team during lunch, and she was hoping to get to know him. She studied her teammates. C.J … cute, but too young. Tank licked a foreign food stain from his left sleeve. Sebastian coughed from the dirt in the air around Dusty. Ollie's pants were so high that if his zipper were open you would see his belly button. Cosmo was looking at Kamia, starstruck, but the fact that his right finger was up his right nostril wasn't going to help his cause.

"We have meals together, and general meetings, and of course all the Adventure Challenge activities," said Kamia.

Carson looked at C.J. "At least we don't have to be around the three stooge-balls—Daegel and his goonies," she whispered.

"Everybody ready now?" asked Kamia.

All eyes gleamed with excitement.

"Okie dokie artichokie. Everyone put on your gloves and let's go. Keep up and stay on the trail."

She walked about 20 yards before she turned around to check on the team behind her. They hadn't followed her at all. Cosmo had his arms wrapped around the trunk of a small tree, his body suspended in midair, while the rest of the team locked onto his feet, trying to get his boots off. They were successful, with a little less chaos this time. Cosmo fell to the ground abruptly. He grabbed the gloves, put them on, and looked helplessly at his boots. The team, now expert at the process, pushed the boots back on him easily, with Kamia looking on in disbelief. They set off toward the ruins.

"Whoa!" said C.J. when they arrived at the site. "I had no idea it would be so big."

"You could fit a small subdivision in here," said Dusty.

"You could fit a bunch of houses in here too," added Tank.

The grass-covered mound of dirt that surrounded the site was almost as tall as the trees. Tank couldn't shake the image of the largest potty seat he had ever seen, but he decided to keep quiet about it. Equipment was everywhere, but it was organized; there were wheelbarrows, ladders, digging tools, tables, crates, portable restrooms. Blake Dawson was seated at a computer under a large tent that contained the latest state-of-the-art electronic equipment. Bamboo poles held wires strung from the camp to provide electricity and communication. Kamia gave the group a brief walking tour that ended at the entrance to the underground site. The opening looked like a triangular stone igloo covered with moss and vines. Two great ant statues made of stone guarded the entrance.

"The religious leaders of the Wagapi prayed to the spirits for guidance after treacherous weather destroyed their villages," explained Kamia. "The story goes that the next morning, anthills covered the area where the villages once stood. The chieftain took this as a sign from the spirits to build underground. Whether it was a sign or not, it turned out to be a great idea. The Wagapi went to extreme measures never again to step on ants or destroy their mounds. They even created a dance to celebrate them. We'll teach you many dances, including the ant dance, at our nightly campfires."

"What do you call a burning male bug?" Dusty whispered to Sebastian.

"I dunno," she answered, not sure whether he was serious or joking.

"Flamboyant," snickered Dusty.

"I would rather have a million flaming boy ants eat the eyes from my face than have to listen to any more of your lame jokes during my two-week torture at this camp with you goofs cooing over worthless bones, rocks, and cheap jewelry," said Sebastian.

Dusty stared at her, looking pale. He gulped largely and said, "All righty then."

C.J. nudged Carson and motioned to the tent where the electronics were kept. A man dressed in a black trench coat was talking with the director. Cosmo noticed it also and nudged C.J. The discussion seemed to be heated; Carson looked at the men's body language and decided they were arguing. C.J., Carson, and Cosmo were the only Stingrays to notice, but Kamia saw the men's conversation as well, and she quickly recaptured the trio's attention.

"Time to get started … Crenshaws, Cosmo …" Kamia turned to speak to the team. "We have three hours to work at our first site. The first room we enter is the Dining Chamber; everything from it has been removed and processed. You'll see some large crates in the corners, because we're using this room as a storage area for new finds. The next room is the Ceremonial Chamber, the largest of the open rooms. It has two doorways in the far wall, one that leads to a hallway connecting to sleeping chambers, and another that's sealed. We haven't been able to figure out how to open it yet. We'll be working in the Ceremonial Chamber. You need to put on your headlamps now, and remember always to wear them when you enter here. Feel free to go out for air or for a restroom break whenever you need to. Watch your step going down, and follow me."

A damp, chill air engulfed the team as they made their way underground. Wires fastened along the walls supported dangling light bulbs that illuminated crude drawings of all types of animal life. All that remained in the Dining Chamber were four large stone tables positioned squarely in the center of the room. They were much larger than the entrance opening. Ollie was the only one to notice; he wondered how they had been brought inside. A flickering torch was positioned on one of the walls in case the power went off on the island, an event that happened quite frequently due to the weather.

"I'll bet they threw down some good food in here," said Tank. His stomach growled from the mere mention of eating.

"Keep going through the opposite doorway," instructed Kamia.

As they entered the Ceremonial Chamber, their mouths fell open in amazement. Gold-and jewel-encrusted mosaics glittered on all the walls. C.J. and Carson looked at each other.

"There's a lot more than three jewels down here," whispered C.J. "There's thousands. How will we know which stones are the ones Dad wanted us to find?"

Carson shrugged her shoulders.

The room was as big as a school cafeteria, with brilliant pillars supporting it throughout. Small boxes, treasures in themselves, lay open everywhere. They held items such as jewelry, fragrant bottles, hair ornaments and small utensils. The floor was entirely mosaic, with a design spiraling out from the center. It appeared to spell out a message that started in the middle and worked its way outward. There was an altar of sorts along the back wall, centered between the two doorways, one leading to the sleeping quarters and the other one sealed. Above each doorway, more mosaic messages appeared. Two bronze ant statues faced each other, one on each side of the altar. They resembled the ones at the main entrance, except that their legs extended from holes in their capes. The top two legs of each statue held one side of a golden chest decorated with beautiful jewels. Even Sebastian said, "OK, this is tight."

"Holy hot dogs! This rocks!" Tank's stomach began to growl again. Cosmo knelt down, ran his fingers over the mosaic, and tried to read some of the message in the pictures on the tiles.

"Can you read any of it?" Dusty leaned over Cosmo's shoulder.

"You're … on … my … fingers," replied Cosmo.

"Hey guys, check this out, Cosmo is reading the tiles," Dusty said, excited.

"No, Dusty, you really are on my fingers! Ouch!" Cosmo tugged at his hand.

"I knew that. I knew that." Dusty looked up to see if anyone bought it. They didn't.

"Hey Dusty, I can read this part on the wall," said Sebastian. "It says 'Dusty … is … a … dork.'"

"OK, let's get started," announced Kamia. "I need you to get into groups of two or three. Using the tools in your backpacks, you can collect and label items, draw sketches, take as many photos as your camera will allow, or work on reading the mosaics. However, I want to warn you about the message above the sealed door. We've been trying to decipher it for two years now. We believe it's a code that tells how to get into the passageway beyond. Sonic instruments have picked up some consistent noise that sounds like static coming from within the walls. We think it's an airshaft, but no opening has been found above it. Don't focus all your attention on that, or you may end up wasting your time while you're here. Put everything that you process into that crate near the entrance. I'll be coming around to help all of you, but call me over if you need immediate assistance."

"Time to rock and roll." Ollie threw his backpack on the ground and pulled some pencils and rulers out of it. He and Tank went to work sketching and measuring items from a large chest near the altar.

Sebastian labeled jewelry. When she got to the line for description, she filled it in with either "Totally Cool" or "Tacky."

Cosmo and Dusty tried to decipher the floor mosaic, with Cosmo looking back and forth from the floor to the symbols above the sealed doorway. Above the doorway there was a medium-sized blue sphere on the left, a small white one in the middle, and a large yellow sphere on the right. Above them was a large back oval with a green triangle in its center. The oval was positioned inside of a crown-shaped design.

Carson and C.J. didn't know where to begin, so they decided to stay near Sebastian in hopes they might find three jewels that stood out from the rest.

"Did you see that guy in the big dark coat talking to the director outside?" whispered C.J. to Carson. "Just like the guy I saw on our patio the other night."

"Come on now," whispered Carson. "You saw the blanket like we all did. There was no man. I can see how you could have made that mistake with the lightning and all, but it was not a man. It's just coincidence that a man was talking with Blake and he happened to be wearing a dark coat."

"But don't you think it's a little odd to be wearing a big dark coat on a tropical island where the temperature is 95 degrees?"

"Not necessarily," replied Carson. "Again: we saw the blanket; it was not a man. We saw a man talking to the director. He was dressed oddly, but people can dress how they want to. So what? Big deal. Forget about it and let's have a great time. We have more important things to think about."

"Aren't you even worried about Dad?" asked C.J.

"Of course I am, but what can we do? We can't wander off from the group alone, and we can't be anywhere unless it's on our schedule. If we break any rules, we get kicked out, and then how can we help Dad find the three jewels? The note said to tell no one. If he wrote it, then he doesn't want us to tell anyone. If he didn't, then if we tell someone it could mean bad news for Dad. I'm worried about it, and the only thing we can do right now is to try and find those three jewel things, whatever they are."

C.J. shook his head and accepted his big sister's conclusions for now. He paused and looked around, in awe of the room's treasures.

"This is without a doubt the coolest camp Dad ever sent us to," he said.

"Let me know right away if you see anything special." Carson winked at C.J. He nodded.

Working in the chamber was like opening presents on Christmas morning; the hours passed like minutes. Soon it was time for dinner, where the topic of discussion was learning the evening's ceremonial dance. Tomorrow's schedule included the first team competition, the Animal Trap, but no one had to tell that to Ollie.

6

Competition #1
Animal Trap

The fire crackled and spat out bits of glowing ember because the wood was wet from the storm the night before. Two teams at a time took turns learning the Ant Dance. The counselors played the roles of drummers and dancers and taught the campers the spiritual meaning of every movement. One counselor, dressed as the Wagapi chieftain, wore an elaborate ant mask and a black robe with six stuffed legs extending from it. The student dancers also wore masks, and they mimicked the chieftain as they followed him around the fire. On occasion the chieftain would turn to face the dancing ants that trailed him. This meant they were to drop to their knees and bow, then mold a small anthill in the soil with their hands. The dance would continue, becoming more animated, because the dancers were not supposed to step on any of the tiny anthills.

The Stingrays and the Scorpions participated in the dance while the rest of the campers sat around the dancers and clapped in rhythm with the drums. The Hermits huddled together and laughed loudly from time to time, making fun of the others. A tiny piece of red-hot cinder popped out of the fire and landed in front of Daegel. He scooped it up with a flat stone and held it behind his back. Shortly thereafter C.J. danced in front of them. The chieftain turned to his followers. C.J. dropped to his knees and bowed right in front of Daegel, who reached over and deftly dropped the hot wood chip into the rear of C.J.'s trousers. The chieftain turned back and continued, the other dancers following him in a line.

"Hey, this is actually pretty cool," said Dusty.

"I think so too," added Carson, short-winded. "But I think it's about time to stop. These masks are making me hot."

"It looks like your little bro isn't ready to stop," said Sebastian.

C.J. picked up the pace, with a bit more waggle in his step and a lot more wiggle in his bottom.

"That's totally wicked," said Cosmo. "But not in a good way. Dude, chill."

"Look at Elvis go!" Tank said, pointing. "He's smokin'!"

C.J. now looked like an electrocuted insect. He passed the head counselor and was about to lap the rest of the dancers.

"He really is smoking. Look—his butt's on fire!" screamed Tank.

Tank yelled "Your" as C.J. ran in front of him and looped around the circle. When he came around again, Tank yelled "butt's." The next time around Tank screamed "on," and as C.J. raced around a fourth time, Tank shouted "fire!"

C.J. came to an abrupt halt but continued to waggle and wiggle in one place as smoke billowed from his backside.

"Did you say King Tut's a liar?" C.J. huffed and puffed and shook his stuff like nobody's business. "What does that mean?"

"Of course he didn't say 'King Tut's a liar,' you dweeb." Carson shook her head and pointed to his rear. "He said your butt's on fire!"

C.J. twisted around, saw the smoke rising from his underwear, and let out a yell that could probably be heard from anywhere on the island. He ran in a frenzy around the campsite, looking for somewhere to put out his rear end. Everyone laughed, but none harder than Daegel and the Hermits. Carson looked at them, and her eyes narrowed with anger as she deduced what had happened. C.J. made it to a large trough used to wash off artifacts, and he sat down in it. A rush of steam was released from the water.

"That was an excellent job of dancing," said the counselor who played the part of the chieftain. "We do have restrooms in the barracks, though." The Hermits roared.

"I'm not using the bathroom." C.J.'s face reddened. "Just cooling down from all that shaking and baking. Mainly the baking."

"I'm sure the gods of the Wagapi would be very pleased with you, C.J. You all did a great job. It's time for the teams to go back to your barracks and come up with your plan for tomorrow. On the table in your meeting room you'll find a list of rules and guidelines for the competition, as well as a few extra tools you may need to use in building your animal traps. Make sure your lights are out by 10:30."

Back in the barracks, Ollie laid out his plan for the first competition, one of the plans he had worked on for the past six months. The whole team sat down, except C.J., who held an ice pack to his bottom. Tank held a pastry in each hand, so his mouth was once more a loaded weapon. Dusty sat next to Sebastian.

"Oh, by the way, Dusty, you do know they got the showers up and running, don't you?" said Sebastian.

"I haven't changed my underwear in a week," replied Dusty to Sebastian.

Everybody turned and faced Dusty with an *eew* look. Silence fell on the room for about twenty seconds.

"I'm not sure I wanted to know that," said Ollie.

Ollie unrolled a large blueprint showing several sketches of snares and traps, along with the types of animals each one could catch. He explained the first major competition and looked up to make sure everyone understood.

Still no one moved a muscle or took their eyes off Dusty, who was the only one looking at Ollie.

"We got it," said Dusty.

"Tomorrow we have three hours in the morning to build and set our traps. Kamia will take us through the jungle on the eastern side to an area where we can rig them up. Once they're in place, we'll come back for lunch, and then we'll head back to our area to bait the traps. Then we'll hide and watch. Each team that captures an animal will receive 50 points, but extra points can be scored. Fifty more points go to the first team to catch an animal, and teams get 20 points for every additional animal caught. If we harm the animal, we receive zero points. There are all kinds of animals here on the island, and luckily, no man-eaters like tigers."

Ollie looked up from the chart, and still no one had flinched or changed their expression. They all were looking toward Dusty.

"What?" said Dusty, throwing his hands up in the air. "If it will make everyone feel better, I'll change into my other pair tonight."

"You only brought one other pair for the next two weeks?" asked Cosmo. "Dude!"

"OK, I'm going to vomit now," announced Sebastian.

"When you change tonight, you need to take the dirty one outside and throw it in the campfire," said Tank, pastry missiles flying out of his mouth.

"I say we take it out back and shoot it." Cosmo shook his head in disbelief. "Dude!"

"OK, I'm going to bed," said Sebastian. "And hopefully when I wake up, this will have been one big gross nightmare, and I really won't have been involved in a conversation about dirty diapers, and I won't have been sprayed by bits of pastry coming from someone else's mouth." She headed for her quarters.

"I'm right behind you," said Carson. Everyone else filed off to bed.

"Right." Ollie tried to hold on to a thread of leadership. "I, uh ... yeah ... I was just about to tell everyone that we need to get a good night's rest, so I think we should all go to bed and get a good night's ... Good night." Everyone exited the room. Ollie rolled up the parchment and followed them to bed.

The next morning after breakfast, Kamia guided them to their trapping zone, located deep in the jungle off the eastern trail. All the other groups were stationed nearby in their own trapping zones. Trees marked with bright red ribbon outlined the boundaries of the Stingrays' zone, which was about the size of a professional baseball field. It had a narrow clearing directly down the center.

"Sweet," said Ollie, grinning at C.J. "The winner of this event the last two years came from this area. Both years, the team in this zone captured an animal first."

"What kind of animals are we planning to catch?" asked Carson.

"Without many predators, there are lots of small squirrels and shrews," said Kamia. "There are also some large bearded pigs."

"Ollie, what are we hunting?" asked Dusty, all clean. He was hardly recognizable. Everyone shot double takes at Dusty all morning as they realized who he was. No one had seen him this clean before. No brown cloud of dirt surrounded him. Even Sebastian found him bearable, until she thought about the demise of his underwear.

"We're going for them all." Ollie gave Tank a high five.

"I'm going to leave now," said Kamia. "You have three hours to make your traps, and then I'll escort you back to camp for lunch. After that, I'll bring you back here and you can hide out over there." She pointed at some thick brush. "Then I'll return half an hour after dark to get you. You can always blow the air horn if you're in any kind of trouble or need my assistance. 'Bye for now."

"No time to waste." Ollie pulled out his blueprints. He gave Kamia several glances as she left.

"What is it?" asked Carson.

"I didn't think counselors were supposed to leave us alone," said Ollie. "Maybe the rules have changed. Anyway, I've drawn up some designs of snares and traps. I think we should make as many as we can and place them in that narrow strip of open land over there. Here's a list of the materials we need. Let's get them, and then we can put the traps together." Ollie directed each member to retrieve vines, sticks, twigs, and large palm leaves. The camp had provided a hatchet and a small spade. After about thirty minutes, they all returned with the materials they had collected. Ollie split them into groups of two and explained to each group how to make the snares and traps. Over the next two hours, they turned the narrow passage into an animal minefield.

"Nothing's gonna get through there," said C.J. with confidence. "I know I couldn't."

Everyone gave Ollie "Attaboys" and "Nice jobs." He really had designed an awesome trail of doom. At the far end of the narrow clearing, a cage trap leaned on a stick. Next to it was a three-foot pit covered with palm leaves. The soil was so rich and soft that it wasn't hard to dig out. Digging was Dusty's job, so he looked like Dusty again. On each side were two snares attached by vines to small trees. Locking sticks that Ollie had designed and carved with the hatchet held down the snares. Ollie's masterpiece was the 5-foot by 5-foot net spread on the ground in the middle of the clearing. It was made from vines and attached to a tree, ready to spring up and collect anything that set off its trigger.

"All done and ready?" Kamia emerged from the trail. "Wow! You guys may win every category of the competition with all this." Ollie rolled his bottom lip out with pride. "I'll bet you've worked up an appetite."

"You can say that again," confirmed Tank.

"Let's go eat!" said Kamia.

The Stingrays ate fast, anxious to get back to their traps. Even Sebastian wanted to see if they would really work. Back in the jungle, they placed food in the traps, careful not to trigger them. Then they took their places behind some thick brush, where they all could view the narrow opening without being seen. The first hour was full of intense anticipation. Everyone hardly blinked, afraid they might miss any movement in the clearing. With each passing minute thereafter, doubt and boredom crept ever so slowly into their minds. After the second hour, the group began to fidget and sigh, which brought stern looks from Ollie. Tank fidgeted the most. His face turned purple and he was clearly in despair. Finally he couldn't hold it in any longer, and he had to do what his dad told him to do in times like these.

"Let her rip, tater chip," his dad would say.

With that thought, Tank let out one of the longest, loudest farts that any of them had ever heard. Everyone grabbed their shirts and pulled them over their noses, and they waved the air in front of their faces. Underneath their makeshift masks, the boys laughed silently and the girls made disgusting faces. Cosmo gave Dusty a high five. Ollie was furious. He had not covered his nose at all, and he glared at Tank with an evil look, sure that the sound or the smell of the bomb had scared away the animals. Tank hadn't moved since the big explosion and wouldn't turn to look at anyone. He looked straight into the clearing and acted as if nothing had happened. The boys uncovered their noses after a few more minutes, but the girls kept theirs buried under their shirts for at least the next half hour.

The sun went down, and it was hard to see clearly. The shadows played tricks on their minds as they waited, hoping that something would venture into their traps. At last they heard something move. They all squinted to see what was rustling in the brush. They couldn't tell if the noise came from the clearing or just outside of it, but it was definitely something big, because they could hear the twigs break as the animal stepped on them. The noise got louder and closer, and then there was silence.

No one knew exactly where the animal was. It had sounded like it was coming toward them before the noises stopped. If it could move without making a sound, then it could be right in front of them. It was so quiet that they could hear each other breathing heavily. Then they heard it again. The animal seemed to be much closer, and it was too dark to see anything. Then there was silence again.

Sebastian, sitting on the far left, wanted to scream, but she was too afraid it would give away their location. Tank, at the other end, could feel the breath of the person on his right against his face. He was so scared that it took him a few seconds to realize that no one was sitting at his right. He slowly turned his head, and then he began to scream. This set in motion a screaming panic by the entire team. They tried to escape any way they could, but it was so dark they just ran into each other. Then it all got quiet.

Within minutes a large spotlight illuminated the clearing.

"Is everybody all right over here?" asked Kamia. "Where are you?" She pointed the light toward the thick brush.

"Over here," came a voice.

"Up here," came another.

"Down here," came yet another.

Kamia shone the beam on the clearing. Carson hung upside down, caught in a snare. So did Cosmo, who seemed more concerned with the booger in his right nostril than with getting down. Ollie was trapped under the cage. Tank and C.J. had fallen into the pit. In the center of it all, Sebastian and Dusty were caught in the big net.

C.J. was the first to climb out of the pit. He turned and grabbed Tank's hand to help hoist him out, but Tank was too heavy, and C.J. toppled back down into the hole.

"You go first," said C.J. Tank climbed out, then turned and gave C.J. a hand.

"Check it out!" C.J. pointed down. A small furry animal that looked like a miniature kangaroo bounced around in the hole. "We got one!"

Kamia, Tank, and C.J. helped everyone else down. Finally they were all freed. They stood in a circle around the pit.

"You mean to tell me that you scared the you-know-what out of us because of this little rat?" asked Carson.

"It's a shrew," said Ollie.

"There was something big and hairy right up against my face," said Tank. "I promise."

"Everyone stand back," said Sebastian. "That beast is capable of tearing us limb from limb."

Everyone laughed.

"The Stingrays are on the board," proclaimed Ollie.

No one was upset with Tank. After all, they managed 50 points on a night that had disaster written all over it. They returned to camp, hoping no one would find out about their misadventure, but as with most misadventures, the news spread. It was the main topic at dinner, and the ridiculing continued during the fireside dance that night. Afterwards they retired immediately to their quarters and fell asleep quickly. Everyone, that is, except Tank. He knew that what had scared him so badly was most definitely not a shrew.

7

The Burial Site

At breakfast the next morning, the hot topic was still the Animal Trap competition. The Dragons were the only ones who didn't make fun of the Stingrays, because they were the only ones who were unable to trap anything. However, the scoreboard showed that the Dragons had 100 points.

"So what happened?" Ollie asked Mickey Bolton, one of the Dragons.

"We built a cage like you did," he sighed. "A beautiful Crested Guam took the bait. We pulled the stick, and the cage trapped her perfectly. Johnny No-Brains over there forgot to put a heavy rock on top of the cage. The bird flapped its wings and knocked the cage over."

"That happened to me my first year." Ollie shook his head.

"Luckily a lizard crawled into Patty's shirt pocket. She ran all the way back to camp so fast that we were the first ones to bring back an animal."

"Points are points, any way you can get them," said Ollie.

"I see the Scorpions got 70 points," said Mickey. "Do you know what they caught?"

"I heard two shrews," said Ollie. "What about you guys?" Ollie asked Darla Dewberry of the Dolphins. C.J. joined the group.

"Wimpy over there caught a tomato frog," she replied. "He didn't use a trap, though. He chased the thing everywhere, jumping and diving, and then he made one final leap at it just as the frog was diving into a stream. He got soaking wet, but he caught the frog. What an idiot. I mean, like, who would do something that stupid just to catch an animal?"

C.J. left the group.

"What's worse is that the frog spit in Christina's face. Frank told her it was poisonous and that she only had minutes to live. She fainted, and we spent the rest of our time in the nurse's station, so we didn't get a chance to catch anything else. Turns out it wasn't poisonous at all. That Frank is such a baboon."

"Hey Stinkrays," yelled Daegel from across the tables. "Looks like we're on the way to winning it all again this year. Not only did we get the biggest and meanest animal of them all, the bearded pig, but we got her three baby piglets too. Those little piggies went *wee wee wee* all the way to the top of the scoreboard with 110 points. They should have given you guys the most animals, though, for catching all you turkeys."

"You know, technically, we did catch more than you—" Ollie began.

"Drop it, Ollie." Carson cut him off. "There are still four events left, and we'll show them who's a turkey. Thanks to Tank, we at least managed to get that shrew into the pit."

Tank hadn't spoken all morning. He tried to convince himself that what frightened him was indeed the shrew. He was fairly certain he saw a face with large glaring eyes, covered with hair, perhaps a beard, but it was definitely a face. He was also a bit nervous on account of what was on schedule for the early morning.

"This morning is going to be way cool," said Dusty, who was back to his unrecognizable clean self. "I wonder what the Burial Site will be like."

"We'd better hurry if we want to get there on time," said Ollie. "Everybody get your backpacks and let's go."

Kamia met the Stingrays in the main pavilion and did her best to act like nothing had happened the night before. After making sure everyone was present, she led them a short distance down the eastern trail and then veered north onto another trail marked by a sign.

"What's on that sign?" C.J. walked up to get a closer look.

"Tombstones," said Carson. "That looks like crows flying above them."

"And above us too," said C.J. looking to the treetops.

The jungle was busy with sounds of screeching birds and rustling brush. Everyone stepped closer together.

"The animals are warning us not to go to the Burial Site, or else they're communicating with each other, planning their attack." Dusty tried to frighten everyone so they'd move closer together.

"You're not going to get me to move closer to you." Sebastian said. "Dirtbag."

Kamia stopped suddenly. The team dominoed into her, falling on top of one another.

"We're here," said Kamia, as the Stingrays got to their feet "The Burial Site of the Wagapi."

In front of them was a large clearing with three stone pyramids with flat tops large enough for a person to stretch out on. The one in the middle towered above the others, with a large stone statue on each side. The identical statues were combinations of different animals. They had the body of a bull, the clawed limbs of a bear, and wings on their backs. Each bore two heads, one of a lion, the other of an eagle. The three pyramids and the two statues were the only structures in the clearing.

"Boy, talk about your split personality," said Cosmo, looking at the statues.

"Animals meant everything to the Wagapi," Ollie explained. "They spent a lot of their time thanking the spiritual gods for all the animal abundance given to them. Many other tribes in this area weren't as blessed."

"How right you are," said Kamia.

C.J. leaned over to Carson and whispered, "I wonder if Ollie knows about the Book of Life?"

"Where are all the graves?" Dusty looked around, confused.

"There are none," Kamia said. "The Wagapi felt that their tribe would last forever on this island and realized the importance of using only a small amount of their limited space for burials. They held ceremonies for people who had passed into the afterlife and burned them on one of the three stone structures you see here. The larger one in the middle was for the high chiefs and their family members. From some of the artifacts we've recovered in the main site, we think they gathered the ashes and stored them somewhere safe. So far I haven't found ... I mean, we've found nothing of the sort, and that's why we're here. We're going to dig around the structures in search of artifacts. Perhaps we can find something that will lead us to where the ashes are. Ollie has explained to you the proper procedure for digging carefully, and if you need any assistance, I'll be right here to help."

"This rocks!" Tank exclaimed, discounting the previous night.

"So we're grave digging." C.J.'s eyes got wide. "Wicked!"

"Come on, C.J." Carson winked at him. "Let's work together."

"Want to work with me?" Dusty asked Sebastian.

"I would prefer being placed on a stone, doused with kerosene, and burned to ashes," said Sebastian.

"So, is that a no, then?" asked Dusty. Sebastian rolled her eyes and walked away.

Cosmo and Ollie threw down their backpacks and started sifting soil at the base of one of the statues.

"I've been thinking about the meaning of the mosaic above the sealed chamber," said Cosmo quietly to Ollie. "The big round yellow one is the only easy one. It's obviously the sun. The oval is weird, though."

"The sun makes sense," said Ollie. "I wish I could help you more but ... I ... I ..." Ollie sneezed.

"I ... eye ... That's it!" Cosmo exclaimed. "The big oval is an eye! Way to go Ollie! You're the man!"

Ollie straightened with dignity, looking at Cosmo. "Did you figure out any more?"

"Not yet," said Ollie, beaming with pride from his ignorant burst of brilliance. "But I'll keep working on it."

Carson and C.J. sketched the statues. "I think we're going to have to tell someone about the note," whispered Carson.

"No way!" Some of the others turned and looked at C.J.

"Shhh!" Carson shushed her brother. "Keep it down. I don't know what we're even looking for, or where we're going to find it. I was thinking Ollie might be able to help us. He's been here a couple of years now, and he may know what stones or jewels we need to find, or maybe even where they are. I don't know; I just know that between you and me, we know nothing. We don't know if Dad needs the stones, or even if he's in trouble. What if Dad has been kidnapped? We're going to have to find a time to break away from the group and look for the stones somewhere. Do you have a better plan?"

C.J. sketched so hard he ripped the paper.

"If we tell Ollie, he might turn us in," said C.J. "If we get caught wandering around, we can get in a lot of trouble, and that might hurt the team's chances to win. Ollie isn't going to let us wander around. All he cares about is that Challenge; he prepared all year for it."

"We have to do something—" Carson said, but she was cut off by a growl from the jungle near the entrance to the Burial Site. It attracted everyone's attention, and Kamia looked toward the sound with concern on her face. She pulled on her bulky backpack. Again they heard a growl, followed quickly by another.

Grunting and snorting noises accompanied the shifting of the jungle brush. The sounds became louder. The team stood still, nervously listening and staring at the brush.

"Gather your backpacks! Now!" Kamia never took her eyes off the moving jungle.

"What is it?" C.J. looked up at Carson in fear.

"I don't know, but there's more than one. The vines and brush are moving in lots of places now. They're spreading out."

"I've never heard anything growl like that before." C.J. stepped behind Carson.

"It's bush dogs." Kamia's voice quivered. "We were told they had all been taken from the island. They're smart hunters. They're spreading out to surround us before they make a charge. Run! Take that trail in the woods behind us. I'll stay and distract them away from you. Not far down the path is the northern beach. Wait for me there; I'll come as soon as they leave. Hurry, you must go before they surround us."

Calmly, Ollie assumed the role of leader and hustled the team to the narrow path.

"Quick! Run to the beach. Don't stop."

Kamia jumped on top of the center structure and shouted to get the animals' attention. Her screams sent the dogs into a frenzy, and they all emerged from the jungle at once. There must have been fifty of them, and they charged, yelping and barking, toward Kamia. They quickly surrounded the central pyramid. They clawed at the sides to get to her. One of the dogs in the back sniffed the air, then the ground, and followed the scent to the narrow trail the team had taken. It raised its head and barked loudly to some of the dogs nearby, who galloped over, sniffed, and barked back. Five of them set off down the trail after the team.

Up ahead, the team raced through the brush and stopped for a moment every so often to make sure they were still on the trail. Vines and limbs blocked their view from time to time, and trees had fallen across the path. They followed Sebastian, who, being the fastest, left the pack and blazed the trail. Tank brought up the rear. C.J. was behind Sebastian, but he lost sight of her when she disappeared around some leaves that dangled across the path. He pushed them aside and found Sebastian. She was standing at the edge of a bluff, looking down a steep incline that disappeared into the jungle below. They were trapped. Their only options were to slide down the incline or go back the way they came. One by one, the team emerged from the woods. Tank finally hustled in from around the branches.

"Go! Go! Go!" Tank motioned. "I can hear them."

"We can't!" yelled C.J.

Everyone looked back. They could hear the dogs grunting and barking.

"I'll hold them off! Just go!" Tank pulled out his slingshot, loaded it with a small rock, and aimed it back down the trail toward the oncoming dogs. Their barks increased and became higher pitched. Tank looked up for an escape route and saw a tree that had fallen partway to the ground. He could see that it was snagged by a vine. He reached into his pocket, pulled out a smooth stone, and shot at the vine to break it in half. He fired a direct hit, but the vine continued to hold. He pulled out another stone and whacked it again in the same spot. The stone nicked the vine again.

"One more." Tank chewed on his tongue.

He pulled back his slingshot, took aim, and struck the vine in the exact same spot. The shot split the vine in two and released the tree. It thundered to the ground in front of the dogs, blocking their way. He knew he had bought the team only a few more minutes before the dogs would find their way around the tree.

"We only have one choice," said Ollie. "I'll slide down the hill first. As soon as you can't see me any more, someone else go, and then everyone do the same. Ready?" Ollie looked around at everyone to make sure they would come with him. Tank was the only one who paid him no attention. With his slingshot loaded and ready to fire, he turned to face the fallen tree. Ollie gingerly sat at the edge of the bluff, pushed off, and slid down the steep path.

"There is no way I'm going down—" Sebastian said, but she didn't get to finish because Cosmo pushed her over.

Dusty jumped over as soon as Sebastian was no longer visible.

"Dude," said Cosmo, and he jumped, going down headfirst.

The dogs found a way around the tree. Tank fired rapidly, stone after stone. Each one struck a dog squarely on the head. When they were hit, the dogs stopped, yelped, and shook their heads, but then they charged, angrier than before. C.J. jumped down the bluff, followed by Carson. Tank picked up a stick, hurled it off to the side of the dogs, and yelled, "Go fetch!" It got the dogs' attention, which gave him enough time to collect some more stones for his slingshot.

The slide down was more like a water slide. It curved one way and then the other, and at one point, luckily, it lifted them airborne, where they sailed over a small patch of briar bushes. Ollie was standing at the bottom brushing sand from his clothes when Sebastian shot out and landed in the sand on her backpack.

Almost instantly, Dusty flew out headfirst and landed right on top of Sebastian. Dusty smiled.

"Help!" screamed Sebastian. "One of the dogs managed to get down here and his butt is in my face!" Dusty puckered up for a kiss. Sebastian shoved him off, stood up, and shook out her clothes, not worried about the sand, but very concerned about where Dusty had come in contact with her.

C.J. shot out next, then Cosmo.

"Hey! Wait a minute, little dude. How'd you get in front of me?" Cosmo looked confused.

"You snooze, you lose," said C.J. "Man, that was totally radical! We need to do that again."

Carson flew out and landed face first in the sand.

"So, how was it?" Cosmo asked Carson as he slid his backpack over his shoulders.

"A little bumpy, and those curves hurt my hips." Carson stood up and spat out sand.

"No, I meant, how was the sand? How does it taste?" joked Cosmo.

Carson wanted to say "better than boogers" but she had never actually put a booger into her mouth.

"Where's Tank?" Ollie looked at Carson with concern on his face.

"He was shooting rocks at the dogs." Carson still spat sand as she talked.

Everyone faced the slide and waited for Tank to come out.

"We should have stayed and helped him," said Ollie.

"I think I broke a nail." Sebastian looked at her hand with her fingers outstretched.

Everyone stared at her.

"What?" Sebastian innocently shrugged her shoulders.

"Do you hear that?" asked C.J.

"Yeah, I do," said Cosmo. "It sounds like a train."

"It's coming from the slide," said Carson.

"That's no train," said Ollie. "It's T—"

Tank shot out and started yelling.

"RUN!" he screamed. "The dogs are coming!"

They turned and ran as fast as they could. They were on a small beach on the northern shore of Crater Island, and they quickly found themselves trapped between the ocean and the dogs, who were running down the mountainside toward them

"Over there—a boat!" Ollie pointed to a small fishing boat that sat upside down at the edge of the water. Cosmo and Dusty tried to push it over, but it was too heavy. The dogs emerged from the mountainside and raced across the beach.

"They're coming!" yelled C.J.

C.J. and Carson tried to help turn the boat, but its weight kept it firmly stuck in the wet sand. Finally Sebastian, Tank, and Ollie joined in, and the small craft flipped over. They slid it into the surf, and once they got it out far enough, they all jumped in. Ollie picked up a long bamboo pole that had lain next to the boat and used it to push them away from the shore. The dogs stepped into the surf, growling and snarling, but a large wave doused them, and they retreated to the shore.

"That's why I'm a cat lover." Sebastian looked at the defeated dogs.

Everyone sat quietly and looked back at the island, breathing heavily. Ollie stood in the back of the boat, pushing them out over the shallow reef.

"Where are we going?" C.J. asked Ollie.

"There." Ollie pointed. Everyone looked and saw a small island a quarter of a mile away. "Black Reef Island."

8

Black Reef Island

Black Reef Island, a small island not far from the northern coast of Crater Island, looked like a giant slug sitting on top of the water. It was long, about two miles or so, and narrow, with a hill at one end that was covered by heavy tropical plant life. It got its name because most of the coral surrounding it was dark purple, but it appeared black on days when the sun didn't shine, which was most of the time. The island rarely had visitors because it was so small, with only patches of sand instead of beaches.

The children tugged the boat ashore, secured it, and then plopped down to rest. They focused on the dogs, who still paced back and forth on the opposite shore.

"Tank, I guess we owe you a big one." C.J. said, and everyone chimed in to agree. "That slingshot is cool. Can I see it?"

"Thanks to you too, Ollie," said Carson. "You took charge when we really needed it."

"I think we all pitched in," said Ollie. "Everyone will get their chance to do a lot more before we leave."

C.J. wandered around and aimed the slingshot at trees and rocks.

"Carson." C.J. pointed at the sand beneath his feet. "Look."

"Footprints," said Carson. The rest of the team came over to see what Carson and C.J. had found.

"Some go up the hill," said Ollie.

"Here are some coming down," said Cosmo.

"What about this?" Dusty pointed to another impression in the sand.

"That looks like someone or something was dragged." Ollie knelt down to get a closer look.

"Maybe someone's here and can help us." C.J. looked at Ollie, who nodded in agreement.

"It could be someone our age, perhaps a male, with good looks and no girl-friend," Sebastian wished out loud.

"Yeah, and maybe they haven't seen a girl in ten years or so, so they just might be desperate enough to find you attractive." Cosmo couldn't resist. He had listened to about all he could take from Sebastian.

"I'm desperate." Dusty winked at Sebastian. "From where I stand, you and I are the only two people on the planet."

"OK, could someone take me back over to the main island, tie a steak around my neck, and leave me with the dogs, so I can die a slow and painful death?" asked Sebastian.

"Who cares if these tracks lead us to people or not?" Tank rubbed his belly. "Let's just hope there's some food wherever we end up."

"Oh, brother," said Carson. "Whaddya think, Ollie?"

"Well, we might as well follow the footprints up into the bushes to see where they go. Someone will need to stay here and keep an eye on the boat and the dogs. Carson, C.J., Tank, and I will follow the footprints. The rest of you stay here. It's not far to the top of that hill, so it should be a short hike."

Everyone agreed, with some reluctance from Sebastian because she had to stay behind with Dusty and Cosmo. She positioned herself on a rock in the surf where no one else could get near her and faced Crater Island. Dusty and Cosmo surveyed the area to see what they could find. Ollie and the others followed the footprints up the hill and past the tree line. Much to their surprise, the path was heavily worn down. Ollie exchanged concerned glances with Carson. They walked a short distance and came upon a cluster of dead palm leaves that hid something beyond it. C.J. pulled the leaves away and exposed the entrance to a cave.

C.J. gulped. "Holy hideout! It's a bat cave!"

"You guys go check it out." Tank gulped even louder than C.J. "I'll wait here and keep a lookout."

"No, you come with us," said Carson. "We may need you and that slingshot."

"I don't have it," said Tank. "C.J. does. Don't you, C.J.?"

"Have what?" C.J. shoved the slingshot down into Tank's back pocket. Tank gave C.J. a squinty stare.

"We all go." Ollie pressed his finger to his lips and stepped in, followed quietly by the others. The narrow cave turned suddenly just inside the entrance. After that it opened into a large room with a flaming torch positioned on a side wall. Sitting in the middle of the space were two stones about five feet tall with a large, flat stone lying across the top of the two, angled like a podium.

"I know what that is." C.J. pointed to the structure in the middle of the cave. "That's the altar Dad told us about. You know … the book … the chieftain." Carson nodded and looked quickly to see if anyone had heard C.J.

"What book?" asked Ollie, surprised that someone might know something that he didn't about the Wagapi. "What chieftain?"

"I, uh … you know, the, uh … Mother Goose. Dad says that, uh, the leaders used to read bedtime stories to the children, like the Three Little Pigs, and Humpty Dumpty, and …" C.J. sputtered. Ollie looked at Carson for a better explanation.

"Hey, do you guys feel that?" Carson quickly changed the subject. "It's cold air coming from there." She pointed to her right, where another torch flickered in a passageway that led farther into the cave. Judging by the position of the glow, it looked as if the cave led downward, deep under the island.

"I hear something," said C.J. Everyone froze, listening. The sound was definitely a voice, but the words were hard to make out. Carson moved closer to the cave entrance.

"I think it's saying *The eyes that glow, remind us of the lore*," said C.J. in his best I-know-what-I'm-talking-about voice.

"Good grief." Carson stood near the main entrance. "That's not what it's saying. It's Sebastian calling us from outside. She's saying 'Hey guys, let's go! Kamia's on the shore!' I guess the dogs have left. Let's get out of here."

"Wait!" Ollie's tone made them stop and turn around. "I think we need to make some things clear. This is weird. I'm not sure we should tell anyone, except our team, about this or about what we saw. We don't know who has been here, or if we're supposed to be here or not. We might get in trouble for being here, and they might not let us continue with camp. Tonight, after we learn our new dance, I think we should have a team meeting and talk about it. Some things are happening around here that are a bit too strange."

"I agree," said Carson.

"Me too," said C.J.

"I'm starving," said Tank. "We're not talking until we get plenty to eat."

They re-covered the entrance with the palm leaves and made their way down to the shore, where Sebastian sat in the boat. They all pushed off and then jumped in one by one. Ollie explained what they had found and told them not to speak of it to anyone. Kamia rushed to meet them and nervously checked them over to make sure they were all right. She covered her face with her hands and began to sob.

"Hey, Kamia, It's OK. We're all OK." Carson rested her hand on Kamia's shoulder. "What about you? How did you get away from the dogs?"

"They couldn't climb up on the center altar where I was, so they finally gave up and disappeared. I was just so worried about you guys."

"It got a little scary, but for the most part it was pretty fun. Right, guys?" When no one responded, Carson turned and repeated, a tad louder, "Right, guys?"

"Sure thing, Kamia," said Dusty.

"We're fine," said Ollie.

"A barrel of fun," said Cosmo.

"The puppies were sweet," said Sebastian.

"I know you guys are safe and OK," said Kamia through her tears. "That's not what I'm upset about. I'm certain that I'll get fired as a counselor. Blake will kill me for this. I let you guys get away from me during an outing, and you were in danger. This is terrible, just terrible." She broke down and sobbed even harder than before.

"Kamia, listen to me ... look at me." Ollie grabbed her by the shoulders. "You did everything you could for us back there. We're all safe, and as near as I can tell ..." He looked up to locate the sun. "We're due back at camp right about now. I say you take us back, and we act like nothing ever happened. No one will know, and we won't tell. You're a great counselor. You saved our life back there at the Burial Site. We owe you one." Everyone else confirmed Ollie's sentiments, and Kamia gathered her composure.

"You guys would do that for me?" she asked in disbelief.

"I'll do it for a kiss," said Dusty. "Ouch!" Carson kicked him in the shin.

"You guys are the best," said Kamia. "I'm going to do everything I can to make sure you have the best time of any team here at the camp." She lifted her thick backpack and slung it over her shoulder. "One more thing."

"What is it?" asked Carson.

"Did you guys find anything at the Burial Site before the dogs chased you away? Anything at all?"

"I found out how fast I could run," said C.J.

"We didn't find anything." Ollie shook his head, along with everyone else.

"We'll try again another time, then." A determined look flashed across Kamia's face.

"Wicked," said C.J. "I hope the dogs come back so we can go down the mountainside again. That was sweet."

Everyone grabbed their backpacks and followed Kamia along the shore. She knew a hidden path that led into the jungle and took them back to the north end of the huge horseshoe, better known to the campers as the big potty seat. They made it past the ruins and almost back to the trail when they were stopped by a loud shout.

"Kamia! Where have you been? I thought you were scheduled for the Burial Site."

Blake Dawson emerged from the tech tent and headed their way.

"Yes sir, it's all my fault, sir …" Kamia began. "You see, sir, we were—"

"We were following some important clues that we discovered at the site." Ollie interrupted. "And they led us back in this direction."

"What clues?" asked the director.

"You tell him, Tank," said Ollie.

"Huh?" Tank was caught off guard.

"You know, Tank." Carson nodded firmly at Tank. "The clues that led us back here … the reason we're here instead of there. You know … the ones that looked really important."

"Oh, yeah, yeah, yeah. Well, it's like this … you see … we were at the site and saw some clues … and we said 'Hey, look, some clues,' and we decided we would follow them, and so we followed the clues, and they kind of led us to here."

"Yes, I understand that, but—" The director tried to get his answer before he was cut off again.

"We thought we interpreted some etchings on the side of the main burial stone that told us to follow the shadows of the sun at the exact time we were there. We did, and we ended up here." Sebastian stood with her arms folded.

Everyone turned to face her with an expression of disbelief.

"And?" questioned Dawson.

"And it turned out to be nothing," Cosmo filled in.

"It appears these clues led you through some water." The director pointed to everyone's shoes and shorts.

"That's where the search stopped," said Carson. "On the north shore. A wave blasted us."

"All of you?"

"It was a really big wave." C.J. spread his arms as far apart as he could.

"I see," Dawson acknowledged suspiciously. "Well, then. I hope you enjoy your dinner this evening. I will see you at the campfire later on. Good evening to you all."

"Good evening." They all shouted.

"Later, dude," said Cosmo.

Tank led the way back to the barracks, driven by his stomach.

"That was close," said Kamia. "You guys are really great for sticking up for me. I owe you big time."

As the team walked back, they thanked one another, but Carson and C.J remained quiet and drifted apart from the crowd.

"We've wasted a whole day and we've come up with nothing about the three stones," whispered Carson. "I think we have to let the team know about this. We need help."

C.J. nodded in agreement. "When?"

"Tonight," she answered, and put her arm around her brother. "We'll tell them tonight."

Thunder rumbled, adding to the feelings of uncertainty that occupied Carson and C.J. They were about to take a leap of faith and trust their teammates. They could only hope the team would turn out to be true friends. They would find out very soon.

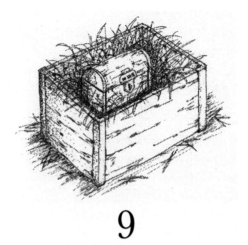

9

The Lost Shooter

A late evening storm settled over the island, cancelling the campfire dances. This meant, as Ollie pointed out in his best leader-like fashion, that everyone would follow an alternate schedule for the evening's events.

"So we all meet under the pavilion," said Carson as she read the new schedule.

"What for?" asked C.J.

"It just says TBD and bring your backpacks." Carson shrugged her shoulders and lifted her eyebrows.

"TBD … The Big Dance, huh?" said Dusty, who had managed to get dirty only five minutes after his shower. "How about you have the first one with me?" He addressed Sebastian, doing a dance that looked like a cross between the twist and the hokey pokey.

"No, Dusty," responded Sebastian. "There is no dance. Didn't you get the message? This night was especially planned to honor you. TBD—The Big Dork." The team laughed.

"Aw, man, Einstein. She dogged you." Cosmo pointed at Dusty. "Don't you know that TBD stands for To Be Determined? That means they didn't have it planned out when they made the schedule. That's why everyone's talking about it. They say it's something exciting, but no one knows what the something is."

"Of course I knew that. What do you guys take me for? A moron?" said Dusty.

Everyone opened their mouths to say yes, but before they could do so, he shouted, "Don't answer that!"

Carson emerged from the girls' quarters and quickly made eye contact with C.J. Both of them wore serious expressions.

"OK, everyone is here now," declared Ollie. "Let's go. I've been watching the pavilion, and they've brought in some large crates. There's no telling what we're going to do tonight. In the three years I've been here, they've never done anything like this before. This is going to be tight."

Everyone was making their way to the door when Carson yelled, "Wait!"

"C.J. and I have decided … what it is, is … the other day …" Carson stumbled over her words.

"I'll tell them," said C.J. "No, I'll tell them," said Carson.

"Tell us what?" the team said in unison.

"The other day, when we were coming back from taking our tests, C.J. and I saw someone walk into the thick brush behind our barracks. When we walked over to check it out, a note and our dad's pocket watch were lying on the ground." Carson held out both for everyone to see. The note says to find three stones, and that we couldn't tell anyone. It was signed *Dad*."

She handed the note to Ollie. The team looked over his shoulder to read it.

"We think the stones are jewels. We haven't been able to figure out what three jewels we need to find," Carson explained. "We don't know if Dad wrote it or not. We don't know if someone has Dad, or if he's in trouble, or if he just wants our help."

"I don't know what I can do, but I'll do anything I can to help," said Tank in his most sincere voice, and for the first time since camp started, no missiles fired from his mouth.

"Me too," said Cosmo.

"Count me in," said Ollie. "We'll figure this out together."

"Us too." Dusty pointed back and forth between himself and Sebastian, as if they were an item. Sebastian glared at Dusty and buried her face in her hands.

"I think there's something really strange going on here," said Carson.

"You guys laughed at me," said Tank. "But I promise, that was a guy's face, not a shrew, looking over my shoulder the other night at the animal trap competition."

"And I think it was pretty odd to see all those fresh footprints at the cave entrance on the island today," said Ollie. "That's dogged me all afternoon."

"On our first day I noticed that a strange man was arguing with Blake at the tech tent by the main site," said Cosmo.

"I think I might have seen him before at our beach house." C.J. looked up at Carson to make sure he hadn't told them something that he shouldn't have.

"But what about the jewels?" asked Carson.

"Why would your father want three jewels?" asked Cosmo.

"He's an archaeologist." Carson explained the reason that her father came to Crater Island. The team listened in awe as she talked about the Book of Life, and she told them about the crabs on the beach.

"That explains the bats!" shouted Ollie.

"And the dogs, too," said C.J.

"The Book of Life must exist," said Cosmo. "And someone is using it to scare us off the island. We need to find out why!"

"Maybe the jewels have something to do with the Book of Life," Carson suggested. "Or maybe they don't."

"Guys," Ollie looked out the door at the teams gathered under the pavilion. "I hate to break this up right now, but we're really late for the meeting. We need to talk more later. We can use brainpower to figure it out. One thing for sure, we can't tell anyone else. Agreed?" Everyone nodded. "Carson, C.J., don't worry. We will get to the bottom of this, and everything will be OK."

All the Stingrays echoed Ollie's words, and they headed to the pavilion. The meeting had already started, so they found seats at the tables in the rear as Blake Dawson, who looked worn out, discussed the large crates positioned at the front of the pavilion.

"... were discovered only a few weeks ago," he was saying to the group. "We found them in the Ceremonial Chamber, and they haven't been opened yet. We did technological analyses of the crates, and they were all found to be safe, so you need not worry when opening them up." The campers fidgeted and whispered with excitement.

"Your counselors will help you open the boxes and identify the artifacts and their purposes. We've never done anything like this with the campers before, and I hope you have a great time being the first to see the items in these chests since they were placed there by the Wagapi people thousands of years ago. Remember—be scientists, record your findings, make sketches and photographs. You have one hour only, then back to the barracks for lights out. The Target Shoot competition begins in the morning."

The Stingrays stood and walked toward Kamia, who waved and directed them to a large crate. Directly in their path stood Bane, Ven, and Daegel.

"Hey, Stinkrays, we're still a bit hungry. Do you think you could go and trap us something good to eat?" Daegel laughed with the other bullies.

"We'll see if you're running your mouth after tomorrow," said Ollie. "Tank's going to toast you guys at the target shoot."

"One big toasted bagel." Dusty looked for someone to give him a high five, but no one wanted to get their hands dirty. He did get lots of laughs from the team.

"Toasted with what?" responded Daegel with a frown. "That slingshot in his back pocket? Ha! We won't be shooting at tin cans. The targets will be moving. It doesn't matter what you use. Ven is going to win anyway—he's deadly accurate with the crossbow."

"Guys," Kamia called to the team. "Come on! Let's get this party started!"

"Losers." Daegel and his bullies plowed through the Stingrays toward their counselor. Ven and Bane bumped Tank from both sides and almost knocked him to the ground.

"Double losers," snapped C.J.

Daegel stopped and looked straight into C.J.'s eyes. His stare was frightening, but after only a moment he slowly turned and walked away. The bullies immediately started to laugh and give each other high fist fives, looking back at the Stingrays as they joked. C.J. pounded his fist into his palm.

"I was about to come and get you when you didn't show up on time," said Kamia as the team approached her. "You didn't miss too much. Here's where the real excitement begins. Ollie, you're the captain. Go for it."

"Grab those pry bars and let's open her up." Ollie motioned to Cosmo and Dusty. They popped off the top. The crate was full of cotton and straw.

"Wow." Dusty looked amazed. "The Wasabis grew hay and cotton. They were farmers! Someone write that down."

"It's *Wagapi*," said Ollie.

"I knew that," said Dusty.

"That's packing for what's inside." Carson rolled her eyes at Dusty.

"I knew that too," said Dusty.

"Hey, Dusty," Sebastian laughed. "I'm writing it down in my notes."

Cosmo pulled out the packing, and he and Dusty lifted the chest from the crate.

"Those serpent handles are amazing," said Ollie with huge eyes. "I'll bet they're solid gold."

"Now you're talking." Sebastian was finally impressed. "Those are sapphires, pearls, and emeralds, all set in solid gold and iron."

"I thought the chest would be smaller," said C.J. It was two feet high, two feet deep, and three feet wide.

"There's an inscription on each handle." Carson noticed. "Can you read it, Cosmo?"

"Something something 'Dark Sun.' That's not right—it doesn't make any sense," said Cosmo.

"That's the most beautiful chest I've ever seen," said Sebastian softly.

"Thanks!" said Dusty "I try to take care of myself, stay in shape and all."

"You have a nice chest," said Sebastian, "For a bird."

"Open it, Ollie," said Tank. The fact that doughnuts awaited the teams when they finished had nothing to do with Tank's trying to hurry things along.

Ollie stuck out his bottom lip until it was three times its normal size and reached for the corners of the chest. As the seal opened, it made a hissing sound as centuries-old air escaped. Ollie let go of the lid, and everyone jumped back.

"Wow." Ollie coughed. "The Wagapi actually breathed that stuff."

Ollie gripped the lid again and pushed it back. Inside were five large beveled mirrors, about the size of a sheet of paper, set in black wrought iron frames with long handles. Two hinges were positioned in each handle so that the mirrors could be turned to face any direction.

The counselors were explaining the significance of the items in the crates, but they didn't know what the mirrors were used for.

"They must have been really important to someone," deduced Ollie. "Or they wouldn't have placed them in this marvelous chest."

"I'd have to agree," said Kamia. "You guys make a few notes about the chest and the mirrors, draw one in your sketchbook and we'll call it a night. Tomorrow is the second part of the Challenge, and I think Tank needs to get plenty of rest."

Tank smiled proudly, but only for a few seconds. He reached around to touch his slingshot in his back pocket, but it wasn't there. He looked all around on the floor. It was clear to Carson that something was wrong.

"What's the matter?" Carson asked Tank.

"I don't have my slingshot."

Ollie turned quickly with a look of horror.

"Maybe it's with your stuff in the barracks," suggested Cosmo.

"He keeps it with him at all times," said Ollie very seriously.

"When is the last time someone saw it in his pocket?" asked C.J.

"I'm so sorry, but I haven't been going around staring at Tank's butt, nor do I intend to." Sebastian shook her head firmly in the negative.

Everyone looked over at C.J. and Cosmo to see if they had noticed.

"Hey! Don't look at us," said Cosmo defensively.

"I don't recall seeing it either," said Carson.

"I'm sure it will show up." Kamia tried to calm everyone down. "Tank, you and Ollie go look for it, and we'll finish up here. This shouldn't take long."

Tank left, deep in conversation with Ollie. Shortly thereafter the rest of the gang arrived at the barracks and found the two of them with flashlights, looking in every corner.

"It's not here," said Ollie. "We've got to go out and backtrack from today and hope we find it. I'm going back to the main site."

"We can't do that," said Carson. "What if we get caught? They could send us all home."

"You all don't have to go," said Ollie. "Tank and I will go." They walked out the front door.

"Ollie, stop! You're not thinking this through." Carson followed them down the main path toward the ruins, with C.J. right behind them.

"If we don't win this part of the Challenge, we're doomed," said Ollie. "It's our only hope." Bunched together in the darkness, they whispered and tried to stay in the flashlight beams. As they reached the entrance to the horseshoe, Carson grabbed Ollie.

"You can't do this," she said in a bold whisper. "We have to go back before we're caught. We have no idea what has happened to my dad. If our team gets kicked out for breaking the rules, I won't be able to find whatever it is he needs me to find. He could be in danger. The Adventure Challenge is just a game. I know it's important to you, but don't you think my father's situation is more important?"

The group heard voices coming from the ruins. They dashed into the brush and turned off their flashlights. Two people emerged in a heated discussion.

"That's Blake Dawson on the right," whispered Ollie. "I don't know who the other one is."

"I do." C.J.'s eyes locked onto the other man. "That's the guy I saw outside the glass doors at the beach house. I know, because his face is covered with bandages."

"Shhh," whispered Carson. "Let's listen."

"They're looking as hard as I can make them," said the director.

"They must look harder!" The cloaked figure's voice was deep and raspy. "The eclipse is only days away."

"We're doing everything we … What was that?"

Someone stepped on a twig and caused a loud crack. The two men walked over to the path and peered into the brush. "So! Who are you and why are you hiding?" The man in the cloak reached forward, grabbed an arm, and pulled someone out of the bushes.

"What are you doing here?" asked Blake.

"I … I was, um, just going to make sure things were squared away at the site and the artifacts were put away properly." It was Kamia. She had seen the group sneak away from their barracks and followed them.

"This makes the second time you have been here today, and you weren't supposed to be here either time," said Blake. "Go back to your quarters. I will speak to you first thing in the morning, before breakfast. Now go."

Kamia fled. The group remained silent, hidden in the bushes.

"Do you think she overheard?" asked the man in the dark cloak.

"It's possible," responded Blake. "We can't have any risk of interference." They walked back down the path and entered the high-tech tent.

Ollie and the rest quietly crept out of the brush and hurried back to the Stingrays' hut. The other members of the group were still up.

"Did you find it?" asked Dusty.

Ollie told them what happened. Cosmo paced back and forth in deep thought.

"I'm sorry." Ollie looked at Carson and then at C.J. "You're right. The Challenge isn't important compared to someone who may be in trouble. Judging by what we just heard, there is definitely something strange going on, and it looks like the director is in on it."

"We need a plan," said Carson.

"We have about two hours after breakfast to find the slingshot, and some free time on our schedule after the competition is over," said Ollie. "Let's sleep on this right now, and maybe one of us will figure out what's going on by the time we wake up."

"I agree," said Carson. "We all look frazzled and worn out."

They shuffled to their separate quarters and were asleep within minutes, with the exception of Cosmo. He lay in bed with his flashlight and studied his sketchbook page by page.

No one heard him when he sat bolt upright and yelled, "That's it!"

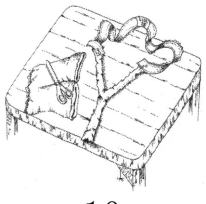

10

The 28 Special

The next morning the Stingrays continued to search for the slingshot.

"It must have dropped out somewhere," said Tank in a depressed tone. "It could be anywhere … in the boat, on Black Reef Island, anywhere. The last time I used it was to fire at those dogs."

"I'm pretty sure I saw it last night before we opened our crate," said Sebastian.

"Aha!" said Dusty. "You were looking at his butt!"

"It's not like that." she blushed. "It's kind of hard to miss. It's kind of like when you drive down the road. You can't miss the billboards on the sides."

"Yo! Tank!" said Cosmo. "I think she just called your butt a billboard."

"No—I didn't mean …"

"I heard it too," said C.J. "Yep, she called you Billboard Butt."

"I didn't say …"

"It's wide and all." Dusty looked at Tank's bottom. "I'm not sure it's as big as a billboard. Almost, but not—"

"Will everybody quit talking about my butt?" yelled Tank.

"Are we all sure that no one has any idea where his slingshot is?" asked Ollie.

Everyone stood still, thinking.

"I have something to say but it doesn't have anything to do with the sling—" Cosmo began.

Ollie cut him off. "Let's keep the discussion on the slingshot right now."

"But—" Cosmo tried to speak again.

"Butts are exactly what we don't need to talk about right now." Ollie looked angry.

"Whatever, dude." Cosmo shook his head.

Tank squinted his eyes in anger. "Sebastian says she may have seen it last night. I'm pretty sure I had it then. When we're at the pavilion eating breakfast, we should look really hard for it."

Tank's stomach told him that eating breakfast was a much higher priority than finding the shooter. He started down to the pavilion, and everyone else followed. As they walked toward the dining area, they saw Kamia. She sat on a stack of luggage down by the main entrance to the camp. The team raced down to see what was the matter.

"I was fired," she said angrily.

"What?" asked Carson.

"Oh no!" said Sebastian.

"You've got to be kidding!" said C.J.

"Why would they do that?" asked Ollie.

"Who fired you?" asked Carson.

"Mr. Dawson," she said. "Last night I saw some of you heading up to the ruins. It seemed like you were looking for something. I went to get you because I knew you might get into trouble; I was right behind you when you darted into the bushes. I knew something was wrong, so I did the same. Somehow he spotted me; he fired me first thing this morning. He'll regret it."

"Kamia!" said Ollie. "It's my fault! If only I hadn't been so selfish and gone out last night. The others told me not to, but I didn't listen. I'm sorry."

"I agree," said Dusty. "It's Ollie's fault."

"It's our fault too," said Carson. "No one was dragging us out by the arm."

"You're right," said Dusty, who didn't have a dog in the race. "It is your fault."

"No, you didn't have to go," continued Ollie. "And you never would have gone if it hadn't been for me."

"Good point," said Dusty. "It was Ollie's fault."

"If I hadn't lost my slingshot, we wouldn't have had to go looking for it in the first place." Tank now took the blame. "It was my fault."

"No doubt about it," said Dusty. "It was Tank's fault."

"Will you shut up?" They all screamed at Dusty in unison, including Kamia.

"Easy, easy," said Dusty, with his hands in the air. "Somebody woke up on the wrong side of the bed this morning."

A large SUV pulled up. The driver got out and loaded Kamia's things into the back. "Good luck in the Challenge today. I saw some Hermits practicing with their slingshot already this morning."

She hugged everyone and climbed into the SUV. She rolled down the window as the driver pulled away. "Good luck in finding whatever you're looking for." The truck bounced away down the rocky road.

"Hey! Didn't she say she saw some Hermits practicing with their slingshot?" C.J. looked puzzled.

"Yeah," said Carson. "So what?"

"Last night the goonies told us that they were using a crossbow. They must have found Tank's slingshot."

"They didn't find anything." Tank was steaming. "I'll bet they stole it from me when they bumped into me last night."

"Well, we don't know that for sure," said Ollie. "We need proof."

His words were a little too late. Tank was already at the Hermits' table, quizzing them about his slingshot. Ven, Bane, and Daegel stood up and surrounded him. Cosmo and Dusty raced over to pull Tank out of the circle before anything happened.

"They said they didn't know anything about my slingshot," huffed Tank. "Liars."

As if someone had flipped a switch, Tank's demeanor changed 180 degrees. His nose caught the scent of bacon, and a calm engulfed him. His tummy was going to be happy, and that was all that mattered for now.

"They say music soothes the savage beast," explained Ollie. "For Tank, it's bacon."

A whistle got their attention. It was the director. "I need all the Stingrays over here for a moment." He waved his hand in the air. The team lumbered over to him. They weren't happy with him after what happened to Kamia, and it showed.

"Judging by the expressions on your faces, I assume you've heard the news. Kamia is no longer working at the camp. She was asked to leave for violating several standard procedures that a counselor must abide by to ensure the safety and welfare of the campers here at Camp Remnant."

"That's bull," said Sebastian under her breath.

"I want to assure you that this will not change your experience here with us. You will still maintain the same schedule, participate in all our events, and be provided with ample supervision to meet your needs. I will be your counselor and will escort you from place to place for the remainder of the camp. I assume you selected someone for the competition this morning. Right after breakfast, you'll have a couple of hours to practice in the clearing directly behind the pavilion, right over there. I'll meet you there when it's time for the Target Shoot. Is everyone excited?"

The team just stared blankly, frozen as if the whole group were a stone sculpture.

"Yes, well, then … enjoy your breakfast, and I'll see you later." Blake walked away.

"He's just a big fat pile of cow-patty," said C.J.

"He is not," argued Dusty. "He's more like elephant dung."

"This is all a bad dream," said Sebastian. "We've lost our counselor, one of our parents, and a slingshot, and strange people are all around us." She finished the sentence staring at Dusty.

"You calling me strange?" asked Dusty.

"What are we going to do without a slingshot?" asked C.J.

"We can always throw rocks if we have to," said Carson.

"I have an idea!" said Ollie. "I need to know what kind of underwear everyone is wearing."

Everyone stopped eating and froze, except for Tank. They all looked at Ollie. Sebastian pinched herself. "Wake up! Wake up! Wake up!" she repeated.

"Ollie, you're a sick puppy," said Cosmo. "A good dude, but a sick puppy."

"I need some elastic." Ollie frowned at Cosmo.

"You can use mine," said Dusty, but everyone conspicuously ignored him.

"Boxers here, with a Brittany Spears picture on them," said C.J. innocently.

The team looked at Carson and she nodded, confirming that it was probably true.

"I can make a slingshot. We still have the hatchet to chop a branch for a handle, but we need some elastic that can stretch really far," explained Ollie. "Like the kind in the waistband of our underwear, or maybe a …"

"Maybe a what?" asked Carson.

"You know … a girl's thing, her top. You know." Ollie couldn't look Carson in the eye. His face was as red as a ripe tomato.

"What?" she asked again.

"A bra," he said, and turned away from her in embarrassment.

"I have—" Dusty began.

"You wear a bra!" said Cosmo. "Dude!"

"No, I mean I wear underwear with elastic." Dusty explained, and again everyone acted as if they didn't hear him.

"She doesn't wear one yet," said C.J., looking at Carson out of the corner of his eye.

Compared to Carson's, Ollie's face didn't look so red any more. All the anger in Carson rose to the top of her head, and it was right in C.J.'s face. She held the front of his shirt in her fist.

"As a matter of fact I do, and unless you want me to tell how many years it took you to get potty trained …"

"OK! OK! She does," C.J. confirmed. "She does."

Carson let go of him and returned to her seat. When she looked the other way, C.J. motioned to everyone and silently mouthed "She doesn't."

"Is anyone wearing, or does anyone possess, underwear that has the elastic I need?" asked Ollie, the picture of patience and leadership.

"Boxers," said Cosmo, shaking his head.

Carson and Sebastian shook their heads also.

"I do," said Dusty. "But if you use them, it's going to leave me with only one pair."

"Fine. Desperate times call for desperate measures," Ollie rationalized.

"That's pretty desperate," said Sebastian. "Not to mention gross, despicable, revolting …"

"I'm going back to the barracks to make the slingshot," said Ollie. "As soon as I'm finished, Tank will need to practice."

Ollie rushed down to the barracks and found Dusty's other pair of briefs in a trunk under his bed. He ripped off the top ring of elastic and cut it in half. Outside, he found a small, stiff branch with the right size fork at the top. He used the hatchet to cut the handle to the right length and sandpaper to smooth off the knots and slivers. He tied the elastic to each end of the fork, pulled on it to test its elasticity, and retied it a few times. The slingshot was ready. The team made their way outside to see Ollie's contraption, with the exception of Tank, who continued to eat. C.J. picked up the slingshot and snapped the elastic.

"This is tight," said C.J. "Hey, what's this tag in the middle of the elastic? It says '28.'"

"That would be my underwear size," said Dusty with a smile.

"I've heard of a gun called the 38 Special," said C.J. "Let's call this slingshot the 28 Special."

"That'll work," Cosmo agreed. "I like that. It does look pretty good, considering."

"Well, it's not as nice as Tank's slingshot," said Ollie humbly. "But it will have to suffice. He's pretty upset about not having his real one. We need to figure out a way to settle him down."

"Food," said Sebastian. "I'll go back up to the pavilion and sneak a few pastries. We can give them to him right before he starts. That should do the trick."

"Want to hold it?" C.J. reached the slingshot out to Sebastian.

"No, thanks," she said. "I'd have to put my hands in scalding water to kill all the germs from that thing."

"Everyone needs to gather a dozen pebbles about this size." Ollie held up a small stone. "That should give him enough for practice and for the competition."

They gathered pebbles and took them to Tank at the practice area. C.J. set cans and plastic bottles on some rocks in the distance and stepped off to the side. Tank tucked one of the pebbles into the slingshot, took aim, and fired. He missed by five feet, but he squarely hit C.J.'s hat off his head.

"Oops," said Tank.

"No problem." Ollie motioned for C.J. to come back and stand with them to ensure his safety. "Take your time, Tank."

Tank placed another pebble in the 28 Special, right on the size tag, and pulled back again. The pebble hit one of the large boulders and ricocheted everywhere. The team hit the deck, belly down on the grass. When it finally stopped, they stood and dusted themselves off.

"No problem, no problem," said Ollie. "That was closer."

For the next hour the team dodged so many missiles that they were drenched in sweat. Tank didn't hit a single object. This was made more humiliating by the fact that Cosmo kept pulling bottles and cans from the trash can to increase the number of targets.

"It's no use," said Tank, defeated. "Let's just go get this over with." As he spoke, a small piece of bacon shot from his mouth and struck one of the bottles, knocking it over.

"Oh, brother," said Sebastian.

They walked to the eastern trail and met Blake Dawson, who escorted them to the shooting range.

"Cheer up." Carson patted Tank on the back. "Here's some pastries in case you get hungry while you're waiting. We know you'll do the best you can. Don't worry."

"He'd better worry," a voice said from behind them. It was Daegel, with Bane cackling at his side. "Terrible thing about that slingshot. I'm sure the one you have now is much better." Both boys laughed uncontrollably. Ollie gritted his teeth. Tank gave Daegel a look that would petrify most people, but the bully just walked away.

The targets were shaped like wild animals and birds, attached to wheels that rolled along a wire suspended in the air between two trees. Fifty targets would glide down two at a time. Sixteen different wires were strung at different places in the shooting range. The shooter could shoot any one he wanted, and one point was given for each target hit. When a shooter was prepared to fire, he or she would signal Stuart Davis, the Dragons' counselor, by saying "Ready." Stuart would push a button and release two targets.

First up were the Dolphins. Hunter Blankenship, the Dolphin shooter, used a spear. For the first eight drops, Hunter's spears found their mark dead center, and it looked like he was true to his name. But his shoulder tired quickly, and he managed only four more hits over the final seventeen drops, bringing his score to a respectable 11 points.

Next were the Scorpions. Aubrey Meadows used a bow and arrow. Like Hunter, she started on a roll, with ten targets hit after the first ten drops. However, while she waited for the next drop with her arrow fully cocked and pointed downward, her fingers slipped and she shot herself in the foot. She was raced to the nurse's station. Another Scorpion, Kayla Kingsly, stepped in to finish. It was clear she would not score another point when she nocked her arrow backwards and pointed it at her chest rather than the target.

The Dragons took the lead with Thomas Frankenfield. He used a boomerang to score 17 points. It was a good weapon to choose, because if it missed a target on its first pass, there was always a chance it would make contact on its way back, which it did quite frequently.

Then it was Bane's turn. He spit into his hands and rubbed them together to get a better grip. He pulled his crossbow up and cocked it against his shoulder.

"I'm ready," he told Stuart.

Indeed he was. He scored a perfect 25 out of the 25 drops. He teased the campers on the final one as his arrow struck it at the last moment. Daegel and Ven, along with the rest of the Hermits, rushed in to congratulate him. Daegel sneered at Tank as they returned to the grassy slope where the campers sat.

Tank walked up to the firing line with his bag of danishes in one hand and the bag of pebble ammunition in the other. He set the bag of cream-filled delights at his feet and spilled the pebbles out next to it. He pulled his slingshot out of his back pocket and placed it in his left hand. He loaded it with his right hand and pulled it back hard near his left eye. "Ready," he said to Stuart, very seriously.

He fired directly at the bird that slid down from the left and waited to hear the impact as the two targets descended. Silence. A miss. The Hermits roared.

Again Tank readied, took aim, and fired another miss.

The Stingrays looked furious. They were upset with the Hermits, who shifted from their victory celebration to laugh at Tank, who reached down and pulled out a third stone. "Ready." He motioned to Stuart.

As the two targets rolled down the wire and came close to passing each other, Tank fired, struck the one on the left and shattered it to pieces. The Stingrays stood and cheered to encourage him. Tank, instead of smiling, looked puzzled.

On the fourth drop, Tank fired and missed again. It was after the fifth shot, which broke the target in half, that a look of confidence formed on his face. "Now I'm ready," he said. True to his word, he scored on the next fifteen drops. With five more to go, Tank had a score of 17. One more meant second place. The Stingrays stood and yelled words of encouragement, while the Hermits quieted considerably. Tank reached down for a pebble and paused a second in thought. Instead of taking one pebble, he picked up two. He tucked one into the patch of the 28 Special and left the other in the palm of his right hand. "Ready."

The two targets slid down the wires, and the one on the left was struck almost instantly. Tank reloaded, and before the target on the right could disappear, he fired and splintered it as well.

"Unbelievable!" said Stuart, though Tank could hardly hear him, because everyone but the Hermits had joined in the applause. "No one's ever done that before. I guess that counts as two."

"Now we're rockin'," said Tank. He hit the next two and then two more. With two drops to go, he was in second place with a score of 23. Daegel approached Stuart in a rush.

"That's not fair," said Daegel. "No one ever told us we could shoot at both targets. Bane would have gotten a 50 if he had known that."

"No one ever asked if they could," said Stuart sternly. "No one has ever done it before, either. Now go sit down."

Daegel turned with a frown and walked back. He mumbled words that sounded like *cheater* and *not fair*.

"If you hit two more targets, you'll be tied for first," said Stuart.

"There's not going be a tie," said Tank, full of confidence. "Tying is like kissing your sister. Time to lock and load. Ready."

The target on the right shattered before it could reach the halfway point of the fall. The opposite target slid safely down to the end of its wire, unscathed. With the exception of the Hermits, the campers went bananas, giving each other high fives and screaming with joy. Their screams merged into a chant. "Tank! Tank! Tank! Tank!"

Tank was oblivious to it all.

"No!" Tank looked down in disbelief.

The makeshift slingshot lay on the ground, split in half. One more time was all he needed. The first one to see it was Ollie, and he pointed to get Carson's attention. One by one the campers' eyes made contact with the fractured 28 Special, and soon all was silent.

Tank suddenly remembered what Carson said earlier.

We can throw rocks if we have to.

Tank looked down at the ammunition at his feet and made up his mind. He reached down, grabbed two cream cheese pastries and crammed them into his mouth. He chewed for a few seconds. "Weigh" he said, lodging a pastry missile in Stuart's ear.

"What?" Stuart stuck his finger into his ear and pulled out a wet drippy chunk of cream cheese.

"Weighey," Tank said and a piece fired into the counselor's other ear.

"OK! OK! I get it! You're trying to say *Ready!* Just don't shoot me again!" Stuart pushed a button and the final two targets slid down the wires. At the instant before they crossed, Tank shouted, "Thingthays." Two pieces of cream cheese struck both targets and disintegrated them upon impact. Their fragments fell like confetti in the wind.

Tank found himself on the bottom of a pile of Stingrays. Carson and Sebastian clapped. Daegel and his boys argued with Stuart about the fairness of the competition.

Tank explained what happened all the way back to the barracks. "The first target I hit on the left was an accident. I was aiming at the target on the right. It took me a couple more times to figure out that the slingshot fired to the left of my aim. From that point on, I just aimed to the right of my targets."

"You saved the day." Ollie put his arm around his best pal.

"No, Carson saved the day. I was thinking about what she told me about throwing rocks if we had to. That's when I thought of the pastries."

"We could never have won if Sebastian hadn't been kind enough to bring you the pastries." Carson wasn't going to accept all the credit.

"Or without Ollie making a wicked slingshot," said C.J.

"Or without my underwear!" said Dusty.

There was about five seconds of silence while everyone realized that Dusty was down to one pair of briefs for the remainder of camp.

"Cosmo and C.J. set up the practice range," said Ollie. "Looks like we all did something. I told you! I knew we would make a great team."

"That reminds me," said Cosmo. "I have some big news we need to talk about. I think it's going to make you all happy."

"Is it about our dad?" Carson asked. C.J. looked up, excited also.

"Well," said Cosmo, "Not really, but it could maybe help find the three jewels." Cosmo's voice quieted as campers from the other teams walked up to congratulate Tank and the gang. "I want to study my drawings a bit more tonight, but I may have found out what the mosaic means above the sealed doorway. I guess it's possible that the jewels could be in there, if we can figure out how to open it."

"Do you think they're there?" asked C.J.

"Who knows? They could be. Let me look over my notes again tonight. If I'm right, we'll talk it over at breakfast and figure out a way to open that door."

"So you think we can open it?" asked Carson.

"I don't want to tell you yes until I check everything out tonight and we discuss it at breakfast," said Cosmo. "Don't get your hopes too high. I could be wrong."

"This is awesome," said C.J.

"Wow," said Carson. "This could be it."

"It could be," said Ollie. "Or it might get us kicked out of the competition. It might get us kicked off the island. It might get us all killed."

11

Missing in Action

The Adventure Challenge board listed the scores of the individual teams and tallied the totals for the overall competition. That night after dinner, the kids all huddled around the scoreboard. After two rounds of the contest, the Stingrays had moved from fourth to third place and gained some respect from the other teams, with the exception of the Hermits, of course, who were still on top with 135, followed by the Dragons at 117. Thanks to Tank's performance, the Stingrays were third with 101. The Scorpions weren't officially out of the race yet with 80, but it looked like a wait-till-next-year for the Dolphins, who had managed a token 62 points.

Ollie duct-taped the 28 Special back together. Everyone wanted to see the slingshot contraption, which meant they had to touch it or actually sling a pebble at a tree. Sebastian shivered at the thought of all the invisible diseases being spread as it was passed around the campfire at the ceremonial dance that night. The counselors explained the Burning Thunder dance, but many of the campers tuned out. They talked and pulled down their trousers just enough to compare the type of elastic on their underwear. C.J. bragged about how Ollie made the slingshot and revealed that Dusty had only one pair of undies left for the remainder of camp. Some Scorpions tagged Dusty with a new nickname, Uno, which Dusty actually liked. At the end of the dance, Blake Dawson appeared.

"I hope everyone enjoyed the target shoot earlier today and had fun learning the new dance tonight."

You could almost see forked tongues and hear hisses coming from the Stingrays' mouths.

"How could he have fired Kamia?" Carson shook her head.

"We've been monitoring the weather this evening, and as usual we're the target of a major storm system that should arrive in the morning. I've decided that we'll work underground at the main site for the entire day tomorrow. I'll have assignments for you tomorrow at breakfast; we'll rotate duties from room to room. Some will pack and label items, while others will decipher mosaics. As you have all seen by now, the Ceremonial Chamber is extremely large, and there's plenty of room and enough work for all of you. Working underground should provide, as it did for the Wagapi, sufficient protection from the inclement weather until it passes over the island by tomorrow evening. Any questions? No? Then it's off to bed. See you in the morning." He gave the Stingrays a see-you-later salute.

◆   ◆   ◆

The next morning, the sun remained lost behind the clouds that swiftly moved in. By the time the others arrived at the pavilion for breakfast, Tank was on his third bottle of milk and had filled his plate for the second time with iguana egg omelets.

"All that stress and energy you put out for the competition really worked up an appetite, eh?" Cosmo sat down next to Tank.

"I think just existing and breathing air is enough for Tank to work up an appetite," said Dusty, clean from the shower. Tank kept up his rhythm of chew-chew-chew-swallow without missing a beat.

Carson, the last to collect her food, sat down eagerly and interrupted all conversation. "What's the big news, Cosmo? You said we'd go over it at breakfast, and I hardly slept a wink last night."

"I couldn't sleep either," said C.J.

"What?" Dusty looked dumbfounded. "I'm the one who didn't sleep on account of all that snoring you were doing."

"I don't snore," said C.J.

"Oh, right." Dusty smirked. "If you weren't snoring, then you were riding a motorcycle in our room all night long."

"Tell us, Cosmo," said Carson.

"You guys said you overheard the director or the guy in the dark coat say something about an eclipse." Cosmo quietly leaned into the table. "I think that's what's pictured in the mosaic above the door in the Ceremonial Chamber—an eclipse."

"Wow!" said Ollie in amazement. "Of course."

"So what does that mean?" asked Carson. "Can we open it?"

"I haven't figured that out yet." Cosmo looked frustrated.

"We'll figure it out together," said C.J.

"I don't think we should tell anyone," said Dusty. "Not even Chief Dawson."

"What a great idea, Mr. Brilliant," said Sebastian. "I sure am glad you're here to help us when we need it."

"He-Who-Must-Not-Be-Named," said C.J.

Everyone turned and looked at C.J., puzzled.

"He who what?" asked Cosmo. "Who's that?"

"Him!" C.J. pointed to the edge of the eastern trail. "Scaredy-Pie." The Australian Shepherd was hiding in the brush at the edge of the trail, with only his head visible.

C.J. stood and stared. Carson pulled him back down quickly. "We don't want anyone else to see him." She looked around to see if anyone was looking in that direction. She told the rest of the team about the dog. Carson wondered why he wouldn't come on out for everyone to see.

"What's that around his neck?" asked Dusty, squinting.

"Oh my gosh!" said Carson. "That's Dad's bandanna. He always wears it."

"Let's go get—" C.J. stood up again. Carson pulled him back down again.

The dog stared straight at C.J. and Carson, never flinching. Thunder echoed from the direction of the ocean where the storm was about to come ashore.

"It sounds like it's time to move on to the main site," commanded Blake Dawson through the microphone. "The rain will start any minute. I see that some of you have your backpacks and some don't. If you don't, then please hurry back to your barracks and get them. Meet us at the western trail entrance. Go, everyone."

"We're going to get our backpacks," said Carson. "And then check out the dog."

"If you get caught, you'll be kicked out like Kamia," said Cosmo.

"We have to," said Carson. "That dog is wearing Dad's bandanna."

"I'll go with you," said Dusty.

"Me too," said Cosmo.

"We can't all go," said Ollie. "All the campers will be working in the ruins, and there will be a lot of commotion. This may be a good time for you to sneak away. Dusty, Carson, and C.J. didn't bring their backpacks, so they can go get them and hang out here until everyone is out of sight. The rest of us will cover for you as long as we can."

"Thanks, guys," said Carson. "Let's go."

"Good luck," they all chimed in.

"And be careful," said Ollie.

The three blended in with the crowd of campers who had forgotten their backpacks. As they walked, the dog stayed close to the brush and never took his eyes off Carson and C.J. They donned their slickers and waited inside until the coast was clear. Then they hustled to the eastern trail. As the three of them neared the dog, he sprang to its feet and headed off. They chased him, softly calling and whistling for him to come back. Scaredy-Pie stopped, barked loudly, waited for them to catch up, and dashed away again. He was never out of sight.

◆   ◆   ◆

While C.J., Carson, and Dusty followed Scaredy-Pie, the rest of the campers walked down the western trail toward the main site. Ollie heard Daegel say, "Did you hear that? It sounded like a dog."

"Whistling, too," said Ven.

Ollie and Tank were close behind and saw that others had also heard the sounds.

Ollie whistled a nursery tune. Tank coughed, doing his best to make the coughs sound like the barks in the distance.

"Oh! It's you!" said Daegel. "Didn't you get enough doggie biscuits at breakfast?" Everyone chuckled and decided that it was indeed Tank who was barking. "There's a toilet over there if you need to lap up some water to wash those biscuits down." Daegel and his goons stepped down into the ruins and disappeared below.

"Quick thinking." Ollie patted Tank on the shoulder.

◆   ◆   ◆

"Here, boy," C.J. beckoned the dog. "Come here, Scaredy-Pie." The three of them stopped to catch their breath, hands on their knees.

"He's not coming," said Dusty. "I had a dog when I was younger, and my sister Misty named him Sid. It wasn't a good name, because the dog always thought we were calling him *Sit*. When we tried to call him, we would say, 'Come 'ere, Sid! Come 'ere, Sid!' but Sid thought we were saying 'Come 'ere, sit! Come 'ere, sit!' If he was on the other side of the backyard, it would take about twenty minutes for him to get to us. We tried to change his name, but it never worked. I wanted to change it to Rollover, but Mom said it would make him too dizzy and he might pass out. I don't think this dog would come to us right now even if we knew his name. He wants us to keep following him."

The dog led them farther down the trail. Carson motioned for the others to hurry. The brush got thicker, and it was clear they were no longer on a major trail, but on a path that wasn't well traveled. They pulled branches down to clear the path. Carson grabbed a long, dangling tree limb and held on as she walked forward. When she let go of the branch it shot straight back. C.J. ducked quickly; the limb would have taken off his head. Dusty wasn't so lucky. His face caught the full force of the limb, and he was knocked at least ten feet back. He lay flat on his back with his arms outstretched and didn't move.

"Nice try." C.J. didn't realize that Dusty had just been slammed silly and lay motionless behind him. "I'm a little too fast for that old trick. I mean, really, you'd have to be pretty stupid to get hit like that."

Carson pointed back at Dusty, who sat up, rubbed his jaw, and gave C.J. a stern look.

"You'd have to be pretty stupid to get hit like that from a tree back home, because the trees back home are way slow, but it's impossible to dodge the trees here. They are lightning fast." C.J. said, smiling hopefully at Dusty.

Almost instantly, lightning struck. Ground-shaking thunder came seconds after the flash, and before C.J. could take his arms from the top of his head, Dusty ran in front of Carson to follow the dog.

"Don't mention lightning again." Carson jabbed her index finger into C.J.'s chest.

The pace of the chase quickened, as did the frequency of the lightning. The dog sped up as he sensed the need to get to their destination before the storm engulfed them. The wind gusted, and they could smell the coming rain. The brush grew thicker just before they reached a small clearing bordered by a wall of cane. The dog leapt into a narrow gap in the cane, and Dusty rushed ahead, bursting through the brush headfirst. The next sound Carson and C.J. heard was a scream so loud it stopped them in their tracks.

◆   ◆   ◆

"I think your hypothesis is correct," said Ollie. "Those appear to be symbols of an eclipse."

"No doubt, dude," said Cosmo.

"Remember the mirrors," said Sebastian. Maybe if we reflect some light down here into the eye, the door will open."

"I've played video games that made you do that," said Ollie. "I never thought it could be real, but you could be right."

"We need to get the mirrors." Tank sent bacon shrapnel flying and hit a few nearby Scorpions in the back of the head. They scratched their hair and continued to work as if nothing had happened.

"They've been packed; they're probably in one of the boxes stored in the next room." Ollie pointed to the Dining Chamber.

CRACK!! BOOM!!

The lightning strike caused the power to go off instantly, and only the flickering flames from the torches lit the cavernous rooms. The campers screamed and squealed.

"Silence!" The director stood in the middle of the Ceremonial Chamber. "If you keep screeching you're going to attract every wild hog on the island. There is no need for fear in this room, nor is there any place for it. All your backpacks are equipped with two flashlights, one to hold in your hand and one with a strap so that you can wear it on your head and keep your hands free. I suggest you use the latter so we can continue our work. Carry on."

Cosmo and the gang were in a remote corner that was extremely dim. Cosmo opened his backpack and walked near a torch to gain some light so that he could find his headlamp. He glanced up at the torch, looked down, and then glanced back at the wall beside the torch. It was hard to see because of all the mosaics in the room, but there was a small hole in the wall. He touched it and then called Ollie over to see it.

"Look at this," said Cosmo. "I think it may be a hole for one of the mirrors. The ends of the mirrors are about this size, and I'll bet one of them fits right into it. We need to find the holes for the other four."

"Hmmm." Ollie placed his finger over his lip and looked into the Dining Chamber. "This would be the only one needed in this room to make light hit the eye above the door. The other four must be near the entrance or in the Dining Chamber."

Almost all the campers had located their headlamps, and the room was filled with beams of light moving in all directions. Some campers stopped their work altogether and simply rotated their heads, watching the beam in awe. Others giggled and pointed their headlamps directly onto someone else's bottom. Ollie and Cosmo walked into the Dining Chamber and found three of the remaining four holes. They were about to ascend the stairs to find the final hole when they were stopped by a voice from behind them.

"Where do you think you're going?" asked Blake Dawson. "The weather is way too bad to go out there right now. What are you looking for?"

"Nothing at all sir," said Ollie.

"We weren't going anywhere sir," said Cosmo. "We just wanted to check out the weather. We weren't going outside, though."

"I assure you that you don't want to go outside in a Crater Island spring storm. They can get very nasty, and I pity anyone who may be out in this weather right now."

Cosmo and Ollie both turned toward the entrance.

"I have been checking in on you from time to time ... the team, that is, and I don't recall seeing the Crenshaws, or the other boy ... I believe his name is Dirty."

"Dusty, sir; it's Dusty," said Ollie quickly. "They're around here somewhere, sir."

"I am aware of how many people are down here, Mr. Patrolli, and it appears that a few are missing. Return to your group, and I will find the Crenshaws and Dingy. Everyone must be accounted for."

"Dusty, sir," said Ollie in a low voice.

"I beg your pardon?" said the Chief.

"His name is Dusty, sir, not Dingy."

"Yes." The chief looked around at faces in an attempt to locate Carson, C.J., and Dusty. Cosmo and Ollie hurried back to Sebastian and Tank.

"Bad news," said Ollie. "The Chief is looking for our friends."

"We're doomed," said Tank.

"No," said Sebastian. "Dusty and the Crenshaws are doomed. No one, not even the big chiefy-wiefy, is going out in this weather. It sounds like one mean storm, and our teammates are out there in it."

◆   ◆   ◆

C.J. and Carson stood motionless after they heard Dusty scream, listening for any sound. What could have happened? Did he run into someone on the other side who captured him, or worse? Carson finally signaled C.J. to walk toward the cane wall. Black clouds loomed above them. The dry scraping of the cane leaves made them feel even drearier. They could hear the rain coming. Carson stepped up to the wall of leaves, with C.J. directly behind her, peering around her waist. She reached out with both hands as if she were about to dive into a swimming pool and spread the cane apart.

"Do you see them?" C.J. screamed over the howling winds.

"No!" she yelled back. "I don't see Dusty or the dog! It's a cliff! They've fallen off a cliff! They may be dead!"

12

The Doldrum Diver

The storm hit with all its fury, but down below in the Ceremonial Chamber the weather wasn't on anyone's mind as campers gathered and catalogued the endless golden treasures. Others analyzed the mosaics that covered the walls. Saber-like beams from their headlamps shone in all directions.

"The walls are like books," said Cosmo. "Over there it says *We are one with the land, sea, and sky.* He pointed to a glyph of three people. "That one says *Our spirits will live forever.* This one I can't quite translate; it starts with *The Great King will return to gather his ...* but that's all I can make out."

"Are you sure about the one over the sealed doorway?" Tank pointed.

"I think he's right," said Sebastian.

"Me too," agreed Ollie. "It's an eclipse. The mirrors fit into the holes in the wall to reflect a real eclipse into that oval eye. We have to find out from Chief Dawson when the eclipse is going to occur."

"Speak of the devil." Sebastian pointed at Blake, who was headed toward them.

"Are we getting anything done over here?" asked Blake.

"Yes, sir," they all answered.

"Mr. Dawson, sir," said Ollie. "Are we allowed to come down here and do more work when we have free time? We really enjoy studying this stuff. Cosmo is teaching us what the mosaics mean. The ruins are always open, aren't they?"

"I appreciate your desire for knowledge, Mr. Patrolli. It's nice to know you think so little of our other activities that you'd cast them aside just to come down here. Maybe we should do away with the Adventure Challenge?"

"No, sir. That's not what I mean, sir."

"Teams may come when they are scheduled to be here, or if I say otherwise. And no, the ruins are not always open."

"We just enjoy learning about all this cool stuff," said Ollie.

"I'm sure your team would learn a lot more if they were all here. I have searched everywhere and found no trace of the Crenshaws or Mr. Pickles."

"They weren't feeling good," said Tank.

"Yeah, they were sick to their stomachs," Sebastian filled in. "I think it was something they ate at breakfast. They went to the barracks to lie down."

"They're probably all right now," said Ollie. "I'm sure as soon as the weather calms down a bit they'll come right over."

"I wasn't aware of their condition," said Mr. Dawson. "Why didn't you tell me before?" He looked at Ollie and Cosmo, who looked at each other.

"They didn't know, sir," blurted Sebastian. "Carson told me, and I didn't tell anyone else. I didn't think it was important."

The director gave them a suspicious look, and then a greasy grin came across his pale face.

"Thank you for informing me. I don't want to go out in this storm, but they are my responsibility. Perhaps I should get them some medicine. A tummyache, did you say?"

"Yes, sir," said Ollie.

Dawson turned and walked briskly into the Dining Chamber. The team watched him speak briefly with Kirk Christianson, the Dolphins' counselor, who also served as the head counselor. Dawson threw on a large black raincoat and left.

"That didn't turn out so good," said Cosmo.

"It wasn't all bad," said Ollie. "When he mentioned our schedules, I remembered there was a big slot blacked out for the ruins when no one was supposed to be here. That has to be when the eclipse is. The rest of the time it's booked solid with campers."

"What about Carson, C.J., and Dusty?" asked Tank. "We better think of something fast, or they're in a heap of trouble, if they aren't already."

◆   ◆   ◆

The rain fell in torrents. Carson raised her arm to block C.J. from going any farther. They stood a short distance from the edge of a large circular canyon approximately a hundred yards across. It looked as if an enormous pole had been driven into the earth and then removed again, leaving a gaping hole behind. Trees filled the canyon, and their tops reached almost to the level of the land where Carson and C.J. stood. There was no way down—at least no safe way. Carson knew Dusty must have fallen into the chasm. There was a long slide imprint in the mud that began where she stood and ended at the edge of the canyon. The pawprints continued around to the right, near the rim. She shuffled her feet in the mud, getting closer to the edge of the gigantic pit, and peered down to look for Dusty. She leaned her head over ever so slightly and readied herself for the worst.

"Dusty!" she screamed, trying to hear over the roar of the driving rain.

"Carson!" a voice came back.

"Dusty!" Carson leaned over a little more, expecting to find him standing down below on a ledge, all safe and sound. What she saw was not what she expected. Dusty had indeed plunged over and fallen into the gigantic pit, but luckily, a tree growing out from the side of the canyon snagged his britches. Dusty dangled by his underwear.

"Dusty! We're here! Are you OK?"

Dusty raised his head slowly and nodded yes. As he did so, his weight shifted and the large branch that held him cracked and dropped a few inches. He bobbed up and down, held by the elastic in his underwear.

"Don't move! Don't move! We'll get you! Don't move!"

Carson dropped down onto her chest in the mud and crept over to the rim of the canyon. She stretched one arm out as far as she could, but she was unable to reach him. Her fingers were a foot short. She pulled herself forward a little bit at a time, her body sliding smoothly in the mud.

"Grab my feet!" she screamed to C.J. "I've almost got him!"

C.J. sat down and held onto her ankles as tightly as he could. Carson reached down a little more and called out for Dusty to grab her hand. He slowly lifted his arm, and as their fingertips were about to touch, the branch cracked again, dropping him another six inches.

"We have to do this now!" Carson shrieked. "The branch is going to break in half. Help me lean over some more."

C.J. braced himself as best he could in the mud. He dug his feet into the saturated soil, but he could manage only so much traction as the rain pounded and water rushed over his boots. Carson's whole upper torso extended down into the canyon.

"On three, I want you to go for it!" shouted Carson. "It's our only hope! I can't reach over any farther! Ready?"

Dusty didn't dare move, but he gave her a tiny thumbs up.

"Here we go! C.J., hold on tight! Ready! One ... two ... three!"

Dusty lunged up as high as he could, which caused the branch to snap in half and fall into the trees below. He grabbed Carson's arms tightly with both hands. The additional weight caused Carson to slide over the edge and she screamed in terror. C.J. wasn't strong enough to hold them both, and he flopped over onto his belly, but he didn't let go of his sister's ankles. Then he started to slide. Carson was now completely over the rim, and soon C.J. would be also.

Something began to tug at C.J. He stopped sliding, but he wasn't being pulled back. It was the dog, and he had a death grip on C.J.'s raincoat. He frantically clawed backwards in the wet mud. The dog struggled to get a grip with his paws, but to no avail. The most he could do was prevent them from going any farther, but eventually he too began to lose ground. C.J. was now halfway over the cliff.

"I'm going to let go and save you!" yelled Dusty.

"You do and I'll kill you!" screamed Carson.

The dog's paws were now at the lip of the canyon, and he whipped his feet into the mud, desperate to find footing. Dusty finally felt himself being pulled back up, slowly at first, then a little faster. He tried to look up to see what was happening, but the rain interfered with his vision. Someone pulled C.J. up by the legs and then let go of him to grab Carson's ankles and lift her to safety as Dusty hung onto her for dear life. Finally, Dusty felt two large hands grab him by the arms and heave him to the top. The three of them lay there in the muck, panting with exhaustion. By the time they recovered and looked around, the dog and the stranger were gone. Carson looked for footprints, but it was raining so hard that all traces of their rescuers had disappeared.

"Did you see who it was?" she asked C.J. He shook his head.

"Dusty?"

"The rain was blinding me, but I think he was real hairy. I could feel his beard rub against my arms as he pulled me up."

"What in the world happened here?" C.J. pointed at the enormous canyon. "What caused this? A meteor?"

"The sides are too steep for a meteor," said Dusty, "and it's not tall enough to be a volcano."

The rain slowed, and within minutes it was down to a sprinkle. Distant thunder declared that the storm had left the island. One by one, they got to their feet, making sure they stood on solid ground.

"Look!" C.J. pointed to the center of the canyon, where a structure protruded from the treetops.

"What is that?" asked Carson.

"The tail of a small plane," said Dusty. "It must have crashed into the canyon. There are words on the back, but I can't make them out."

"Here, I'll tell you," said C.J., reaching into his backpack for his binoculars. "Oh my gosh, Sis, you're not going to believe it!"

"What?" she asked.

C.J. lowered his binoculars. "It says *Doldrum Diver*."

◆   ◆   ◆

"I feel terrible just sitting around in here, not able to do anything," said Sebastian. "Not only are they in big trouble and probably kicked out of camp, but there's no telling what happened to them in that storm. I don't like dogs anyway. Dogs just lie around all day drooling and licking their butts, and then they turn around and try and lick you in the face right afterwards. They're so nasty. Do you like dogs, Cosmo?"

Cosmo just picked his nose and tried to locate the result on his finger with his headlamp to get a better look at the size or shape of it.

"No doubt," said Sebastian.

"I like dogs," said Tank. "Cats are too bossy. You feed them and feed them, and how do they reward you? They let you give them a neck massage."

"Well, they don't keep you awake all night barking at the moon!"

"Will you guys knock it off?" asked Ollie. "Carson and C.J. are in trouble. What are we going to do about it? No one has any ideas? Fine. Let's go see if we can find them, then."

"And how are we going to get past Mr. Dawson?" asked Sebastian.

"I don't know. Let's just go," said Ollie.

"Kirk Christianson is at the entrance." Tank pointed into the Dining Chamber.

"I'll get Captain Kirk's attention," said Sebastian. "You guys leave while his back is turned."

The four of them entered the Dining Chamber and pretended to examine materials that were itemized in crates.

"Mr. Christianson," called Sebastian. "This item looks very similar to something I saw on the wall in the Ceremonial Chamber. Can you come with me for a moment so I can show it to you? I'd ask Mr. Dawson, our new counselor, but I can't find him right now."

"Certainly," said Kirk. "No problem. Let's see which one you're talking about."

She pointed out a gold figurine in a crate, then guided him to the other room and out of sight to show him a mosaic. Then she apologized for being mistaken about it being similar. The trio shot up the steps, pausing at the top to survey the situation. Their luck was twofold. The rain had stopped, and Blake Dawson hadn't gone to the barracks yet. They spotted him entering the high-tech tent and rushed to the trail, being careful to step on branches and leaves so that their footprints wouldn't be left in the mud. They stayed on the foliage at the edge of the trail and reached the barracks within minutes.

"They haven't made it back here yet." Ollie came out of the boys' quarters.

"No sign of Carson either." Tank emerged from the girls' side.

"They're still out there somewhere," said Cosmo. "We don't have much time. Let's go find them."

Cosmo walked out the door with Tank and Ollie right behind him. Before Tank could step outside, Cosmo turned and shoved them back into the meeting room.

"It's Dawson!" said Cosmo. "He's here! And he's heading this way!"

Blake Dawson stepped onto the front porch of the barracks and removed his raincoat. He shook it briskly and threw it across a bench.

C.J., Carson, and Dusty were almost out of the woods on the eastern trail, deep in a discussion of who might have saved them, when they stopped dead in their tracks. They saw Dawson on the porch. He stepped inside.

"I don't know why he's going into our hut, but lucky for us he is," said Carson quietly. "Let's hurry back to the ruins before he comes out." They took off at a sprint and vanished down the western trail.

No one was in the meeting room. Blake walked slowly around the table as he searched for signs that someone was in the hut. He turned, looking stern, and approached the boys' quarters. There in Dusty's bunk was Cosmo, covered from head to foot by a blanket.

"Mr. Pickles," asked Blake. "Are you not feeling well?"

The blanket mumbled back, "Unh unh."

Mr. Dawson turned to the bunk next to Dusty's, where Ollie was completely covered, pretending to be C.J.

"And you, Mr. Crenshaw?"

C.J.'s blanket just moaned.

Blake Dawson squinted, stepped briskly out of the room, and hurried to the girls' quarters to check on Carson.

"Is everyone dressed in there?" He waited and got no answer. "I'm coming in to check on Miss Crenshaw."

Tank lay all covered up, but he looked a little suspicious due to his size.

"Miss Crenshaw." The director listened for a response.

Tank hesitated, and then in his best high-pitched girly voice said, "Yes?"

"Miss Crenshaw, are you not feeling well?"

"No."

"What happened?"

"I think I drank some bad moo juice." Tank whimpered.

Mr. Dawson gave the lump in the sheet a puzzled look and then slowly reached for the edge of the blanket to pull it off. He was about to yank it back when Tank fired off a stink bomb from his bowels that made the covers vibrate. The startled director let go at once and covered his mouth and nose with his arm.

"Dear Lord, you are sick! I'll find Mrs. Snookembockem, our nurse, and send her right over."

"No! No!" Tank squealed like a pig. "I'll be fine."

"I insist," said Mr. Dawson. "You need medical attention." He rushed out of the room, picked up his coat, and left the barracks. No sooner had he stepped outside than Cosmo, Ollie, and Tank ran to the door and watched him head straight for the clinic.

"He's going to get the nurse," said Tank in his high-pitched voice.

"You don't have to talk like her any more," said Ollie.

"I kind of like it," said Tank.

"Dude." Cosmo shook his head and gave Tank a that-ain't-right look.

Before they could put a foot out the door, Dawson stepped out of the clinic and walked down the western trail. He slung his coat over his shoulders; it flapped in the wind like wings.

"We have to follow him and hope we can get back in there," said Ollie. "And we have to go now, before Mrs. Snookembockem comes."

"What about Carson and the others?" asked Tank.

"Maybe since the storm has passed, we'll have some time to sneak away at lunch," said Ollie. "Right now, if we don't figure a way to get back into the ruins without Dawson catching us, we'll all be doomed."

Dawson entered the ruins and made a beeline for the Ceremonial Chamber, where Sebastian, Carson, C.J., and Dusty sat in a corner. Three of them still wore raincoats covered with mud. Sebastian had filled them in on where their teammates were. Dawson stopped in front of them and curiously looked each one in the eye before he began to speak.

"Did Mrs. Snookembockem see you already?" asked the director.

"No sir," said Carson. "Our stomachs are all feeling better. Must have been a mini-virus."

"I think it was something in the moo juice, sir," said C.J.

"I feel better now," said Carson. "I have so much energy, I think I could just explode!"

"Please spare us," said Dawson. "An explosion of that nature would call for immediate evacuation of these confined chambers." He paused for a moment to survey the campers around them. "I don't see several of your teammates. I hope they have not fallen ill also."

"No, sir," Ollie stood behind Dawson. "We're all right here."

Dawson whipped around. Behind him stood Ollie, Tank, and Cosmo.

The electricity popped on and the room filled with the sound of small clicks as the campers flipped the off switches on their headlamps.

Blake looked at the team members suspiciously and then spoke to the rest of the campers.

"Attention, everyone. I see you managed to get a lot done here today. I would like everyone to return your tools to your backpacks, and then let's go to lunch." He walked out into the Dining Chamber and exited the ruins.

They all collected their things and headed back together.

"We were almost kicked out of the camp," said Tank, who then proceeded to tell the entire story. The team walked and listened as Tank explained. Suddenly Carson stopped and slapped Tank across the back as hard as she could. The rest of the team laughed so hard that their stomachs really did ache.

"It worked, didn't it?" asked Tank. "Besides, we were there trying to save your rumpelstilkins while you were off on some crazy adventure in the woods. What happened to you guys, anyway?"

"Oh, we were just on a wild dog chase." Carson grinned at C.J. and Dusty. And then she told the other Stingrays what really happened.

13

All Fired Up

"I told you so," Tank declared, as they sat in the meeting room. "Next time the Tankster talks, you'd best be listening."

"OK, Tank," said Carson. "You can stop rubbing it in. We believe you. It probably was a man who made you scream like a two-year-old girl at the animal trap. And he's most likely the same man who rescued the three of us." Tank didn't respond.

"We don't know who he is," said C.J. "But he can't be a bad guy. He saved our lives."

"True," said Ollie. "So that's not anything we need to worry about right now. I think we've discussed this enough over the last few days. We have more important things to talk about right now. Today is the eclipse, or at least we think it is."

"Different teams are scheduled for the ruins at different times, except when the Challenge is going on," said Carson. "The eclipse has to be around noon today."

"Let's go over our plan one more time to make sure we've got it straight."

"Not again." Sebastian moaned and rubbed her eyes. "We stayed up till midnight last night, going over it again and again."

"Get over it," said Carson. "C.J. and I have sneaked out every night. We can't find any dog tracks or anything. We still don't know if Dad is safe or not. The only thing that keeps us sane is that we tell ourselves he's all right."

"I don't think there's any reason to think he isn't," said Ollie. He turned to Sebastian with a withering look, and then began to speak. "Dusty and Carson will do the Fastest to the Fire competition." Ollie tossed Carson two copies of a tropical plant field guide. "You'll need these. Where's Dusty?"

"I don't know," said Carson. "I hope Dusty can do most of this. My mind is fried. I need rest."

Her hope turned to hopelessness as soon as Dusty stepped into the room.

"Well, I'm not wearing underwear, because I don't have any more," he announced to the gang. "Ollie made that slingshot with one pair, and the tree ripped my last pair to shreds."

"Everyone wait here one second," said Sebastian. She walked to the door and stepped out onto the porch. She screamed loudly for a solid ten seconds, then reentered the room.

"I'm OK now," she said.

"I might have to try that," said Tank. He turned to Dusty. "Mine are too big, or I'd give you a pair."

"Mine are too little," said C.J.

"I have a towel." Ollie's inventive juices flowed again. "If we can find two safety pins, I can make a diaper. I've done it dozens of times for my baby sister Mollie."

"I'm not going to wear a diaper," said Dusty. "Although that could come in handy. I mean, if I couldn't make it to the bathroom in time, I could just go in my diaper."

"That would be normal," said Sebastian.

"Dude," said Cosmo. "There is nothing normal about a kid our age doing the deuce in a diaper."

"Ya think?" Sebastian rolled her eyes.

"I'm not going to change him," said C.J.

"I suppose I could wear a pair of panties if one of you girls doesn't mind," said Dusty.

Tank stood up, walked out onto the porch, and screamed.

"Dude." Cosmo shook his head.

"Maybe they'll have some at the supply store or at the nurse's station," said Ollie. "Let's just not worry about that right now."

"Yes," said Sebastian. "Let's please change the subject and talk about more important things."

"Let's go eat breakfast," said Tank.

Tank led the way, and before they could all sit down with their plates, he downed two full containers of milk and loaded his missile launcher with two pieces of bacon. Ollie sat down between Carson and Dusty to discuss their strategy for the Fastest to the Fire competition. While the competition was going on, the rest of the Stingrays planned to sneak away and attempt to open the sealed doorway during the eclipse.

After breakfast the team's schedule took them back to the Burial Site for a couple of hours. They didn't collect much information from the site, because Ollie constantly rotated among them to make sure they knew exactly what they were to do, both for the competition and for opening the sealed doorway.

"For the two hundredth time, I've got it already!" said Sebastian. She recited each word of her assignment to Ollie verbatim and then turned to continue working on an inscription carved on a rock that was firmly stuck in the ground. Leaves and debris had covered it; she tripped over it when they entered the site. Like the rest of the team, she didn't watch her step. Her eyes and ears were locked onto the surrounding brush, looking and listening for wild dogs. Before it was time to go, she discovered two more rocks with inscriptions.

"It's time," Ollie announced. He was not only the captain, but also a counselor of sorts. Blake Dawson came around only at the beginning of each activity on their schedule. As quickly as he appeared, he vanished again, leaving Ollie in charge. Ollie liked the extra responsibility. It made him feel important, especially compared to the other team captains.

For the Stingrays, the best thing they saw when all the teams got together was the crowd of campers. This, along with the fact that they no longer had a real counselor, allowed them to move around Camp Remnant under the radar. Slipping away unnoticed was what they planned to do at the Fastest to the Fire competition.

Not this time, though. Unexpectedly hampering them today was Blake Dawson. He was at the competition, and he rooted himself near the Stingrays. He had an unpleasant expression on his face, and he repeatedly looked down at his watch, then up at the sky, which Carson and the others noticed.

"All righty! Here we go!" said a petite girl with short, dark brown hair and big cheeks. It was Ashley Sturbridge, the Dragons' counselor. She motioned for the campers to quiet down. "Will the two contestants from each team step up to one of the five fire pits, please?" She gave her two Dragons a wink and a good-luck thumbs up.

Carson and Dusty took their places.

"As I come by each group, I need one of you to pull an envelope out of this hat. The paper inside the envelope will tell you the method you must use to try and start a fire."

Levi Tucker of the Scorpions reached in, picked an envelope, and ripped it open. "Iron and flint," Levi announced. The Scorpions cheered; they knew it was easy to start a fire with iron and flint.

Mindy Lipscomb of the Dragons was next. "Gunpowder—yes!" This was one of the easiest ways to start a fire. They would remove half the gunpowder from a bullet casing and pour it on some tinder, then put the half-full casing back into a special cap pistol, without the bullet, and fire it at the powder on the tinder. This method was guaranteed to work every time.

"Congratulations," said Ashley.

Darla Dewberry of the Dolphins pulled out the next envelope. "Steel wool."

It was basically the same as the iron and flint method. They were given a six-volt battery to ignite the iron shavings, rather than flint.

Dusty took out the next envelope. He handed it to Carson. "Ladies first."

"No." Carson couldn't believe how dirty the paper had gotten when he held it for only a few seconds. "You go ahead."

"Magnification," said Dusty. Ollie nodded, satisfied. He had rehearsed this method again and again with Carson and Dusty.

"They can do it," Ollie said. The rest of the Stingrays applauded. To use a magnifying glass and create a focal point bright enough to ignite wood chips was easy enough, but chancy, because you needed sunlight. Ollie looked up. There were no clouds at all today.

Ashley Sturbridge handed Samantha Dungston of the Hermits the final envelope. Talon Cleaver opened it up. "Stick friction."

None of the Hermits made a sound. It was the most difficult way to create a fire. They were given two sticks, and they had to rub them together and create enough heat, through friction, to ignite the tinder.

"Yes!" Ollie made a tight fist. "This is our big chance to bury the Hermits and leave them in the dust."

"I'll give you five minutes to discuss your plan with your teammates," said Ashley.

"Here," said Ollie. "Take my glasses for backup, in case you lose the magnifier. I can hardly see without them, but I'll manage."

Dusty put them on and said, "Look!" His eyes looked as big as a horse's.

Sebastian whistled a flirty tune and said, "Ooh, I like a man in glasses." She gave Dusty goo-goo eyes.

"Fer real?" Dusty inclined his head toward her.

"No." She looked away, satisfied that she had just grabbed his heart and thrown it on the ground.

Ollie pulled his glasses off Dusty's face and handed them to Carson. "You'll need to look for the flavican lichen. Make sure it's a bit on the dried side. It's perfect for fuel because it resembles a miniature bush about the size of your hand and should catch fire quickly in the focused light."

"What's a lichen?" asked C.J.

"It's kind of a cross between a fungus and an algae," Ollie explained.

"Oh, you mean like Dusty," said Sebastian.

"Hey, do you know what the fungus said to the algae?" asked Tank. "It said, 'I've taken a lichen to you.'"

Cosmo gave Tank a high five.

"If you can't find any, then try to get bark chips," said Ollie. "You can find them at the base of tree trunks. But remember, don't bring back any other type of lichen. The blue bangula lichen has explosive properties, and the red nausetica releases narcotic fumes when it catches fire. Do not bring back either of those."

"I've got it." Carson assured everyone they would get the right kind. "I've looked in the field-guide books and I know what to look for. Are you guys ready for the doorway?"

"As long as we can locate the mirrors in time," said Cosmo. "I think between the five of us, we ought to find them pretty quick. All the crates are in the Dining Chamber, and we remember exactly what our chest looked like. Then all we have to do is wait for the eclipse. I think we can sneak away by …"

"Shhh!" said Ollie. "Here comes trouble." He motioned with a nod in the direction of Daegel and his crew, who were headed their way.

"Hey, Scumrays," said Daegel. "I want you to know there are no hard feelings over anything we may not have agreed on here at camp. Good luck in the Challenge today. Oh, by the way, does this belong to anyone?" Daegel held up Tank's slingshot.

"Give it!" yelled Tank. Bacon bits went in all directions.

"Whoa!" Daegel ducked and tossed the slingshot to Tank. "You don't need it anyway with a pucker like that."

"Get lost!" said C.J.

"You gonna make us?" threatened Daegel.

Carson stepped in between C.J. and Daegel.

"Lucky you have a big sister around—again!" Daegel turned away. "You're going to need a lot more than luck to win today's game."

"We don't need luck to beat losers," said Carson. "You're the one who's gonna need luck rubbing those two sticks together. I can't wait to see you try it."

"Well I guess it's good that I have my lucky rabbit's foot." Daegel held up a rabbit's foot and spun it around his index finger. Ven and Bane broke into a mischievous laugh as all three walked off.

Carson looked down at the magnifying glass, checked her pocket to make sure she had Ollie's glasses, and then looked up at the sky, where the sun glowed with no clouds at all. On the opposite side, Samantha Dungston and Talon Cleaver kissed Daegel's rabbit's foot, and Talon put it on like a necklace.

"Remember the rules," said Ashley. "You must stay on the trail at all times. All items you gather must come from the edge of the trail. You may go down the trail only once, so you will need to gather enough material to keep your fire going for the full fifteen minutes required. I have a stopwatch for each team, and I will start them the moment you get a fire going. The team to receive the most points will be the one that can start a fire first and keep it lit for fifteen minutes.

"You can do it!" yelled C.J. to Carson.

"You too," she said back.

"Everyone ready?" asked Ashley. Each team's duo returned to their fire pit. "Then, on your mark, get set, go!"

The competitors raced for the eastern trail and were out of sight in no time. The remaining campers engaged in small talk and kept their eyes on the trail entrance. Twenty minutes later, the first two returned. Ashley smiled as Mary and Mindy Lipscomb, the twins on the Dragons team, ran up with their arms loaded down with different types of foliage. As they worked to separate the bullet from the shell casing, the two Scorpions sprang into the campsite. They carried so much foliage they looked like two moving bushes. Right behind them were the Hermits, Samantha and Talon. Carson and Dusty raced in next. There was no sign of the Dolphins yet.

Carson's arms were full of dried flavican lichen and wood chips. Dusty collected just as much, but it was harder to see because it blended in with the cloud of dirt and dust that surrounded him.

"He needs to leave." Ollie motioned to C.J. and nodded toward Blake Dawson.

"What do we do if he doesn't?" C.J. asked.

"I don't know," said Ollie. "Let's wait a few more minutes."

BOOOMM!!

A powerful explosion erupted in the Dragons' fire pit when Marcy fired the gunpowder at the tinder. Both girls stood there with their faces and fronts covered with soot. Their blond hair was singed and dyed a coaly black.

"Blue blangula," said Ollie. "I'm surprised their counselor didn't warn them about it. I hope Carson and Dusty listened and didn't bring any back."

"Look." Tank pointed at the western trail. During the confusion, Blake Dawson had slipped away and was walking toward the ruins.

"Oh no," said C.J. "Here we go again. Why is he always in the way?"

"Now's our chance too," said Ollie. "We have to go. It's almost 11:45—we only have fifteen minutes."

Thanks to the twins' distraction, the group slipped away unnoticed. The explosion not only gave Dawson and the Stingrays the diversion they needed, but it also gave one to the Hermits. Samantha positioned some of her bark chips in a hole in the center of a flat stone. Talon unscrewed the end of the rabbit's foot. Inside the hollow paw were match heads snapped off wooden matches. She poured them onto the bark chips and quickly dropped the ends of their two friction sticks down into the hole. Samantha placed the sticks between her palms and began to roll them back and forth briskly. Smoke rose from the hole as the match heads ignited the chips of wood.

"Mrs. Sturbridge," said Samantha. "Start our timer."

Ashley gave the Hermits a faint look of disappointment and clicked on a stopwatch. A loud roar came from the Hermits as they patted Daegel on the back.

"Oh, for the love of mercy." Carson looked up to the sky. A puffy, white cumulus cloud approached the sun.

"If that thing covers the sky we're all in trouble," said Dusty. "No fire and no eclipse!"

"Quick." Carson placed some of the dried branches into their pit and focused the light onto the pile.

Next to them, the Scorpions put some wood shavings into their pit and smacked flint with a rock in an attempt to throw sparks at the clippings.

Carson held the magnifier steady. Smoke started to coil up and around the glass.

"Yes!" Dusty said. "Hurry! The cloud is almost blocking the sun!"

Without warning, a chunk of flint flew out of Levi Tucker's hands and struck the magnifying glass to the ground. Carson picked it up quickly to refocus the light, but there were large cracks in the middle, and it was no longer useful.

"The glasses!" yelled Dusty. "Quick!"

The sun flirted with the edge of the cloud.

"Sorry." Levi retrieved the flint.

Carson pulled Ollie's glasses out of her pocket and focused the light on the lichens. She moved the spectacles up and down to find the brightest point. Smoke started to swirl from the fire pit.

Levi returned to his pit. Being frustrated, he gave the flint a pounding blow with the rock. This caused a flourish of sparks, which instantly ignited his material.

"Mrs. Sturbridge," said the Scorpions.

"I see," she replied. "Congratulations. You are on the clock."

"Almost," said Carson. "Almost … almost … come on …"

"We only have a few more seconds … oh, no." Dusty looked up as the sun snuck behind the big cloud. Their tinder smoked, but with no flame.

Carson pulled the glasses away and let out a big sigh of disappointment. The lichens burst into a crackling fire.

"You did it!" said Dusty. "Just then when you blew on the stuff. That set it off! Way to go, Carson. Mrs. Sturbridge! Mrs. Sturbridge!"

She waved and gave them the thumbs up. Carson dropped more pieces of lichen onto the fire so that it would last fifteen minutes.

"I can't believe it," she said. "We did it, and how close was that? I hope the cloud is gone before the eclipse. What do you think?"

Dusty didn't reply.

"What do you think?" she asked again. This time she stood up and looked behind her.

There on the ground lay three boys, one of whom was Dusty. The others were the two Scorpions, and their fire had diminished to a smoking pile of rubbish. She saw the problem at once—red nausetica. The tranquilizing fumes had knocked them out cold.

"Mrs. Sturbridge." Carson waved her over. "We have a small problem over here."

"Oh, dear," said the Dragons' counselor. "What's happened?"

"I think they passed out from the fumes coming from what they were burning." Carson pointed at the pile of red foliage.

Mrs. Sturbridge tugged at Dusty's shoulder, got no response, and motioned for some of the other Scorpions to help. They picked up all three boys and carried them to Mrs. Snookembockem.

A timer went off and the Hermits rushed their teammates in celebration of another victory. Minutes later, Carson's timer beeped. They too had completed the task successfully.

"We're here!" came a voice from the edge of the eastern trail. It was the Dolphins. They had finally returned with large sticks and limbs, so large that it would take hours to light them by using steel wool and a battery. They got some of the outer bark to smoke but then the battery died and that was that. Later at dinner, the Dolphins were given a token round of applause from all the teams for their efforts.

The Fastest to the Fire competition was over. The Stingrays were successful again, although Dusty would have little memory of it. He was back, along with the Scorpions, by the time everyone walked over to the scoreboard to see the totals being posted. The Stingrays passed the Dragons and moved up to second place, but they still trailed the Hermits.

"We did our part." Carson held out her hand to Dusty for a shake.

"If you say so." He shook her hand. "We were lucky you didn't catch wind of any of their fumes."

"Lucky is right." Carson looked toward the western trail. "I hope the others have been lucky too."

"Yeah," said Dusty. "I'm sure they have been. I can't imagine what's behind the sealed doorway."

"Yeah," said Carson, frightened by Dusty's comment. "I can't imagine what could be behind there either."

14

The Eclipse

C.J. and the group barely stayed out of Dawson's line of sight as they followed him along the western trail. They stopped at the edge of the main site entrance while the director walked into the equipment tent.

"I think it's safe to say that our hunch is correct," whispered Ollie to the gang. "Did you see the way he kept looking at his watch and then looking up at the sky?"

"If he knows what we know, he'll be going down into the ruins any minute," said Sebastian.

"C.J. and I will go in there right now," said Ollie. We're the smallest, and if we need to hide, it'll be easier."

"Are you saying I'm fat?" asked Sebastian, glaring at him.

"That's not what he was saying," said Cosmo. "It's just safer. Besides, the only thing fat about you is your fat mouth."

"Watch out, Cosmo," said Tank. "It's a good thing Dusty isn't around to hear you talk trash about his lady."

"I am most definitely not Dusty's lady," said Sebastian. "I'd rather date a little dweeb like C.J. than something like Dusty."

"Hey!" yelled C.J. "Who're you calling little?"

"Guys, hold it down," said Ollie. "Sebastian, you can come with us if it will make you feel any better."

"What about me?" asked Tank.

All of them took a step back and glanced at Tank's round belly, partially exposed above his belt.

"You don't like my figure?" He smiled and turned sideways so they could get a better view of his bulging stomach. "Momma says I'm just big-boned."

"It's now or never," said Ollie. "Tank, you stay here as a lookout with Cosmo. If you see anyone coming, fire some stones down into the ruins to warn us."

"Got it," said Tank. He pulled out his slingshot.

"Cosmo," continued Ollie. "Keep an eye out behind you for anyone else who might be coming. C.J., Sebastian, stay close to me."

Ollie checked to make sure Dawson was still inside the tent and then dashed across the clearing. He came to a halt right at the entrance and tumbled down the stone steps as Sebastian ran into him from behind. She hadn't looked where she was going because her eyes were on the tent. Ollie crashed into a crate full of jeweled bowls and urns, making a racket that caught even Tank's and Cosmo's attention. C.J. and Sebastian glanced over at the tent and saw a shadow inside move toward the doorway. C.J. pushed Sebastian on inside. They hurried down the steps and met Ollie below.

"I couldn't run straight on in," explained Ollie. "It's quite dark down here compared to up there, and I can't see very well without my glasses. From now on, I'll follow you two."

"Mr. Dawson heard the noise, and now he's coming," said C.J. "What are we going to do?"

"Ow!" yelled Sebastian. She grabbed the back of her head.

"Shhh!" said Ollie. "That was a rock from Tank's slingshot. Ow!" Tank fired a second warning sign that caught Ollie squarely in the forehead.

"Shhh, yourself," whispered Sebastian.

"Let's hide in the next room," said C.J.

They all rushed into the Ceremonial Chamber. Not only was the room still full of artifacts and jewelry, but it was also littered with equipment left behind by the campers. Sketchpads, gloves, and headlamps lay about here and there. They could hear footsteps as someone descended the stone stairway, so each one epoxied himself to the nearest pillar. They heard voices. Blake Dawson was not alone.

"We have only five minutes," said a raspy voice. "Move quickly."

"They're in that box over there," said Dawson.

The three Stingrays were silent as they listened to the scuffling sounds of a crate being opened. Blake Dawson moved back and forth, placing the mirrors in their predetermined positions. C.J. pressed his hand over his heart to muffle the sound of its beating. One person made his way into the Ceremonial Chamber and stood a few feet away from C.J.'s pillar. His knees were shaking. He looked over at the next pillar and saw Sebastian. She could see the dark figure from where she was standing, and her eyes widened with fear. She saw a man in a black cloak with his entire head wrapped in bandages. C.J. looked at another nearby pillar and saw Ollie, standing stiff as a board with his nose against the stone.

"Last one," said Dawson, entering the room. Ollie could tell by the sound of scraping rocks that Dawson was placing the final mirror into the position Cosmo had discovered near the torch.

"Align the light," said the cloaked man.

"Yes, father," said Dawson.

Father? Ollie and Sebastian exchanged glances. Ollie could hear the joints of the mirrors squeak, metal grating on metal, as the mirrors were adjusted. The rooms filled with bright light as the beams reflected from one mirror to the other. The last one in the Ceremonial Chamber was out of alignment. Dawson adjusted it, but before he could aim it at the eye, the beam disappeared.

"A cloud!" Everyone sat motionless in the dark and waited for the sun to shine again. C.J. could hear Dawson's father breathing through the bandages. As the cloud passed, Dawson quickly moved to the final mirror and focused the beam directly onto the eye. He and his father walked over to the sealed doorway. Again the beam faded to nothing.

"Clouds again," said Dawson.

"The spirits will bless us with light at the exact time of the eclipse," said the man in the cloak.

"What do we do?" Tank asked. He pointed at the mirror on the outside of the ruins. Clouds hadn't turned off the beam. In fact, there wasn't a cloud in the sky. Unable to support its own weight, the first mirror had shifted to the side. The notch that held it in place had become weathered over the years.

"Stay here," said Cosmo. "I'll fix it."

"Wait," whispered Tank. "They'll catch you." But Cosmo was already halfway to the entrance. He walked up to the mirror and pressed it as firmly as he could back into the hole. The beam shot down and ricocheted from one mirror to the other. The first lens immediately slid to the side again. Cosmo straightened it up and let it go, over and over. Down below it looked like someone was turning a light switch off and on.

"I'll check it out," said Dawson.

Cosmo heard footsteps coming as Blake entered the Dining Chamber. He quickly reached into his right nostril with his right index finger. He thrust it up in his nose farther than ever before. He pulled out a massive booger, stuck it around the base of the mirror, and cemented the beam back into place, just as Blake Dawson looked up into the stairwell. The light temporarily blinded him.

"Is someone there?" Blake held up his hand to block the beam. He walked up to the top of the stairs and looked around. Cosmo hid on the right side of the ant statue and tried not to move a muscle. Blake glanced up at the sky, where there were no clouds, and he rushed back down below.

Cosmo raced back to Tank.

"That rocked," Tank whispered. He held up his hand for a quiet high five. Cosmo gently slapped Tank's hand, and then looked down to see his hand coated in chocolate. Tank looked down at his hand and flicked off the boogers that Cosmo had so kindly transferred to him. The two of them wiped their hands on a nearby bush. Then the sky went dark.

"Whoa!" said Cosmo. The bright sunny day switched over to twilight as the moon covered more and more of the sun. Tank looked up and pointed at the brilliant halo that surrounded the moon when it blocked the sun. Dust rose from the entrance to the ruins. An eerie blue beam of light reflected off the first mirror into the tunnel. It bounced from one lens to the next and landed dead center on the oval mosaic. The oval eyelid rolled back into the wall and exposed a brilliant golden eye with an emerald green iris. The sealed doorway opened and slid sideways into the wall. The rumbling of its slow movement shook the foundation of the underground structure. Dirt and sand sifted through the cracks in the ceiling. A large amount of silt fell directly on Sebastian, turning her black hair to sandy brown. Dawson handed his father a lantern, and they entered the dark corridor. C.J. motioned to Sebastian that they should leave, and she passed the warning to Ollie, and they quickly ran back across the field to join Tank and Cosmo.

"Let's get out of here." Ollie waved toward the barracks. They ran back to the campsite, unnoticed by everyone except Carson and Dusty. The Fastest to the Fire competition had just finished, and everyone was looking at the leaderboard and the scores.

"Ollie!" Carson waved her arms. "Over here!"

The group merged together, and Ollie, even after all that had happened, squinted at the posted scores.

"Oh, your glasses." Carson reached into her shirt pocket. "Did you find the jewels? Tell me you found the jewels."

"Thanks," Ollie wiped his glasses with his shirttail before he put them on. "No, we didn't." He stepped closer to read the numbers. Carson looked disappointed.

"You took over second!" Ollie said. "Awesome! What happened?"

"Way to go, Dusty! Tell us about it!" said Tank.

"Well, um … we gathered the lichen … lots of it, the kind we needed, and, uh … Carson, you tell them." Dusty didn't want the others to know he had spent most of the time passed out in the clinic.

"Your glasses saved us!" said Carson. "The magnifier broke." Carson told the story of each team, ending with the Hermits. "They cheated again, and they weren't caught," she said, sounding discouraged.

"We're getting closer," said Ollie. The Stingrays took second place from the Dragons and were only 44 points behind the Hermits. The Hermits started their fire first and kept it ablaze for fifteen minutes, so they received 50 points. The Stingrays earned 40 points for successfully completing the task, even though they weren't the first. The Scorpions scored 30 points because they actually started a fire. The Dolphins and Dragons picked up the 20 attaboy points for good effort. With two competitions to go, the Dolphins' ship had hit an iceberg, and it was all but sunk. For the others, there was still hope.

"Now!" said Carson, frustrated. "What happened with you guys? Don't leave out any details."

"The guy in the black cloak is Blake Dawson's father," said Ollie.

"What?" said Carson, blinking. Cosmo and Tank were stunned.

"Let's go back to the barracks," said Ollie. "We can talk about it there. We don't have anything scheduled until lunch."

They strolled across the campground. Blake Dawson appeared from the western trail, slightly out of breath, and approached the group.

"Mr. Patrolli." Dawson was out of breath. "If I might have a word."

Ollie walked over to the director; the rest of the team stayed close by.

"I have noticed that …" Dawson began. He looked up at the team and caught them all with their ear to the wind. They quickly looked away, shuffled their feet, and whistled. Dusty didn't see the Chief looking at them, and he remained slightly bent over with his ear turned to listen. When he saw Dawson, he improvised and slapped his right ear as if something was going to fall from his left ear. Then he started to scratch behind his left ear, which caused his right leg to shake uncontrollably.

"How appropriate." Sebastian looked at Dusty with disbelief and then acceptance.

Dawson turned his attention back to Ollie.

"Mr. Pa ... Ollie. I noticed what a superb job you're doing with your team, and I have some things of great importance that need my attention. I am going to ask that you take over the counselor duties entirely. Do you think that would be a problem?"

"No problem, sir," said Ollie.

"Fine. I'll still check in with your team from time to time, and if you need anything immediately, you can contact one of the other counselors. I'm sure Kirk Christianson can assist you with whatever your team needs."

"Fine," said Ollie smartly.

"Fine," said Blake.

"Fine," said Ollie.

"Fine," said Blake.

"Fine," said Ollie.

Dawson hesitated and then gave Ollie a stern look. "Fine." He stretched the word out, and the look on his face ended the conversation. He turned and walked back up the trail.

"Fine," said Ollie as soon as the director disappeared around the brush.

"Fine!" said a loud voice from the trail. Ollie stopped. He couldn't believe Dawson heard him. Ollie folded his arms, mouthed "fine," and stuck his tongue out. The group made their way toward their barracks.

"That's the limit," said Sebastian. "First we have a counselor who can't find her way out of a paper bag, and she gets fired. Next we have a counselor who hangs out with Count Dracky. He goes and quits on us. Now we don't even have a counselor. No offense, Ollie, but you're supposed to be one of us. Carson has received a mysterious note, and we aren't sure if it was actually from her father or not. Oh yeah, there's a caveman who scares us to death, but then he turns around and saves our lives. We have no phones! Oh, and don't forget the dog without a real name."

"When did you dye your hair sandy brown?" asked Dusty.

This time Sebastian walked into the barracks and screamed. The rest of the group followed her in.

"I think Blake found something," explained Ollie. "It might be the three jewels mentioned in the note from Carson's father, or it might be the Book of Life, but it's definitely something big."

"You know what I think?" added Carson. "I think there's more than one strange thing going on around here."

"You can say that again." Sebastian looked over at Tank and Dusty. Tank licked chocolate from his shirtsleeve and from the empty wrapper in his hands. Dusty pulled the waist of his pants out in front and stared down as if he hoped underwear would suddenly appear.

"I think that caveman-looking dude is Baron von Nickleburg," said Carson. That's definitely his plane we saw crashed in the trees. He survived."

"How did he climb out of that massive hole?" asked Dusty. "Trust me. I saw from up close how far down it was, and there's no way anyone could climb down into it or climb up out of it."

"Good point," agreed Carson.

"What about Black Reef Island?" asked Ollie. "We saw that the cave went down deep into the ground, but we didn't go down there."

"And there was that boat," said Cosmo. "With tracks leading to and from the cave. Remember? It looked like something had been dragged up the hill."

"So, do you think this caveman guy, this Baron fellow, has anything to do with Dawson and his father?" asked Dusty.

"No," said Ollie. "I think the Baron is alive, and that's who we keep running into. I think Dawson has been running this camp for three years now, looking for something, and he's found it, but he had to wait until the eclipse to get it. As for the mysterious note for the Crenshaws, I don't think it has anything to do with the Baron or Dawson, unless Dawson has found what Mr. Crenshaw was looking for. What do you and C.J. think?" Ollie looked over at Carson.

"I don't know," said Carson. "C.J., what do you think?"

There was no answer. Everyone looked around. He wasn't there.

"Did he go outside?" asked Carson.

"Nope," said Sebastian, who was close to the door.

They looked out at the scoreboard. All the teams had dispersed. There was no one in the campground.

"Ollie, didn't he come back with you?" asked Carson.

"I can't say for sure; I was leading the way," said Ollie.

"I was right behind Ollie," said Sebastian.

"I was right behind Sebastian," said Cosmo.

"I was right behind ... well, OK ... I was way behind Cosmo," said Tank. "I didn't see anyone behind me. I just figured I was last."

"You mean he never came out?" said Carson anxiously. "He's still in there? What if he's gotten caught?"

"What are we going to do, Ollie?" asked Dusty.

Ollie lowered his head in thought and then looked across the campground at the scoreboard. Victory was in sight. It had taken three years to get within reach of the championship. It was almost lunchtime, and they would all be missed if they didn't show up. He looked down at his shockproof, rustproof, waterproof, GPS, weather-band, LCD, impact-resistant, MP3-capable wristwatch.

"We're going to have to make this quick," he said. "Let's go get him."

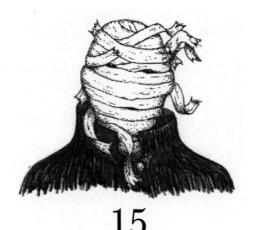

15

Rest in Peace

At last C.J. stopped trembling. He surmised that Dawson and his father had
retrieved some treasure and left for good. C.J. never saw Sebastian and Ollie take
off. He looked around with his flashlight beam to see if the coast was clear, but
when he looked back they were gone. He froze up, unable to decide if he should
make a dash for it or stay put. By the time he felt brave enough to scram, the
scuffling of footsteps and a lantern glow were coming from the newly opened
room. He found a hiding place and used his ears to learn what his eyes could not.

"He won't be able to get in without these," C.J. heard Dawson say as they
passed him on the way out of the Ceremonial Chamber.

C.J. heard Dawson's father respond in his deep, dead voice, "He's still alive. I
can feel it."

C.J. decided it might be too risky to try and go back to the barracks at that
moment. He walked to the newly opened chamber, picked up one of the lan-
terns, and cautiously stepped inside. A moth followed his light into the corridor
and became entwined in a spider's web, or what was left of it after Dawson and
his father had walked through.

C.J. jumped back a step, startled by the iridescent blue, eight-legged creature that descended upon the moth, entrapped in the web and unable to shake itself free. With grace and precision, the stationary spider spun the moth in a circle and released silk that entombed the moth and brought it to a standstill. C.J. clenched his teeth as he saw the spider bite the moth again and again before it attached the motionless bug to one of its hind legs and carried it, already decaying, to its lair. C.J. ducked under the remaining threads of the web and started trembling again from what he saw next.

Lining both sides of the corridor were stone statues unlike any statues he had ever seen. They weren't all the same height or size, and although the faces were similar, C.J. could tell they were different people. Sections the size of small shoeboxes standing on end was missing from the chests of the stone men. Golden urns rested in the hollow spaces. Clay vases with lids marked by inscriptions surrounded the base of each statue. At the end of the corridor was a small room with a large square platform in the middle, on which were three golden chests decorated elaborately with jewels. The chests were the size of cinder blocks, shaped like treasure chests with arching lids. In front of the platform was a similarly decorated chest, square and flat. C.J. opened the square one first, because it was closer and easier to reach. He put down the lantern, knelt in front of the chest, turned the latch, and lifted the lid.

Empty. He put down the lid and stood to examine the other three chests. He set the lantern on the platform, climbed up, and opened the center chest.

"Empty," he said out loud. He guessed as much for the other two but figured he should check to make sure. Both were empty. He surveyed the room to see if there was anything else to investigate. The walls were covered with inscriptions and drawings, none of which he could interpret.

Feeling lucky not to have been caught by now, he jumped down, retrieved the lantern, and left the room. He trotted past the statues and reentered the Ceremonial Chamber. He tiptoed to the doorway that led to the Dining Chamber. He poked his head around the corner, stepped in, and continued toward the exit. He looked back and accidentally kicked over a crate. The contents spilled and made a racket.

"That's the same stupid crate." He remembered that Ollie had bumped into it earlier.

He decided to make a run for it and darted toward the stairs. Before he got to the first step, black-gloved hands reached out of the shadows and grabbed him by the shoulders. C.J. yelped and jumped back. He saw a tall figure dressed in a long dark cloak. White bandage strips dangled from the face, which was concealed in the shadows.

"What are you doing down here?" said a low, crusty voice.

C.J. was too frightened to answer. It wasn't only that he was caught in a place where he shouldn't be; he knew that voice. He couldn't see the face, but he knew what it looked like. He had seen it on the porch at the beach house. He knew it was the same man Carson spotted at the tent in discussion with Dawson, the same man Dawson addressed as "Father" less than a half hour ago.

"Answer my question," demanded the man in the cloak.

"I … I left something in here … in there … the other d-d-d-day, and I came back to find it," C.J. answered, and waited a full ten seconds for a response.

"What?" the man asked in a loud, ghostly whisper.

"My headlamp and my sketch pad," answered C.J.

"I don't see them with you."

"When I got down there, I got scared and decided to get out of here."

"Are you scared now?" Dawson's father paced back and forth, still in the shadows.

"Yes, sir," said C.J. "But a different kind of scared."

"What do you mean?" hissed Dawson's father.

"I'm scared I'm going to get in trouble for not being with my team."

"Where are they?"

"Probably at lunch right now, sir," answered C.J. It crossed his mind that the team surely missed him by now, and there was a good chance that they would barrel down the stone steps at any moment.

"Then I suspect you'd better join them, Mr. Crenshaw." The man stepped out of the shadows and into the light. His face was fully wrapped in bandages, with hollow black holes where the eyes should be. Around his neck hung an animal charm necklace adorned with bones, teeth, and feathers from different animals and birds.

"I'll be sure my son doesn't catch wind of our little meeting. Go!"

"Yes, sir. Thank you, sir." C.J. leapt up the steps. At the top he slammed straight into a pile of Stingrays who had come to find him.

"C.J.! Are you OK?" Carson grabbed him by the shoulders.

"Yeah," said C.J. "I'm fine." He looked back into the entrance. "Why wouldn't I be?" he said a bit louder. "I was only looking for my headlamp and sketch pad. I couldn't find them." He winked for everyone to play along.

"Oh, right," said Tank. "Well, time to eat now. We'll find them later."

"Yeah," said Cosmo. "Don't worry about it. We'll find them later."

"Right," said Ollie. "Let's go eat."

"You didn't leave your sketch pad, I saw it in your—"

Wham! Sebastian slapped Dusty across the back of the head.

"He was looking for his headlamp and sketchpad, but couldn't find it, so now we're going to eat." Sebastian gave Dusty a go-along-with-us-or-you're-going-to-get-it look.

"Oh, yeah." Dusty rubbed his jaw. "The sketchpad and the head slap … I mean headlamp."

The team gave Dusty a stern glare as they pushed past him toward the dining pavilion.

"Huh hittin haf hany heis?" Tank tried to speak and munch a loaded cheeseburger at the same time.

"Open mouth, remove burger, chew, swallow, talk," said Sebastian with a sigh, as if she had said these words before. Tank responded, going through the steps of Eating 101.

"He didn't have any eyes?" Tank asked.

"No, he didn't," said C.J. "Just big black holes."

"I'm sure he had eyes," said Carson. "You can't see without eyes. It was probably too dark to see them."

"What happened to him?" asked Dusty. "Why was he wearing all those bandages?"

"How would I know?" answered C.J. "We didn't exactly sit down for a friendly discussion or anything. I've told you everything he said."

"What I can't get is how he knew your name," said Ollie.

"Maybe he's the one who wrote the note," said Carson. "Maybe he has our dad and is using us to try and find something for him."

"I'd say no to that idea," said Cosmo. "When he wanted to find something, he and Dawson didn't need any help getting it."

"I agree," said Ollie.

"So all the chests were empty?" asked Cosmo. "And there was no other door?"

"Right," said C.J. "But I did feel some kind of air whishing around in there. I couldn't tell where it was coming from. I almost brought back one of the vases from one of those statues. It's a good thing I didn't. If I had been holding one of those when Mr. Creepy caught me … boy."

"Those are canopic jars." Ollie explained. Everyone stopped eating and turned to face him. "Many ancient civilizations mummified their kings and pharaohs. They would remove their organs and preserve them in jars, all but the heart, because that's where they believed the essence of the person dwelled. If the tribe or group believed in gods, usually the jars would have a lid shaped like the head of one of those gods to protect the person."

"These jars didn't have any specially shaped lids," said C.J. "But the ones at their feet were made of clay, and there were inscriptions on them."

"I don't think the Wagapi embalmed their leaders," said Ollie. "They probably embalmed their main organs, and that's what's in the jars, except that the larger jar in their chest is probably their ashes gathered from the Burial Site. They would burn the bodies, hoping to release their spirits to an afterlife or some other realm or something."

"If you'll excuse me," said Dusty. "I'm going back to the barracks to use the restroom. I need to release something back to the underworld myself."

No one said anything for a full minute.

"This is hopeless," said Carson. "We know bits and pieces about this and that, but we don't know everything about anything."

"I have a plan." Ollie called for everyone's attention again. "I think we need to finish out today's schedule to perfection. After C.J. was seen in the ruins, they may be watching us closely. We have a trip to the Burial Site again at 1:00, then a war paint and jewelry-making workshop at 2:30. Dinner is at 5:30. Planning time for tomorrow's competition after that, then learn the new ceremonial dance by the campfire. I think we may have a shorter planning period tonight, because I'm hearing that they want to make up for missing a dance the other night due to weather, and we may learn two dances tonight. One is a welcoming dance the Wagapi performed when other tribes visited their island for trading. We have to dance with other teams for that one."

"I'm not dancing with a Hermit!" said Carson.

"We may not have a choice," said Ollie. "Anyway, here's the rest of my plan. Tomorrow is the fourth competition, the Medicine Man. Cosmo, you'll be on your own for this one. That's your specialty, given your family's history."

"No problem," said Cosmo.

"As for the rest of us, it's time to find out some answers while the Challenge is going on. That means a trip to Black Reef Island."

"That place is creepy," said Carson.

"Well, we only went a little way into the cave, but it continued on down; I think we need to go and check it out. There were a lot of suspicious tracks around the cave entrance. We might find something or someone there that will help us make sense of all this mess."

"Can I have everyone's attention for a moment?" The teams slowly became quiet and turned to see Blake Dawson standing patiently with his hands folded.

"I have something remarkable to share with you. For three years now we've been trying to solve the mystery of how to enter the sealed doorway in the Ceremonial Chamber. I'm excited to tell you that it was opened this morning. This chamber is the Wagapi's Hall of King's Souls, a room where all the kings of the Wagapi were entombed and their spirits sent to join their spiritual gods. You only have a few days left here at Camp Remnant, and we want you to take pleasure in our discovery, so we are asking your counselors to find a time slot on your schedule so that you may visit this sacred room.

"There is much to see, and I'm going to ask you not to touch any of the statues, or items within the statues, for it would show tremendous disrespect to our ances ... to the Wagapi people. We haven't been able to find any descendants here on Crater Island, but we are confident they're here. So, with that said, I'll let you get back to your lunch. Enjoy the rest of your day, and we'll see you at the dances tonight."

Dawson spoke to Kirk Christianson before leaving. The pavilion was abuzz with anticipation.

"I wonder what he's talking to Kirk about?" said Ollie, curious but also slightly jealous. "I can tell you more about this camp in my sleep than he'll know in his lifetime."

"Settle down, Muhammad Ollie," said Carson. "We've got more important things to talk about. Did you guys catch some of the things Dawson said?"

"Nothing we didn't already figure out ourselves," said C.J. "I pretty much described it all to you."

"No," said Carson. "There was more in what he said. He slipped up one time and referred to the statues as his ancestors. I think he might be descended from the Wagapi, which means his father is too."

"That doesn't change anything," said Sebastian. "And it doesn't solve any of our problems, either."

"That's not all," continued Carson. "He also said 'We haven't been able to find any of them here on Crater Island,' meaning he's been looking for them. Why? Why would he be looking for descendants of the Wagapi?"

"Great," said Sebastian. "Why don't we add that to our list of questions? You know, the ones we're answering instead of having fun?"

"I just thought of something," said C.J. "What if the boat isn't there? It may be over on the island if someone is using it, which they obviously are, judging by the footprints."

"Hang on." Ollie picked up his backpack and pulled out a small booklet. He thumbed through it, and his eyes followed his fingers down a page.

"Here it is; we're in luck. This book list the times for high and low tides around the world, and it says here that in the morning, when we go to Black Reef Island, it'll be low tide. I noticed when we went across on the boat that there was a sand bar close to the surface that stretched from Crater Island to Black Reef Island. If the boat isn't there, then we'll just walk across the sand bar. It might even be above water at low tide, I'm not sure."

"Well," Dusty returned to the table. "I got 'em."

"Got what?" asked C.J.

"New bloomers," said Dusty. "Three new pairs. A truck delivered them to the supply store today. I've asked them every day if they'd have some delivered up here. They were on my bunk."

"Good for you. They'll last you until we leave camp," said Cosmo.

"What are you talking about?" asked Sebastian. "They'll last him until next year, maybe the next three years."

"One problem solved, fifty more to go," said Tank.

◆   ◆   ◆

They were ten minutes late for their second trip to the Burial Site. They arrived at the entrance marked by the gravestones and hesitated for a moment. Then they huddled close together, ran down the path, and stopped as one when any sound echoed from the thick jungle. When they arrived, they were still a little on edge. Soon, though, they realized that if there were any wild dogs in the area, the Stingrays all would have been eaten by now. Or at least Tank, the slowest person in the group, would have been eaten. Except for Sebastian, everyone focused on the areas around the three flat-topped stone pyramids. Cosmo and Dusty sketched the animal statues. C.J. and Carson dug delicately around the base of the smaller pyramid on the left, while Ollie and Tank did the same at the one on the right. Sebastian dug around three similarly-shaped rocks lodged securely in the ground, their rounded tops exposed. They were the same ones she had stumbled on during their last visit. It wasn't long until Ollie announced that they needed to wrap things up.

"That wasn't much time," said Dusty.

"Well," said Ollie, "We got here late, and then it took us twenty minutes to walk down the path to get here instead of the normal five minutes because you guys were scared of all the sounds in the trees."

"Oh, and I suppose you weren't scared?" Carson emphasized the last few words. "I thought someone was cooking popcorn until I realized it was your teeth chattering. What is it with guys? You never can admit you're scared."

"I was scared," said Dusty.

"That wasn't my teeth," said Ollie.

"Then what was it?" asked Carson.

"It was my knees," said Ollie with a grin. The Stingrays chuckled at Ollie's surrender, except Sebastian, who stood up and looked at the backside of one of the three rocks.

"Hey, Cosmo!" she said. "Come take a look at this before we leave."

Cosmo and the group stared at the three rocks for a moment, and Cosmo finally said what they were all thinking.

"It looks like three rocks."

Sebastian let out a sigh, looked upward, and shook her head. She slowly looked over at Cosmo.

"I'm not talking about that side. Around here, on this side. This middle one has something carved into it. Do you know what it means?"

Cosmo walked around the rocks, bent down, dusted away some dirt, and ran his fingers along the lines carved into the stone. He stood up with his mouth open and his eyes shifting back and forth among the three rocks.

"What does it say?" asked Sebastian.

"It says *Rest in peace, the spirits are with you*," said Cosmo. "These aren't ordinary rocks. These are tombstones."

16

The Calm Before the Storm

"How do I look?" Dusty blinked his eyes.

"Dude!" Cosmo shook his head. "We're supposed to learn how to put on war paint and make it spiritually pleasing, not try to look like girls."

"They are." Dusty pointed at Carson and Sebastian.

"Dude! They *are* girls."

"As I was saying," Ollie tried to help as best he could, thinking about earlier war paint sessions at Camp Remnant. "By grinding these green leaves with this pestle, you can make a juice that can be used as a green paint, and as you can see on Carson and Sebastian, it makes ... oh yeah, and on Dusty, too ... it makes great eye shadow, but that's not what the Wagapi used it for. They mainly used this lighter shade of green to decorate their bodies for their dances, especially to try to please the spirits."

"That looks real nice on you three girls." Tank gave Cosmo a high five. Dusty frowned, grabbed a towel, and rubbed his eyes vigorously.

"Over here in this bowl are some red berries," said Ollie. "You can grind them up into a blood-red paint, but red was used only for battles. The Wagapi didn't use red very much, because they were the only ones who lived on this island, and they had no enemies. There's a myth that the only time red was used was when a young man betrayed his brother over jealousy, in order to be king of the Wagapi."

"That's what I want." C.J. reached for the bowl with his fingers outstretched, ready to make a big scoop.

"No! Wait!" said Ollie. "When you put on some paints, like this one, you need to use this stick. It's narrow and flat, and it makes very straight lines on your face as you paint. Indians would whittle sticks this way or sometimes even carve a small design in the end so that they could paint special lines on their face and chest."

"Cool," said C.J. He lifted the stick and dipped it in the dye. He made a scrape across his right cheek. "How's that?"

"Wicked," said Tank. "Put one on the other side to match."

"The other colors here came from different clays found in the soil, usually near creeks," explained Ollie. "They don't need to be ground up."

"What about his one?" Sebastian grabbed a stick, dipped it into a bowl, and made four streaks of blue across each of her cheeks. She accidentally got a smidge in the corner of her mouth. "Yuck! This isn't poisonous, is it?"

"No, but that blue one," explained Ollie, "is obtained from duck droppings."

SPLAT!

Sebastian turned her head, and her mouth erupted like a volcano all over Dusty. Bits of blue duck dung covered his face.

"Oh! Dusty, I'm so sorry," said Sebastian.

"Really?" Dusty smiled with a blue-freckled face and decided that his foot was in the door, even if it was because of duck doo spray.

"No," she replied.

They continued to decorate their faces with the dyes, although no one used the blue one. They ran out of paint, because C.J. and Tank took off their shirts and decorated their chests, and Tank's belly required a large amount of paint.

Then it was time to design jewelry. Each camper was given a long strand of black twine, many silver beads, and a pendant-sized, flat piece of turquoise. Ollie explained how to engrave a picture on the blue-green surface, one that reflected their inner thoughts or their inner spirit, and then he showed them how to construct a necklace with their materials.

"All we get to make is a necklace?" asked Carson. "What about matching earrings or a bracelet?"

"A necklace," answered Ollie.

"That's cheesy," said Sebastian.

The team worked silently engraving their pendants, with occasional glances at the others' carvings. Ollie engraved E=MC squared. Tank tried to chisel out a double quarter pounder with cheese. C.J. spelled out *C.J. was here.* Dusty engraved a pair of briefs with the number 28 in the center. Cosmo replicated the eclipse mosaic above the no-longer-sealed doorway. The girls put a bit more thought into their pieces. They knew they would wear them back home around their friends, unlike the boys, who would throw them into the back of a drawer, never to be seen again until they packed up for college. Carson sat some distance away from the others, to keep her design a secret. Sebastian inscribed an angel.

"Just like me," she held it up to show everyone.

"It's missing a few things," said Dusty.

"Like what?"

"The head needs horns, the face needs fangs, and you're missing your pitch-fork," said Dusty.

The team focused on Ollie as he explained how to finish assembling the neck-lace, but as he demonstrated how to attach the fasteners, a loud screech from the tree above stole everyone's attention. Perched high on a moss-covered branch was a beast of a bird some 40 inches high, with white feathers on its head and breast and deep blue wings. Its talons were as big as a grizzly bear's claws, and it had a large, black, hooked beak. No one said a word. They looked up in awe of the rap-tor that stared down at them as if they might be next on its menu.

"Harpia harpyja," said Ollie. "More commonly called the Harpy Eagle. They are very rare. Beautiful, absolutely beautiful." Everyone agreed.

"The Wagapi held them in high regard. The Harpy Eagles were supposedly protectors of the kings. One story tells of a king's infant son who had come under attack by three gila monsters. A Harpy Eagle swooped down, killed the lizards, and swallowed them in one gulp. The king then decreed that Harpy Eagles were never to be harmed because they possessed the protective spirits of kings past."

"Why is it looking at us like we're about to become its next meal?" asked Carson.

"It shouldn't bother us," said Ollie, "although it does sometimes feed on small monkeys and slow-moving sloths."

C.J. stepped behind Carson.

The bird let out an ear-piercing screech and flew off gracefully through the vines and branches of the jungle, despite its twelve-foot wingspan.

"She's probably off for dinner," said Ollie.

"Us too," said Tank. "Time to eat." His internal alarm clock growled.

After dinner, the team took turns grilling Cosmo about how to remedy an assortment of body malfunctions using jungle flora and fauna. Ollie did his homework when he chose Cosmo for the team; each time they questioned him, Cosmo not only knew the answer, but also told a story about how his grandfather performed a similar medical miracle.

Just as Ollie predicted, two dances were on the menu for the night's ceremonies. One, performed only in the springtime, was the Dance of Innocence Lost, announcing the coming of age of a young Wagapi. The other, the Festival of Peace, welcomed other tribes to the island for trade. Tank was a butterfly in the first dance.

"They can't make wings big enough to get you off the ground," shouted Daegel as the Hermits rolled with laughter.

"I don't want to say you better win tomorrow, Cosmo," said Carson, "but you better win tomorrow."

"My dad says we should kill our enemies with kindness," said Ollie, "except there was that one time when our neighbor was mowing the grass, and his lawn mower hit a screwdriver that had been left in the yard. The screwdriver flew out from the mower and struck my dad's 1967, mint condition, royal blue convertible vette right smack in the windshield and shattered it to pieces."

"What did your father say then?" asked Cosmo.

"Do you want me to leave out the swear words?" asked Ollie politely.

"Yes," said Cosmo.

Ollie paused. "He didn't say anything."

Kirk Christianson spoke to everyone.

"Thanks to all of you who pupated … I mean participated as butterflies in that dance. It was a time of great celebration for the tribe when an adolescent transformed from childhood to adulthood, and more responsibilities were taken up by the young men and women presented at the ceremony.

"Now for our last dance, the Festival of Peace. We changed it by adding a few things so that you might enjoy it a bit more. Before, only the men danced during times of trade among tribes, as a show of fellowship and trust, but times have changed, and we don't think it would be fun for our lady campers if they had to sit around watching the boys do their thing. Since it was originally a dance done in pairs, we have followed that tradition and changed it into a dance done by two or more people. We've decided to allow you to dance with anyone you want, no ceremony and no rehearsal, just a slow dance."

The counselors converged and started to play homemade instruments, such as flutes made from hollowed-out cane and drums made from hog skin wound tightly over hollow stumps.

The girls looked around at each other with smirky smiles.

All the boys sat frozen. Nothing horrified a preteen boy more than being told he must dance with a girl. Each boy's peripheral vision got a workout, since no one dared make eye contact with anyone else. Most of the boys said, either out loud or to themselves, "I will as soon as someone else does." Others reasoned that whichever girl got chosen, that would be the girl they wanted to ask also, so they would be off the hook by forfeit and manage to save face.

The girls got restless as they began to realize that the boys were hopeless. It was going to be up to them if there was to be any dancing and no way were they going to pass up the opportunity to dance. They strategized the who-dances-with-whom decisions and went so far as to make backup plans three to five guys deep in case their first few choices were already taken.

Dusty, all talk and no walk, made time go faster by gazing at the fire and trying to see which glowing bit of ember would drift up into the sky the highest. Then he felt a light tap on the shoulder. It was Dawn Ryebaker, a charming, petite, red-haired girl from the Dolphins who did her best to smile and not show her braces.

"Would you like to dance with me?" She extended a hand to Dusty.

"Who, me?" Dusty answered, realizing how stupid it was to say that.

"Yes."

"Sure." He took her hand. They strolled out near the fire and turned to face each other. They settled into the twelve-year-old's waddle version of a slow dance.

"I was going to ask her, so I guess I can't dance now," said C.J., relieved.

"That was who I was going to ask," said Cosmo.

"Me too," said Ollie. "Looks like we'll have to sit this one out."

"I was just about to get up and ask her too," said Tank.

"You guys are pathetic," said Carson. "You're all a pathetic, immature, shallow-minded, half-witted, nincompoop, blockheaded bunch of baloney."

"That's no way to ask me to dance," said Tank.

Carson walked directly over to the Dragons and asked Thomas Frankenfield to dance, which left a disappointed look on most of the other girls' faces. He was very handsome, with emerald green eyes, and he was also taller than any of the girls.

All the boys gazed as the two couples danced. The girls started to move about and ask boys to dance, fearing that all the best ones would be gone if they didn't act fast. All the girls, that is, except Sebastian. She tried to hide her sulky feelings as she watched Dusty dance with Dawn.

"Excuse me," she said to Cosmo and the others. "I think I'm going to turn in for the night. I'm not feeling well." She rushed off to the barracks.

"What's with her?" asked C.J. The boys shrugged their shoulders. C.J. felt a tap on his shoulder. It was Heidi Ringer, the tallest girl at the camp, from the Scorpions. Before C.J. could react, she grabbed him by the arm and swept him away to dance. His head was barely above her waist, and he looked up to see her smiling down at him. The smile exposed two exceptionally large front teeth, which took up most of her narrow face, which matched her thin frame.

Molly Maples from the Dragons walked up to Tank, smiled with her hands behind her back, and stopped in front of him. Molly looked like Tank's fraternal twin sister in almost every possible way, with the exception of the long, brown hair that draped her backside.

"What?" he asked unenthusiastically. "I can't dance. It's a hereditary thing on my daddy's side."

Molly, being prepared for rejection, brought her right hand into view. It held a super-size Cuda Chocolate Bar, shaped like a barracuda, that she had purchased at the camp supply store. Tank didn't hesitate to accept the bribe. He took the bar and broke it in half to share with Molly. She unwrapped her share, and before they started to dance, she and Tank devoured their candy. They danced the rest of the dances together with chocolate rings around their mouths.

Aubrey Meadows dragged a petrified Cosmo to the dance floor. Like many of the couples, Aubrey did all the dancing, which suited her just fine. Cosmo, like many of the other boys, stood and looked constipated. He shifted a foot here and there, out of rhythm, and he never caught on that his movements were supposed to be in sync with the music. Aubrey might as well have danced with a tree, a fact that she seemed to ignore. She knew that it wouldn't matter to her friends how bad a dancer he was, but rather how good a dancer she was.

By now only two people remained around the fire: Ollie Patrolli, and Patti Eslinger from the Dolphins. Like Ollie, she wore glasses, and the lenses were as thick as Ollie's. They grinned at each other. Ollie gave Patti his best formal bow as he pointed to the dance floor. Patti looked right and left to make sure that he wasn't asking someone else, and then she nodded and took his hand. Ollie introduced himself, and they started the waddle.

"My name is ..."

"Ollie Patrolli!" she interrupted. "I know who you are."

"And you're Patti Eslinger. From Montana, I believe."

"How did you know that?" she asked flattered.

"I know a little about everyone here," he answered. "I also know that you're the captain of your middle school math team, just like me."

"Patti Patrolli," she whispered. She didn't think Ollie could hear her, but he did. Ollie's face turned scarlet red. They danced the evening away, discussing various ways to solve three unknowns in a differential equation.

Afterwards, the Stingrays walked back to the barracks and thoughtfully readied themselves for bed. No one spoke a word of the dance, by reason of either embarrassment or nervousness about what lay ahead at dawn. They settled into their cots and stared at the thatch on the ceiling, mostly thinking about what no one knew: what lay deep in the cave on Black Reef Island. Sleep finally overwhelmed them and stilled their thoughts, except for Sebastian, who hadn't thought of the next day at all.

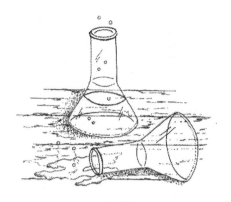

17

'VEN'OM

Ollie was up and dressed before sunrise. Thunder from the latest of the routine storms growled off the coast. The Medicine Man competition started promptly after breakfast and would last until lunch. After that, Ollie penciled in the Stingrays for a three-hour visit to the newly opened chamber, which, of course, they would not show up for. He calculated travel time to and from the small island. He even provided for intangible delays, including the weather, snack breaks, and how well Tank could keep up with the team. As the rest of the crew awoke, he instructed them to check and make sure their backpacks were fully equipped. Everyone was still eerily quiet. The only voice was Ollie's, giving instructions.

"Cosmo," said Ollie. "Remember, stay in the barracks when you finish the competition."

"Got it." Cosmo didn't look up from his notes on natural remedies.

"Right after breakfast, we'll go over to the leaderboard, and I'll keep watch and tell the rest of you when the coast is clear and you can slip down the eastern trail."

Everyone nodded, put on their slickers, and picked up their backpacks. Dusty didn't fully zip up one of the compartments, and his headlamp fell out as he lifted it the bag to his shoulder.

"Here." Sebastian picked it up and handed it back to him. "You dropped this, and you're going to need it." Her eyes focused squarely on his.

"Uh, yeah, thanks." Dusty looked confused.

"Keep your backpack hanging down low, hidden under your raincoat," said Ollie.

Tank waited at the door, and Ollie gave him the signal to lead them down to the pavilion for breakfast. After they ate, they followed Ollie's plan to perfection and disappeared from the crowd of campers, who were busy talking about the competition. Ollie looked back at Cosmo and gave him a thumbs-up before he too slipped out of sight.

When they reached the beach, the shoreline of Black Reef Island was barely visible due to a thin fog that blanketed the ocean and the beach. The team squinted into the fog, looking for the boat. Lightning flashed between the clouds, creating enough light for Carson to spot it lying upside down on the opposing bank.

"It looks like we're going to have to cross the sand bar," said Ollie. "The water shouldn't get any higher than our boots. It's low tide right now, and when we come back, we can take the boat. The sand bar starts over here, but it's very narrow, and you can't really go very far off either way without the water getting deeper. Follow me, and stay close."

Ollie stepped into the shallow water and walked out toward the sand bar. He stepped lightly onto it and began to cross, using the toe of his boot to test the depth of the water and the firmness of the sand before each step. Each person focused on the ripples from the footprints of the person in front of them, trying to step in the same spot. They reached the halfway point, and, as predicted, the water had reached no higher than their ankles. Then the fog thickened, and they couldn't see Black Reef Island or Crater Island from where they were. They could barely make out the person in front of them or the person behind them.

SPLASH!

"What was that?" asked Dusty. "It came from our right."

"Just a fish," said Ollie, not so sure.

SPLISH!

"There's another one," said C.J. "That's a pretty big fish."

SPLASH!

"That came from behind me." Tank brought up the rear.

"What's making them jump?" asked C.J.

Ollie stopped, and everyone came to a halt. Without the sounds of their feet flopping, they could hear what sounded like a small waterfall to their right. The rushing sound got closer and louder every second.

"What is that?" asked Sebastian. "A waterspout?"

"Whatever it is, it's coming this way," said Carson.

Ollie stepped to the right of the team, still on the spit of sand. He shouted directions over the percolating water.

"We need to go, now! Get across quickly!"

The sound was close now, its source still hidden in the fog.

"Why? What is it?" shrieked Carson.

Then Tank saw a large silver flash jump clear out of the water over the sand bar and he yelled ear-piercingly.

"BARRACUDAS!"

C.J. was in front. He ran across the top of the sand path as fast as he could, followed closely by the rest of the team. The fish jumped in frenzy and swiftly gained on them. One leapt into the air, latched on to Tank's backpack with its razor-sharp teeth, and gnawed. Tank reached around, grabbed the fish by its tail, and made it let go of his backpack, just as a second assassin blasted out of the water straight for him. Tank swung the barracuda like a bat and made a solid connection with the other assailant. The blow knocked the fish he was holding senseless and sent the second attacker spinning through the air.

Tank lost his sense of direction and could no longer see Dusty, who had been right in front of him, and then he heard splashes on all sides. He couldn't tell if they were coming from the barracudas or the other members of the team. Then he heard a terrible scream, and he dashed helplessly through the fog toward the sound. C.J. made it to Black Reef. He turned and started to shout so that the others could hear him and follow his voice in the fog. Carson made it to the island next, followed by Ollie. They yelled for the others. Sebastian broke through the fog and plopped down on the sand, her right arm bleeding from a deep gash near the elbow. Carson rushed to help her as Ollie and C.J. continued to shout encouragement to the others.

"Dusty! Tank! Over here! Run this way!"

"Let's get up to the cave," Carson told Sebastian. "It's beginning to rain again and we need to get your raincoat off so we can see how bad you're hurt."

Carson screamed and jumped back as a large barracuda flew through the air and landed near her feet.

"It's dead!" yelled Ollie.

"Take that! And that!" came a familiar voice from the fog, as two dead 'cudas sailed over their heads.

Tank emerged from the watery mist. He still held his fish in one hand and a tattered and torn backpack in the other.

"Hey, Dusty!" he said. "I found your backpack in the water back there."

He saw the horror in the others' eyes and realized that Dusty wasn't there. The crew all screamed his name, but there was no reply. The sound of the flopping fish faded as quickly as it had begun. The falling rain diminished the fog, and the northern shore of Crater Island was now visible. There was no sign of Dusty.

"We have to go back and find him," said Tank. "I'll go."

"We can't risk it," said Ollie. "The barracudas might return. The tide is rising. Sebastian was bitten, and there's blood in the water. Sharks may be around, so even the small boat is too risky. Either a shark or a 'cuda could tear it to shreds. Dusty isn't on Crater Island, or we'd see him."

Rain rolled down their cheeks.

◆   ◆   ◆

The storm moved the competition under the main pavilion.

"You each must draw one of the ailments from the urn, and you will have as much time as you need to collect the proper ingredients and make a remedy," said Topper Billingsly, the Scorpions' counselor.

"All the things you need, and some that you don't need, are in the crates on the shelves. Before you burn or boil anything, make sure you check with me that it is safe to do so. Each team will have its own table with the tools you need, and when you think you have it done, call me over and I'll grade you. The highest score for this competition is 50 points for making a cure to treat the condition you select. No points are awarded for finishing first, and everyone will get a score, provided you don't create something that would kill a person."

The campers laughed and several acted out a horrific and painful poisoning. Topper held out the urn, and each of the five contestants reached in and pulled out a rolled parchment.

"On my mark, unroll your scroll and get started," said Topper. "After you open it, hand it to me and I will write the disease or condition you select on the board for everyone to see. Are there any questions? No? Then you may begin."

Cosmo unrolled his paper. In red letters it said *poisonous bite wound*.

He grinned confidently, handed the scroll to Topper, and went to the ingredient shelf to gather materials.

A very odd thing happened to everyone else in the competition: they seemed to catch a slight case of the ailment they drew. Paul Shuttlebus of the Dragons chose *chronic cough,* and he coughed every minute or so. Bartholomew Jenkins of the Scorpions pressed his palm to his forehead after he drew *headache* from the urn. Veronica Stamps of the Dolphins rubbed her stomach. Ven drew *skin disease* and began to scratch here and there, more on his bottom than anywhere else.

Cosmo didn't feel poisoned at all. He browsed among the tadpoles, skull of catfish, cuttlebone, sweet beer, pine resin, and soot until he found powdered grounds from a dried-up lizard and some Spanish leeks. He took them back to his table, cut the leeks into tiny cubes, and used a pestle to combine the two ingredients, forming a mushy brown paste. Cosmo walked back to the materials to look for a strainer to separate the mixture. Ven returned to the Hermits table with his ingredients. Seeing how far ahead Cosmo was, he conveniently bumped hard into Cosmo's table. The jolt knocked everything off. All the campers, with the exception of the Hermits, stood open-mouthed at the sight of Cosmo's wet paste on the ground.

"Uh … sorry about that," said Ven. "I was holding so many things that they blocked my view, you see, and I accidentally bumped into your table. Looks like everything's ruined." Ven gave Daegel a satisfied wink.

Cosmo walked over and picked up the bowl and pestle. His mixture was spread over the dirt floor of the pavilion. He would have to start over. He kept his wits about him and went back to the cabinets to gather what he needed once again, but the shelves were out of the necessary ingredients.

"Mr. Billingsly," said Cosmo. "There are no more lizard grounds or Spanish leeks."

"I'm sorry." Topper shrugged his shoulders. "You'll have to use what we have."

"But …"

"There's nothing I can do," said Topper. "It was an accident."

Cosmo looked over at Ven, who waggled his fingers in a wave and gave him a sinister smile.

◆   ◆   ◆

Carson wrapped a strap from Dusty's bag around Sebastian's arm to stop the bleeding. The team huddled in the cave, still shaken by the uncertainty of what might have happened to Dusty. Black Reef Island received only the edge of the storm's wrath, until the winds changed and brought thundering fury down on its plant-covered slopes.

"It's too dangerous to cross back over now," said Ollie as he looked out through the curtain of water that fell across the cave entrance. "No one knows we're here except Cosmo, and he won't think we're late until six hours and fourteen minutes from now. We've waited long enough here. I think we should do exactly what we came here to do. We have to see where this cave leads."

"We'll stay here," shouted Carson, thinking of Dusty. "Sebastian and I, in case we hear anything."

"No, I think we should all go together," said Ollie. "It will be safer for all of us. I think it's clear that someone doesn't want us here. Those barracudas didn't appear by themselves."

"You mean somebody may be using the Book of Life?" asked C.J.

Ollie nodded. "Someone's been trying to get us to leave the island since we came here. We may find some of the answers to all this down in the cave. Let's get going."

"Dusty!" C.J. called, turning his ear to the wind. Everyone stood still and quiet. There was no reply.

"Even if he made it back to the other shore, we couldn't hear him in this monsoon!" Ollie tried to speak louder than the driving rain. "Let's go!"

They followed Ollie into the cave and down the torchlit cobblestone corridor. Sebastian, at the end of the line, turned once more to look back at the cave entrance, then started forward. The long slope downward was cold and damp, but the air smelled fresh. A rushing sound echoed in the winding stone hallway, getting louder as they walked. The path widened and formed the entrance to one of the cave's large chambers.

Ollie paused and held up his hand, motioning to the others to stop and be quiet. He saw that the rushing sound came from a wide underground stream that flowed from one end of the cavern to the other. He also heard a voice, but he couldn't make out any words over the noise from the rolling water. He moved toward the cavern entrance, but in doing so he dislodged a small rock that rolled and bounced down the slope of the cavern and plopped into the stream. The voice went silent.

◆   ◆   ◆

Cosmo didn't panic. He tried to remember some of the remedies his grandfather taught him, such as how to apply the brown spit from chewing tobacco to a bee sting. He studied the materials on the shelves. He had used only half of the leeks for his first antidote, so all he needed was ground powder from a dried lizard. He picked up some owl pellets and noticed a tiny brown tail sticking out from one of the casings. He took a closer look and sure enough it was a thin brown scat, possibly from a lizard.

"The owl must have spit out this pellet before it fully digested this lizard," he said out loud to himself.

"What's that?" asked Topper.

"Oh nothing." Cosmo grinned. "Just talking to myself. Sorry."

As he walked to his table, Cosmo meandered past the others as they mixed their prescriptions. Bartholomew bubbled a concoction over a burner; a catfish skull poked out of the top of the pot. The boiling water animated the skull, making it look as if the fish was attempting to escape. Bartholomew's headache worsened. Veronica's mixture of plants, sweet beer, and fruits foamed like a top-heavy shake. She looked paler than normal and held a barf bucket close to her face. Things were no better for Sherri or Ven. Sherri coughed so much that she gagged and gave Veronica's barf-bucket a longing look. Ven was the funniest of all. He scratched feverishly in so many places that he looked like he was being attacked by a swarm of bees.

Cosmo shuffled back to his table and picked apart the pieces of the owl pellet. He separated feathers and small bones to reach the morsels attached to the brown tail. He let out a sigh of disappointment when he realized that it wasn't a lizard's tail, but that of a small mouse. He knew the chance of being able to make something that would suffice without a lizard's tail was zero.

"We're doomed." He spoke low enough that no one heard him.

Cosmo stood up, moping, and shuffled over to Topper, who patted Sherri on the back as if her coughing was caused by something lodged in her throat.

"Mr. Billingsly, sir," said Cosmo loudly so that he could be heard over the coughing and slapping.

"Yes, Cosmo?" Topper turned and walked away from Sherri, glad to be rescued from having to tend to her.

"Is she going to be all right?" asked Cosmo.

"They all will," said Topper. "A weak mind is a powerful tool that can play tricks on the body. By the way, I don't see you acting as if you've been bitten by anything poisonous. Are you finished?"

"Yes, sir ... well, sort of."

"What do you mean?" asked Topper.

"I forfeit. There are no more dried lizards, and I can't make it without that."

"What a shame." Topper shook his head. "And I believe your team was in second place, wasn't it?"

Topper nodded.

"Maybe next time you'll be a little more careful when you're doing an experiment of this sort."

"It wasn't my fault," said Cosmo, surprised. "Ven purposely …"

"Mr. Jeffries," said Topper sternly. "You call an accident exactly what it is … an accident."

Cosmo stared at the ground to hide his anger. He had made a successful remedy, and he could do it again if there were more materials.

"Mr. Billingsly, sir," said Cosmo. "Is it possible to get any kind of partial credit in this competition? I mean, in the Fastest to the Fire, some of the teams got points even though they never made a fire. I can tell you exactly what it takes to make a medicine for a poisonous bite wound and the right way to make it."

Topper brought his hand up to his chin. "Hmmm. That may be possible. I'll talk to Mr. Christianson about it when we finish here. I have some paper and pencils on my table there. Write out your remedy and tell how to prepare it. If Kirk says it's OK, then maybe we can give you some credit."

"Thank you, sir." Cosmo felt slightly better. He took paper and pencil back to his table and wrote out the recipe in detail. He handed it to Topper and sat down again. Under the word Stingrays on the scoreboard, Topper wrote *forfeit* in big letters. The Hermits roared as they saw that another Adventure Challenge championship was in their sights.

18

Death Twice Cheated

The cobblestone corridor was drafty and cold, and it smelled of musk and mildew. The entire team sweated with fear. Their backs were firmly pasted to the wall as they tried to stay hidden from the person who had spoken, who was somewhere in the cave. Ollie listened for footsteps, whispers, anything, but he heard nothing over the swiftly flowing water.

He glanced back at the others, gestured with his hands, and mouthed, "I'm going to look around the corner." Everyone nodded or signaled OK. Ollie turned, took a deep breath, and stretched his head as far out from his skinny shoulders as he could.

"Do you see anyone?" asked Carson, right behind him.

Ollie motioned with one finger that he hadn't finished his survey of the room. The floor of the cavern was a maze of stalagmites, and Ollie checked each pillar to make sure no one was hiding there. A movement in one corner of the ceiling startled him, causing everyone to hop back a step.

"Fruit bats," Ollie whispered over his shoulder.

"Not again," sighed Sebastian. "Did anybody bring any bananas?"

"I'll take one," said Tank.

"Not for us, for the bats," whispered Carson.

"We could share," said Tank.

"I think the coast is clear," said Ollie. "I don't see anyone. Stay alert just in case, though."

He stepped into the cave, followed by the rest of the team. Magnificent stalactites covered the ceiling; some reached the stalagmites on the ground. A bat occasionally flew around the columns, weaving back and forth and then returning to its populated corner. Rimstone lined pristine pools of crystal clear water in other parts of the cave, away from the stream. But however incredible the rest of the chamber was, no one gave it much attention. Instead, they stared at a structure built across the stream. Two triangular wooden supports, one on each side of the water, were connected at their tops by one beam, a rafter that suspended a pulley attached to vines leading into the tunnel through which the water exited the cavern. On the ground were hollowed-out gondolas of sorts, with pedals connected to a paddle wheel in the rear. The boats had two narrow poles attached to one side of the hull that were connected at the top to another pulley, similar to the one over the stream. The apparatus resembled a ski lift.

"Time to take a ride," said Ollie. "It looks pretty simple. I could have designed it better, but it looks like it'll work. We lift the boat, placing the outside pulley on the vine, and when we pump the pedals, the paddle wheel will move us into that tunnel. We should be able to fit into these two boats."

"Are you nuts?" asked Sebastian. "You want us to use these? To go in there? You're telling me that we, the five of us—by the way, there used to be six—are going to risk everything by, let's see, going into that huge icy cavern that's populated by deadly blood-sucking bats … oh, and don't forget the voice we heard … Where was I? Oh, right—we're going to climb into a homemade floaty and paddle into that darker-than-death hole, not having any idea if we're going to be eaten by a monster or killed by a deranged lunatic?"

"Well … yeah." Ollie shrugged his shoulders.

"OK," said Sebastian. "Just wanted to make sure."

They slipped the pulleys on the two boats over the vine and climbed in with their gear. Tank threw Dusty's tattered bag off to the side onto the cave floor before he jumped in the boat.

"I want to go back outside the cave and look for Dusty," said C.J.

"I think we all need to stay together," said Ollie.

"But what if he's hurt and needs help?" asked Sebastian.

"We waited long enough on the bank for him to show up," said Carson. "Like we said, if he swam back to the other shore, we couldn't see him or hear him in all that rain and thunder."

"What if he didn't make it back to the shore?" asked C.J.

"There really is nothing we can do right now." Carson stared at the backpack. "We need to stay together, like Ollie said. It's too dangerous to split up."

"Put on your headlamps," instructed Ollie. "We shouldn't have to pedal much because we're flowing with the current. The paddle wheels are for the ride back."

"What if there is no ride back?" asked Tank. "Ow!" Carson punched him, and everyone gave him don't-even-think-that looks.

As the pulley turned along the vine overhead, the boats drifted with the water and slid into the black hole.

Ollie's light found the folded wings of a kalang dangling upside down, and he kept his beam on it for everyone else to see.

"Whatever you do, don't make any loud sounds in here," he whispered. "It might startle the bats."

"What did you say?" Tank yelled from the back of the second boat.

A roar of flapping wings surrounded them. They ducked and covered their heads with their arms until all the bats had settled back onto the roof of the tunnel.

"Smooth," said Sebastian quietly. "Real smooth one, you are."

There was a circle of dim light up ahead where the tunnel ended. Ollie motioned to the others and pointed to the light, which rapidly widened. A curtain of water blanketed the tunnel exit because the storm still thrashed the island. Lightning flared, followed by resounding thunder that echoed down the tunnel. As they reached the end of the tunnel, the boats came to a stop against another pulley suspended from a support beam identical to the one back in the cavern. The roots, vines and palm trees of the thick jungle swallowed the stream. The only cleared land was off to the left, next to a round, thatched hut at the edge of the forest. Stacked near the entrance were several hand-carved spears. Various animal skins hung next to them. The team climbed out of the homemade boats. They lifted the pulleys from the vines and placed the boats next to a similar one lying on the bank of the stream.

"That boat might have been used by the person in the cave." Ollie pointed at the third craft.

"Carson, look!" C.J. tapped her on the shoulder and pointed to a shape high up in the canopy of trees. "That's the plane we saw—the Doldrum Diver. We're at the bottom of the pit."

"I've read about something like this before," said Ollie. "That underground stream eroded so much of the soil away down here that this whole section of earth eventually collapsed because it didn't have enough support any more, forming this pit. Over hundreds of years, the jungle grew in the middle. There may be plants and animals down here that have never been discovered. This is a biologist's dream come true."

"I smell something." Tank rubbed his belly, sniffed the air, and pointed to the hut. "It's in there."

They all walked cautiously to the hut and stepped in.

"Carson! C.J.!" A familiar voice yelled from the back of the dark room. It was Mr. Crenshaw. He was tied to a chair with his hands tied behind him.

"Dad!" They ran to their father and hugged him hard. Ollie ran to the back of the chair and started to untie the vines. Tank ate some pastries he found in a bag on a small table.

"These are just like the ones we get at breakfast." Tank shot crumbs everywhere.

Sebastian walked over and looked at the pastries.

"I think we should leave right now," she said in a rush. "These came from our breakfast this morning. Someone's been ..."

"No one's going anywhere!" A mangy-looking man with a squeaky voice stood in the doorway holding a machete. Everyone moved closer together, near Mr. Crenshaw. The man at the door was the man who scared Tank and pulled Dusty, Carson, and C.J. to safety over the ledge. He looked like a caveman, with bushy, gray, matted hair and a beard to match, which he stroked with his black fingernails. His yellow teeth ground visibly between his dry, chapped lips. His clothes were torn, and he wore no shoes. A sewn patch on the top pocket of his shirt read *Von Nickleburg*.

"What are you doing in my hut?" The Baron gave Mr. Crenshaw an angry stare.

"You tell me." Mr. Crenshaw rubbed the top of his head. "The last thing I remember, I was walking in the market. Someone must have hit me on the head and brought me here. I assume that someone is you."

"No." The Baron also rubbed his head and looked confused. "Someone tried to kill me by pushing me over a bluff on the eastern shoreline. I landed on a ledge below, but I hit my head, and I was out for days. This morning somebody threw me a rope. I used it to climb up, and all I could find was pawprints left by a dog. I've seen dog prints on this island ever since I crashed here twenty years ago." He rubbed his aching head as he stood at the hut's entrance.

"Why are you hiding and living down here?" asked Mr. Crenshaw. "Why haven't you left the island?"

"I'm looking for the same thing you are, the Book of Life. It's the most powerful treasure in the world. Civilizations have risen and fallen, searching in vain for what it can do. It is what man has frivolously sought since the beginning of time. The Spaniards went to Mexico believing it was there, having been told by the natives that it existed, only to find it didn't. It was over here, on this island, and I'm not leaving until I find it."

"Someone already has it," said Carson. "They used it to kill Dusty."

Mr. Crenshaw looked at Ollie in disbelief. "When?" he asked.

"On our way here, crossing the sand bar to Black Reef Island."

"You murderer!" Mr. Crenshaw turned to face the Baron.

"Back!" The Baron raised his machete. "I've done no such thing. I'm no murderer. I haven't killed and I never will, unless I have to protect myself from you. You're not listening—I don't have the Book, and if I did, I would never use it for that. I want it for another reason."

"I get it," said Ollie. "The Spaniards came looking for the Fountain of Youth, which doesn't exist. This Book of Life can make animals appear in great numbers, like the bats and the barracudas, but it also holds the key to everlasting life."

"You're a smart one, you are," said the Baron. "It can do all of that ... and more."

"You're still going to need something to place in the Book for that to happen," said Mr. Crenshaw.

"The three jewels!" said Carson. "You need to find three jewels, and when you put them into the book, you'll receive everlasting life. That's what you wanted us to find. That's why you left me that note."

"What note?" asked Mr. Crenshaw.

"Then you wrote it!" Carson turned to the Baron.

"Stop your squawking," said the Baron. "I don't have time to write notes."

"The note asked us to find the three jewels," said C.J. "We saw you drop it for us behind our barracks, just before you walked into the brush."

"I don't know what you're talking about." Mr. Crenshaw looked confused. "I didn't write you a note."

C.J. reached into his back pocket, pulled out the message, and handed it to Mr. Crenshaw.

"And here's the watch." Carson held it out.

Mr. Crenshaw read the note and looked at the watch. "I didn't write this, and I haven't seen this watch since I dropped you guys off at the camp. I was looking for information about the Book, not three stones."

"You mean three jewels," said C.J.

"No, this note says three stones," said Mr. Crenshaw.

"Stones indeed," agreed the Baron. "I've looked everywhere, but can't find where they've been buried."

"What makes you think the stones are buried?" asked Carson.

"I didn't say the *stones* were buried," said the Baron.

Sebastian's eyes grew wide.

"We've found out a lot more." C.J. and the others related all that had taken place with Blake Dawson and his father. During the whole explanation, Sebastian tried to help tell the story, but she could never get in a word.

"So it's Dawson and his father," said Mr. Crenshaw. "And they already have the Book, and something else. That can't be good."

"They haven't found the stones yet," said Sebastian.

"How do you know?" Carson asked.

"The Baron said he wasn't looking for where the three *stones* were buried, but where *they* were buried, meaning where people were buried. The stones are tombstones."

"Of course," said Ollie. "The tombstones you found at the Burial Site."

"Know-it-all!" said the Baron, wincing at Ollie.

"Are these tombstones what we're looking for?" Mr. Crenshaw asked, looking at the Baron.

"Almost certainly," he answered. "Judging by the note, which neither of us wrote, someone else is looking for them too."

"What's so special about them?" asked Sebastian.

"They are the tombs of three men considered to be the fathers of the Wagapi chiefs. One ruled the spirit of the wind, one the spirit of the water, and one the spirit of the land. They blessed the kings with the fruits of their domains, until a jealous son of a great king, a son second in line to the throne, violated the covenant between man and the spirits. From that moment on, the spirits have maintained a steady barrage of storms that ravage this island, which eventually put an end to the Wagapi civilization."

"That explains a lot," said Ollie.

"Didn't know that, did you?" The Baron stuck his tongue out at Ollie. Ollie gave him a you-are-one-strange-old-man look.

"So that's why the Wagapi moved underground and started worshipping the ants for saving them," said C.J. "The blocks along the road to the camp must have been structures they built before the covenant was broken."

"And this hole we're in was created by the storms," said Ollie. "The rain and wind probably added water to the underground creek currents, which caused the soil to erode below, making the top collapse." Ollie looked over at the Baron and stuck his tongue out.

"We're wasting time," said Carson. "Someone is looking for those stones, and we know where they are. Dawson and his father probably have the Book, and they might find the graves before we can get there."

"I think you should all stay here while the Baron and I go look for Dawson and his dad," said Mr. Crenshaw.

"No way!" said Carson. "I have been walking around for the last couple of weeks not knowing if you were dead or alive, and I am not letting you out of my sight."

"I'm coming with you!" Tank stood beside her. "As long as I can bring these." He held the bag of breakfast goodies.

"Me too!" C.J. stepped up to Tank.

"That goes for me also," said Ollie.

Everyone turned to look at Sebastian, who scuffled her toes on the floor.

"What?" she asked. "Are you looking at me to see if I really want to go out into that storm, crawl down into a tunnel full of bats, cross back over a sea of barracudas, hang out in a graveyard waiting for Dawson and his father, the grim reaper, to come along, so that we can have tea and chat with them about everlasting eternal souls?"

"Well, yeah," said Ollie.

"OK," she said. "I'm in."

"One thing," said C.J. "What do they need from the tombstones?"

"Not from the tombstones, but from what lies underneath them." The Baron explained with a grim look on his face. "Resin from the hearts of the three spiritual fathers. When you combine them and place them in the Book of Life, you'll receive the gift of everlasting life. It's considered sacrilege to destroy any part of a resting corpse, especially ones of such high importance as these, so we'll have to gather the hearts and keep them well hidden without desecrating the bodies. It won't be easy."

WHAM!

The Baron fell to the ground. A stranger draped in a black cloak stepped into the hut, tossed a homemade oar aside, and picked up the machete. The person's face was covered with a blue scarf.

"Thanks for the information." The voice was muffled by the scarf.

"Too bad you won't be using it," said another voice from behind the stranger.

There stood Dusty in the rain, drenched, pointing a spear at the cloaked figure. He had an animal skin wrapped around his waist where his trousers were supposed to be.

"Dusty!" they all screamed.

"Just back it on out of there," said Dusty. He kept the spear against the stranger's back until they were both outside the hut. Lightning struck the tree that held the Doldrum Diver, and the plane became dislodged. It slammed into one limb after the other and then fell directly toward them. As it crashed into the jungle floor, Dusty dove one way and the stranger the other. The stranger landed in the creek and was swept downstream. The team rushed to help Dusty to his feet. Mr. Crenshaw checked on the Baron. He was still unconscious but had a strong pulse. Everyone came back into the hut.

"He'll be all right," said Mr. Crenshaw. "He's just in for another long nap."

"What happened, Dusty?" asked C.J.

"I had three barracudas chewing on my backpack, so I slung it off and swam down under water for cover, behind some plants and big rocks. I found this deep hole, and a kicker of a current sucked me into it. It pulled off my pants. I held my breath and rode it out until it popped me up in a cave, where I found my backpack. I figured you guys had come this way, so I decided to swim on down the stream and find you, which I did. I'm glad you were all inside when I came out of the stream without any bottoms on. I grabbed one of the animal skins hanging outside. Who's Colonel Caveman here?" Dusty looked at the Baron.

All talking at once, the team filled Dusty in.

"And that's the skinny." Tank said.

"I'm really glad you're OK," said Sebastian. She wrapped her arms around him and hugged him tight.

"We need to go," said Ollie.

"Right now!" said Carson.

"Then let's all stick together," said Mr. Crenshaw. "No one will wander off anywhere by themselves. Agreed?" He looked at each face for affirmation.

"Where are we headed first?" asked C.J.

"To the Burial Site," said Ollie.

"Right," said Mr. Crenshaw.

"So we'll just go and stand guard over the tombstones?" asked C.J.

"Oh, no," said his dad.

"You mean …" said C.J.

"I'm afraid so," said Mr. Crenshaw. "We're going to have to dig up the graves and carefully remove the decayed hearts."

19

The Prodigal Son

"Wake up!" A familiar voice startled Cosmo from his nap, so much so that he flipped his cot and fell to the floor. "What are you doing in here when all the commotion is outside?"

Cosmo stood, shook off his uniform, rubbed his head, and then looked up to see Kamia standing in the doorway. She wore a dripping-wet rain suit and a backpack slung over her shoulder.

"Oh ... hey, Kamia." Cosmo tried to wake up. "What's going on?"

"Oh, just checking in on you guys to see how you've been doing," she replied. "I saw the leaderboard, and it looks like the Stingrays have been doing fine and dandy. I knew Ollie would find a way to win the Challenge this year. I can't seem to find anybody else, though. Where are they?"

"Where's who?" asked Cosmo, stalling.

"The team, silly!" She smiled. "I came back to get a few things of mine and I wanted to tell them hi."

"Oh ... them ... the team," said Cosmo.

"Yeah." Kamia could see that Cosmo might still be half asleep. "You know, Carson and C.J. Tank. Dusty and Sebastian. Ollie."

"That team," said Cosmo. "Um … they're at the ruins right now. Yeah … they're up at the ruins because Dawson figured out how to open the sealed doorway, and the gang is checking out what was inside."

"He opened the doorway!" said Kamia in disbelief. "When?"

"During the eclipse," said Cosmo.

"Of course," Kamia spoke half to Cosmo and half to herself. "Did he find anything?"

"Dawson and his father found something, but we don't know what it is," said Cosmo.

"His father." A look of understanding came over Kamia, and she nodded her head for a moment, looking past Cosmo.

"We were doing great in the Challenge until just now, when I blew it." Cosmo changed the subject.

"What's that?" Kamia didn't hear him at first.

"I said that we were doing great in the Challenge until the Medicine Man part, which I did, but my stuff got knocked off the table and I had to forfeit because I couldn't find any more dried lizard tails. I needed them to make an antidote for poison."

"You can find tons of dead, dried lizards scattered around outside the barracks," she pointed out to Cosmo. "I think they spray under the huts to keep them from getting inside and scaring the campers."

"I wish I had known that sooner. It's no good to me now. I might still get some points, but I doubt it. There's no way we can win the Challenge."

"Haven't you heard?" she asked, surprised. "Come and take a look."

Cosmo and Kamia stepped out onto the porch. Over at the competition, all four contestants lay flat on their backs on their tables, being tended to simultaneously by Miss Snookembockem.

"Back up, everyone, and give them air," said Miss Snookembockem. "They'll all be fine as soon as I give them this shot." She held a syringe with a three-inch needle up in the air, and slightly pulled down Ven's trousers to expose a cheek of his white buttocks.

"What happened?" asked Cosmo.

"They were all disqualified," said Kamia. "For some strange reason, they all took sips of their own medicines, knowing they weren't allowed to do so, and it knocked them out cold. Topper decided that under the circumstances, no team would get any points for this part of the Challenge, and the scores would remain the same going into the last competition."

"Aw, sweet." Cosmo's face lit up. "As Tank would say, that rocks!" Cosmo filled her in with more details about how the Challenge unfolded.

"The Hermits never play fair," she said. "Your team is still a close second to those goons."

"That's the best news I've heard all day," said Cosmo. "And if I know Ollie, he'll have a trick or two up his sleeve for the final stage. By now he's got it all planned out."

◆   ◆   ◆

"I have no clue as to how we're going to handle the last leg of the competition," said Ollie to Tank. "It looks like things will turn out fine for Carson and C.J., though. We found their father, and that's what's most important. So much for the Challenge. I haven't even thought about it lately."

As the team marched back to the graves, they were nervous and apprehensive. They jumped at every unfamiliar sound, even though Mr. Crenshaw was with them. With the exception of the drenching rain, they made it back to Crater Island without incident. No bats. No barracudas. No fog. No wild dogs.

"Something's about to happen," C.J. said as they entered the burial site. "I can feel it."

"I'm getting an eerie feeling myself," said Carson.

"You can almost smell it," said Ollie.

"That would be Tank," said Dusty.

Mr. Crenshaw looked at Tank, who shook his head sadly, as if admitting that he was indeed guilty of creating any smell that was out of the ordinary. They sloshed on through the rain and arrived at the three flat-topped pyramids without any delays.

"They're right over here." Sebastian pointed to a corner of the clearing and led Mr. Crenshaw to the headstones.

He leaned down and dug around the soil at the base of each stone with his fingers.

"This has to be the stones," he said, "and they haven't been disturbed, recently or ever."

"What do we do now?" asked C.J.

"We dig," said Mr. Crenshaw. "Everyone has to help. The soil is wet, so it shouldn't be too hard to dig—muddy, is all. I saw a stack of big sharp rocks over by the main pyramid. We'll use them as shovels."

"Oh, no!" said Sebastian. "I found the graves, but I am not going to dig up dead people."

"I have a pair of brilliant earrings that I bought from a local at the market," said Mr. Crenshaw. "They were probably worn by the wife of one of the Wagapi kings. I'll give them to you if you help."

"Pierced or clip-on?" asked Sebastian.

"Pierced," answered Mr. Crenshaw.

"Studs or posts?"

"Studs."

"Gold?"

"Pure, no less."

"Gemstones?"

"Rubies, diamonds, and emeralds, of the highest quality."

"I'll go get a rock," said Sebastian.

The group divided their efforts among the three graves. The graves were about three feet deep, and in less than an hour a clank could be heard from each hole as rocks met coffin. The team lifted the caskets and placed them gently on the ground. Lightning crashed across the sky.

"Bad news," said Mr. Crenshaw.

"I see that too," said Ollie.

"What is it?" asked Carson.

"They're all locked," said Mr. Crenshaw, "and each one has its own special key. Without the keys, we can't open them."

"I still want my earrings." Sebastian shifted her head back and forth, showing off her ears.

"Let me think," said Mr. Crenshaw.

With the help of the pounding rain, Ollie and C.J. wiped away mud and debris from the lids of the caskets.

"Whoa!" said Ollie. "This looks like it's made of pure jade. Incredible."

"And look! This one is solid blue," said Dusty. "What kind of gem is it?"

"That's sapphire," said Carson. "Truly stunning."

"Is this opal?" Sebastian rubbed the solid white coffin.

"That's moonstone, for the Father Spirit of the Sky," said a raspy voice behind her. "The emerald one holds the Father Spirit of the Earth, and the sapphire holds the Father Spirit of the Water."

Out of the corner of her eye, Sebastian saw Carson turn and run to stand behind her father. She could tell that the rest of the gang did likewise. She slowly raised her head to see everyone on the other side of the graves, facing her. They weren't looking at Sebastian, but at someone behind her.

"That wasn't any of you that just answered me, was it?" she asked with a quivering chin.

They all shook their heads.

"There's someone standing right behind me, isn't there?" Her body trembled visibly.

C.J.'s head bobbed up and down.

"I thought I recognized the voice," she squeaked. "It's Dawson's father, isn't it?"

Carson nodded.

Sebastian turned around and stood face to face with Dawson and his father. Both wore capes, and the older man's face was hidden in the shadow of the cape's hood. She wobbled and swayed before she passed out, fell backwards, and landed in the middle grave. Mr. Crenshaw rushed in to lift her out. He brought her around with small pats on the cheek.

"You have done well in finding these for us," said Dawson. "The last great chieftain buried them himself, leaving no trace or account of where they were. We've been searching this entire island for them."

"Who's in the coffins?" asked Carson. "They aren't spirits. Spirits don't live in dead bodies."

"You're both right and wrong," Dawson's father hissed in the rain. "Spirits can return to earth from time to time, in many shapes and forms. However, these are the tombs of our tribe's first fathers. The spirits instilled in these three the knowledge to unlock the powers that control the fabric of life. They shared this great wisdom with our first king, and future kings in turn passed it down from generation to generation, until one of the wise became careless, which started the collapse of the Wagapi. So the bodies that lie in the tombs before us are known by our people as Father Spirits."

"So the Baron was right, and these are the ones he described," said Ollie to Mr. Crenshaw.

"Man, I'd hate to be that chiefy-wiefy that started the fall," said Tank.

"What a moron!" said Dusty. "They had it made."

"Totally dumbskull," said C.J. "A good leader should know better."

"I drifted off to sleep and left our spiritual gift, a book, laying out in the open," said Dawson's father, with his face still hidden under the dark cloak. "The temptation was too strong for my youngest son, and he took it."

"You're the chieftain," said Carson. "You've come back!"

"Yes, I am the careless one."

"It could happen to anybody," said Tank, trying to reverse his comments quickly.

"It's the same thing I would have done," said C.J.

"It's all your stupid sons' fault, not yours." Dusty wasn't thinking again.

"I would be one of those 'stupid' sons." Dawson stared down at Dusty.

"I'll just go right over here in my animal skirt and shut up now." Dusty walked away from the others and stepped behind Mr. Crenshaw.

"You're one of the king's sons?" Mr. Crenshaw looked for a response.

"I am," Dawson replied with distrust in his voice. "My given name is Praja. The great spirits permitted my return. I created Camp Remnant so that I could protect the artifacts of our people, keeping them here on the island. The only things we shipped away to greedy traders were fakes and replicas. All of our treasures are still here on our island, where they belong, well hidden. No one should violate our altars or our homes. No one."

Dawson looked down at the coffins with a measured gaze.

"We didn't come to do anything to the coffins or take anything from them," said Ollie in a squeaky voice.

"I thought we were going to take out their hearts." Once again, Dusty didn't use his brain.

Carson's eyes blazed as she glared at Dusty. Dusty realized what he had done, so he zipped his mouth and walked back behind the group with his head bowed.

"Liars!" said Dawson.

"It's true." Mr. Crenshaw tried to speak above the thunder. "We came here to do what the boy said. We didn't plan on finding the caskets locked. We know what the hearts can be used for, and we were going to take them, but only to prevent anyone from using them with the Book of Life. You must believe that."

"You have the Book," Carson said. "Don't you?"

"No. We do not have it, but we do have the keys to the coffins."

Dawson's father reached into his pockets and pulled out three small leather pouches. He opened them to reveal three irregularly shaped golden keys, about the size of a man's hand. The bottoms were flat, and the tops were slightly raised and inlaid with jewels that matched the three coffins.

"We seek a greater prize," said the chieftain.

"Everlasting life," whispered Carson to Ollie out of the corner of her mouth.

"No." The chieftain startled Carson.

"Wrong again. We need something from within the tombs, but it is not the hearts. We want to go home, but not until we've found all that we seek."

"You found those keys in the chamber that was sealed," said C.J.

"That chamber is called the Hall of King's Souls." Dawson's father nodded and turned to face Carson. "So you know the Book can give life that never ends."

"Yes," said Carson. "And that it can produce life. That's why we dug up the coffins, not to do those things, but rather to prevent them from happening. We know that whoever has the Book wants the three hearts in these coffins."

"They lie, father!" said Dawson. "They are weak, and without the spirits they have succumbed to the Book's temptations. They wish to use it for their own desires."

"We don't have the Book!" said Mr. Crenshaw.

"Give it to us!" said Dawson's father, unconvinced.

"He told you—we don't have it!" shouted Carson.

"Enough! They must be dealt with. We don't have time for their interference." Dawson took a giant step forward, crossed his arms to his hips, and pulled two long golden swords from under his cape. The group stepped back as far as they could toward the edge of the jungle. Dawson leapt across the graves. A large growl came from behind the group.

"Oh my gosh!" said Sebastian. "Bush dogs!"

"Where is the Book?" yelled Dawson as lightning flashed and struck a tree on the opposite side of the Burial Site. The tree exploded in flames. "Give it to us!"

The barking coming from the other side of the nearby bushes grew more ferocious. The kids looked back and forth, not knowing which way to go. Panic and fear distorted their faces.

"We don't have it! You must believe us!" Mr. Crenshaw stood in front of the team.

"Tell me now, before it's too late!" screamed Dawson.

A large howl erupted from the jungle behind the Stingrays, and out sprang the Australian Shepherd with Mr. Crenshaw's bandanna still around his neck. He positioned himself between the team and Dawson, barking and growling feverishly. His white teeth were exposed with each snarl and snap.

"Feeble animal." Dawson drew his swords to kill the dog.

"No!" shouted Dawson's father. "Put down your blades!"

Dawson lowered the swords, but he never took his eyes off the dog, which slowly became calm and turned to face the chieftain. There was long silence as the dog and the chief gazed at one another.

"My prize!" said the chieftain. "The greatest of my lost treasures has been found."

"What?" Dawson looked confused. "The dog? Nakoda?"

The team stepped out from behind Mr. Crenshaw to see the Australian Shepherd.

"Nakoda is a better name than Scaredy-Pie," said C.J.

The dog walked around the graves past Dawson. It stopped in front of the chieftain and bowed low.

"My son." The chieftain pulled back his hood to get a better look at the dog. His entire head and neck were covered with white bandages, several strips flapping in the wind. He did have eyes, but they were hard to see, hidden in deep, dark sockets, and there were small openings for his mouth and nose. He untied the collar of his cloak and threw it over the shepherd.

"This cloak is to be worn only by a Wagapi chief," he said to the dog. "Naapaaw Nikitaaw Atim"

The chieftain stepped back as lightning crackled all around them. The cloak began to rise in the air as the dog underneath changed from a four-legged animal into a man.

The man pulled back the cowl hood of the cloak and surveyed everyone around him. He looked like a younger Dawson, with long black hair that spilled out from under the hood. "Father," he said.

"Nakoda," Tears rolled down the chieftain's face as he embraced his son.

"I have lived here ever since that terrible day," said Nakoda. "That day when I was overcome by jealousy and watched my brother sail into a sea of barracuda. The spirits would not let my soul leave this place, but forced me to spend eternity with pain and suffering over my betrayal. How could I have been so blind?"

"We have come for you," said the chieftain. "Your brother and I."

"How is this possible?" asked Nakoda. "Why would you come for me? I betrayed you. I betrayed our family, our people, our way of life. I caused the fall of the Wagapi culture. I broke the covenant between man and the spirits. Have the spirits asked you to find me so they can punish me further?"

"You still are blind," said the chieftain. "I begged the spirits to let me return, so that I might find you and bring you home with me. I have been asking them every day from the moment you strayed."

"You would take me back with you after all that I have done?" said Nakoda in disbelief. "How could you?"

"How could I?" ask the chieftain. "You are my son. A father's love for his son never dies, never weakens, but stays strong for eternity. It is stronger than any power the spirits can unleash. I would not abandon you, nor have I ever, even when you fell from the good graces of the spirits. You never fell from mine."

"We want you to come home, brother," said Dawson, placing his hand on Nakoda's shoulder. "At home with us is where you belong."

"It is not possible," said Nakoda. He looked over at Mr. Crenshaw. "They do not have the Book, I'm certain of it, but someone does. I, like you, have been trying to discover who. I found out only today that ..."

"Well, well, well," came a voice from the trail entrance. "I can't believe I wasn't invited to your little family reunion. It almost made me cry. Hey, look! There's a tear ... no, sorry, just a raindrop. Hah! Kudos to the royal family for finding the keys in the Hall of King's Souls. I can't believe I didn't figure out that little eclipse thing myself. Kudos also to my favorite team for finding the three stones. I was beginning to think you had forgotten all about that little note I left you."

It was Kamia. She wore a black cloak and a blue scarf around her neck, flapping in the wind. Her backpack hung on her shoulder, with the Book of Life sticking out from the top.

"You look like you're having such a grand royal shindig. I would have done it indoors, though; this weather is dreadful. Nevertheless, invited or not, I'm afraid it's time I crashed this party."

20

Scorpions, Tigers, and Snakes, Oh My

"Nice to see the old team, and the old boss, eh, Dawson? Or should I call you Praja now?" Kamia spoke as lightning branched across the sky above her. "Let's cut to the chase, shall we? You have something I need, so hand it over, and you all can go on about your merry way, living happily ever after, which is what I plan on doing myself. Living happily *forever* after."

"I should have known," said Dawson. "The counselor who couldn't quite follow her schedule. You never were where you were supposed to be, always snooping around our tent. We knew it—you were up to something, and you were going to get in our way. You even sent those dogs after your team, knowing the kids would head for Black Reef Island, so that you could have a reason to go to the cave and investigate. But you didn't count on the kids leaving you behind. We knew you were lying about the glyphs on the side of the burial pyramids. There are no such things."

"Those little buggers are sharp," said Kamia. "And fast. I hand picked them a little too well. Sorry, Ollie, ol' boy. I know you thought you had something to do with that.

"I found out that the infamous Mr. Crenshaw was coming to camp with his two brats, so I left that note, figuring they could help me find the graves. I had to make it seem real, so when Dad set his watch down on the registration table, my elbow just happened to knock it off and I covered it with my foot until he was gone.

"When Dawson fired me, I needed a place to stay. I knew about the crazy old Baron's hut, because I found it once when I was exploring Black Reef Island. So I followed him to the eastern shore one morning and pushed him off the bluff. Then I heard from some of the locals that Mr. Crenshaw was snooping around, asking about the Book. I hired a friend to gather him up and carry him back to the hut for me. He charged me way too much, that thief! When I came back to check on Mr. Crenshaw, I found you guys snooping around in my new home. I was able to grab a vine and pull myself out of the creek. That's no way to treat a lady, Dusty. Oh well, fate is on my side. I mean, look, here I am, after all that!"

"Why?" asked Carson.

"I am a descendant of the Quatztec tribe who live on an island north of here. Our people have survived famine, raids, starvation, and every type of weather disaster. We heard tales of the Wagapi and how they were so blessed by the spirits, yet the spirits never cast any blessings upon the Quatztecs. We're now a culture of less than one hundred survivors. With this Book, we will be strong again."

"The Book," said the chieftain. "How did you find it?"

"I was able to decipher almost all the glyphs and mosaics in the Ceremonial Chamber," she explained, over the pounding of the rain. "One told how to operate the two statues, and the Book was in the chest held by their outstretched arms."

"I overlooked the glyphs," said Dawson to his father. "I hid the Book in the chest when I recovered it from the cave, but I hadn't counted on treachery from a snooping woman."

"So, carelessness has cost our family once more," said the chieftain.

"The apple doesn't fall far from the tree," Kamia laughed.

Dawson pointed his swords forward and started to march toward Kamia. She flipped off her backpack and opened the Book. In her other hand she held up a scorpion's tail.

"Back away!" she screamed. "I'll do it! No one has to get hurt here. I have nothing to lose and everything to gain."

Dawson stopped and lowered his blades. He looked down for a moment, then back at his father and brother, before he made his decision. He swung around and charged hard at Kamia. She dropped the scorpion's tail into the Book and slammed it shut. A blinding blast of light shot out in all directions from it, causing Dawson to stop and shield his eyes. Then the clicking started. From everywhere in the jungle it could be heard, even over the heavy rain. The sound advanced toward them through the brush.

"Up here! It's our only chance!" shouted Ollie. He ran for the stone pyramids and waved desperately for the others to climb up with him. Everyone sprinted for the structures. Mr. Crenshaw jumped on top of the tallest one and turned to help pull the others up. They all clustered together on top of the tallest pyramid.

The ground quickly turned into an ocean of black scorpions. Kamia stood amid them, untouched, as if the scorpions knew who it was that summoned them. In front of her was a small black hump. It was Dawson, trying to shield himself from the stinging arachnids with his cloak. Kamia shook her head sadly, repeating, "This didn't have to happen." The scorpions started to climb on top of one another to make their way up the pyramids.

"They've made it to the top over here!" Carson shouted and motioned to the pyramid on the right.

"And over here also!" Tank looked at the one on the left. "I need some ammunition."

"They're getting closer!" Sebastian looked down at the scorpions rising higher and higher on the pyramid's walls.

"Enough!" yelled Dawson's father. "You may have the keys! Stop them now!"

Kamia opened the Book and pulled out the tail. The scorpions retreated, scuttling back into the jungle and out of sight. Nakoda leapt down to his brother and pulled back the cloak to find a limp body.

"Brother!" he pleaded. "Talk to me, Praja! Don't leave me."

Mr. Crenshaw rushed in and checked his vital signs.

"He's alive," Mr. Crenshaw said to Dawson's father, "but barely. He hardly has a pulse, and his breathing has slowed considerably. He's been stung over and over through his cloak. The poison is shutting him down. He doesn't have much time."

"So I have come back to save one son," said the chief sadly, "and in doing so, I have lost the other."

Carson grabbed C.J. by the arm, pulled him aside, and whispered in his ear. In the commotion, C.J. slipped away unnoticed and raced down the trail toward the main camp.

"If he dies …" Nakoda clenched his teeth and looked at Kamia.

"You'll do what?" asked Kamia, who held the Book open and shook a snake's rattle in her other hand. "I warned you. Give me the keys now! No one else will get hurt."

The chieftain reached into his robes and pulled out the three leather purses. He threw them down at Kamia's feet.

"What you seek, you will never find," said the chieftain. "Not even with these."

"We will see about that." Kamia attempted to come across as coy and in control. "And we will see right now. No one move a muscle. Your little tap dance with the scorpions was nothing compared to rattlesnakes."

Carson measured Kamia's nervousness by the fact that she didn't notice C.J. was gone. Kamia walked backward to the graves, keeping an eye on everyone. The children stood still in the pouring rain, while the adults tended to Dawson. She put the Book down at her feet, careful to keep it close, and opened one of the leather purses. She pulled out an emerald key set in gold and slid it securely into the slot on the top of the brilliant green coffin. She turned the stone until the latch released the lid, which made an eerie hiss as the air escaped. She glanced up frequently to check on the group as she repeated the procedure with the other two keys.

"Finally, the time is here." Kamia looked exasperated. "The Fountain of Youth itself. I will live eternally from this day on, never aging. Today I will cheat death, and it will no longer have its hold on me. My people will rise in numbers and in strength. They will have hardship no more."

She opened the first tomb. A bolt of lightning hit a tree on the opposite side of the clearing, causing a loud crack of thunder. Kamia looked down at the body lying in the green shell. It was mummified and surrounded by canopic jars, but in the center, where the heart was supposed to be untouched, there was a hole all the way through the chest. Panic-stricken, she looked into the sapphire casket. The body was the same—the one in the third, as well as the one in the white casket on the other side.

"Where are they?" she screamed in mortal fear. "Where are the hearts?"

The chieftain gave her a cold stare that said he knew, but he was not about to tell her.

"You have them!" she screamed, pointing at the chief.

"If my son dies, or anyone else here, you will never lay your hands on them," said the chieftain. "This I swear by the spirits."

"I know they're on this island, and even without your help, I have at least one lifetime to find them, which shouldn't be too hard once I get you and these pests out of my way." Without any reason or thought, she dropped the snake's rattle into the Book and closed it tight. An explosion of crystal blue light burst from the cover. Sounds of hissing and rattling approached through the jungle.

"Let's go!" Carson tugged at her father. "We need to run for it!"

The team took steps toward the trail, but stopped as the path disappeared under a mass of slithering rattlesnakes. The chieftain did not move from his position.

"Hold!" he shouted. He took one of the animal bones from his necklace, placed it to his lips, and blew into it. Huddled around Dawson, the group jumped and danced, dodging the aggressive snakes. From high in the trees came a long, ear-piercing screech, so loud it could be heard over all the other sounds echoing at the Burial Site.

One of the largest of the snakes got in close to Carson and armed itself for the strike. It lunged forward with its fangs ready to sink into her skin. Carson closed her eyes and screamed, and then she felt a great gust of wind across her face. A Harpy Eagle, the one they had seen earlier, swept down and carried the serpent away. It grabbed the snake with its talons, ripped it in half in midair, and released the two limp halves. The eagle swooped down and grabbed snakes by the dozens, killing them with its talons and its beak. Its cries paralyzed the snakes with fear, giving the raptor the advantage it needed to win the fight. The battle continued for several minutes, until the white-winged savior held the last snake's neck in his beak. He flung it through the air at Kamia's feet. The great eagle returned to Dawson's father, extended its twelve-foot wings over him for a moment, and gave a death-defying screech. It flew off and settled on a branch at the edge of the jungle.

The chief leaned down to look at his son. Mr. Crenshaw held Dawson's head and shoulders with a look of despair.

"We're losing him," said Mr. Crenshaw.

"Carson!" C.J. emerged from the trail, followed by Cosmo. "He's got it!" The two of them were winded when they came to a stop. They bent over and held their knees, trying to catch their breath. C.J. tossed a bag of pebbles to Tank.

"Are we too late?" He looked at Dawson's pale face.

"What is it that you have?" Nakoda asked.

Cosmo stepped around C.J. and held out a syringe filled with brown liquid.

"It's an antidote for poison," said Cosmo. "I made it. My ancestors passed down the recipe."

"How'd you get it?" asked Ollie.

"C.J. came to the barracks and told me what happened. He collected rocks for Tank. I ran and got a needle from Mrs. Snookembockem's bag while she tended to some sick campers. All I needed was dried lizard tails, and Kamia told me where I could—Hey, is that the eagle we saw earlier? What's Kamia doing over by those graves with that book? Is that the Book? What's going on here?" Cosmo and C.J. saw the snakes and realized that the Burial Site had been turned into a battlefield.

Mr. Crenshaw inserted the needle in Dawson's arm and squeezed the thick fluid slowly into a vein.

"His heartbeat is weak," said Mr. Crenshaw. "It may take too long to work."

"I've warned you, and this is your last chance," shouted Kamia. "If you don't tell me where you've hidden the hearts, you will all die, and everyone's blood will be on your hands, Your Majesty. Even your precious eagle won't be able to save you this time."

"I want all you kids to go!" said Mr. Crenshaw. "Right now!"

"We're not leaving you, Dad," said Carson.

"I'm not asking you, I'm telling you!" shouted Mr. Crenshaw. "Leave!"

"No way, Dad," said C.J. "If we leave, we may never see you again."

Nakoda stood up between them.

"I suspect your wishes are falling on deaf ears," said Nakoda. "Thinking that you may never again see the ones you hold closest to your heart is a thorn in the flesh that will fester in the soul. I will never separate myself from my loved ones again."

"But they—" Mr. Crenshaw began.

"C.J.! Stop!" yelled Carson. C.J. was running full speed toward Kamia.

"You fool!" Kamia dropped a large tooth into the Book and closed it before C.J. could reach her. C.J. dove for Kamia and tackled her backwards into the center grave. A brilliant beam radiated out from the grave, lighting up the underside of the rolling black storm clouds. C.J. got to his feet, ripped the Book from Kamia's hands, and climbed out of the grave. He darted back to the chieftain and handed him the Book just before the sounds began.

"What was that?" asked Dusty. "Was that your stomach?" he looked at Tank, who shook his head no, serious this time.

Kamia laughed ghoulishly as she splashed her hands in the puddles of water around her in the grave. The jungle was alive with snarls and roars. The foliage near the Burial Site moved and swayed, announcing the approach of some very large animals. Lightning flashed close by, followed by a quaking boom, just as an enormous tiger sprang to the top of the tall pyramid, growled long and loud, and then roared, calling the rest of the pack. More tigers shot out of the brush and paced back and forth in front of the group.

Kamia continued to laugh, never looking up from her grave. The Harpy Eagle positioned himself between the chieftain and the tigers, extended his wings, and screeched bravely in an attempt to fend off the striped beasts.

The chieftain opened the Book and motioned for Nakoda to hold out his hands. He placed the Book in Nakoda's palms, pulled off his animal necklace, and lifted it up in the air in his fist. He looked toward the grave where Kamia lay hauntingly laughing and dropped the leather necklace into the Book. Nakoda looked into his father's eyes and then closed the Book firmly. The tigers roared at the strange light that exploded from the Book, momentarily blinding them. When the light dissipated, the tigers regained their focus and snarled behind their razor sharp teeth.

The ground shook as a rumbling sound came from the pyramids. Tank loaded his slingshot and then stopped dead still, uttering a low croak.

"What's that noise?" Kamia asked, looking up from the grave, no longer laughing.

In front of the main pyramid, the two eccentrically shaped statues came to life. The lion and eagle heads began to roar and screech, which silenced the tigers, who pinned their ears back, ready for war. The Harpy Eagle shrieked, communicating with the golden eagle head on each monstrosity. The fierce intensity on the lion faces showed that they understood the guardian eagle. The tigers swarmed around the two statues, violently growling and snarling as a show of strength. The tiger on top of the tall pyramid vaulted from the platform and was met in the air by the bear claws of one statue, killing it instantly. Both stone warriors flapped their wings and took to the air. They picked the tigers off one by one and sent them away.

Three tigers turned their attention to the gang. Outnumbered, the Harpy was unable to protect them all. Another tiger was advancing on the team from the rear. Mr. Crenshaw and the chieftain saw the tiger sneak into position, about to pounce, so they rushed in together to distract it before it could charge. In the next instant, one of the statues flew across, carried away the cat, and dropped its limp body back down onto the other three, killing them all. The Harpy Eagle screamed victoriously at the pile of dead tigers and pulled her wings back in with pride.

The two statues continued to fight valiantly, relentless in their drive to defend the royal family and their friends. Dawson hadn't moved during the battle, but he was startled by the Harpy's cry. Cosmo's medicine had begun to take, and Dawson began to mumble, unaware of the events around him. A tiger across the field noticed his movement and started an approach, zeroing in on its target. The tiger never broke stride as it leapt into the air, claws extended, eager to unleash a ferocious attack on Dawson. At the top of the tiger's dive, Nakoda came out of nowhere, slammed into the cat, and knocked it to the ground, where the two of them rolled in a fierce struggle. The eagle sprang into action, sank its claws into the back of the tiger, and pulled it away from Nakoda, whose left arm was broken and gashed. The tiger swatted at the eagle and turned back to Dawson.

"Son!" The chieftain tossed Dawson a knife. He caught it by the handle with his right hand and plunged the blade deep into the chest of the beast as it crashed down upon him, killing it instantly.

One tiger remained, and the two stone warriors quickly cornered it. The cat summed up its situation and let out a small meow before it darted off into the jungle. The lion heads sniffed the air to make certain that all danger had passed.

"It's over," said Mr. Crenshaw. He ran to Nakoda to examine his wounds.

"Perhaps." The Chieftain still looked concerned. "They won't stop until all danger is gone from this area."

"But I don't see any more tigers," said Carson.

"There are things more dangerous than tigers," said the chieftain.

"Where?" Carson asked, baffled.

The statues lifted their noses into the air as they moved heavily toward the graves.

"Many dangers with many names," the chieftain intoned. "Greed, jealousy, desire for power, preying on the weak. All are always ready to surface."

Kamia screamed as each statue clutched an arm. They pulled her wet and muddy body from the grave.

"No!" yelled Carson. "You can't let them kill her."

"She is a threat to my family," said the chieftain, "and to yours."

"She deserves to live," said C.J. "Just like Nakoda."

"He's right, father," said Nakoda. "She will have to live with what she has done here. It is a punishment far worse than you can imagine."

"It is difficult to stay on the right path," the chieftain said, "but what is most important is that when you stray, you come back." He opened the Book, removed the necklace, and placed it back around his neck. The statues released Kamia face first into a large mud puddle and returned to their post by the middle pyramid. They cracked and creaked as they turned back into stone. The snakes and tigers that littered the field faded out of sight.

Kamia jumped to her feet and dashed for the trail. C.J. and Carson tackled her before she could get away. Tank and Cosmo grabbed some vines and tied her up.

"Nakoda," said Dawson in a faint voice. Nakoda took hold of his brother's hand. "You saved my life. Stay with me. I have missed you so."

"I'm not going anywhere," said Nakoda as tears rolled down his cheeks. "I will never leave you again."

Nakoda helped Dawson stand and looked up at his father.

"I want to go home," said Nakoda. The chief walked over and placed a hand on each son's shoulder. The rain clouds disappeared, and the sun smiled down from a crystal blue sky.

"If the history books are correct, your name must be Razulu." Mr. Crenshaw shook hands with the chieftain, who nodded. "I think this belongs to you." He was holding the Book. He handed it to the chief with quivering hands.

"You do know where the hearts are?" asked Mr. Crenshaw.

"Yes," said the chieftain, "but we do not need them. It is not eternal life that we want. We need something else from the graves in order to return to our spiritual kingdom."

"What is it you need? No, wait! Don't tell me!" Mr. Crenshaw held up his hands like stop signs. "I think it's best not to know."

"Very wise," said the chieftain. "Not all knowledge is good."

"I do want to know one thing, though," said Mr. Crenshaw. "Is there someone in there? I mean … inside the bandages … a human body? It's … hard to see your eyes."

"What do you think?" asked the chief.

"That's what I thought," Mr. Crenshaw said, rubbing his chin and trying to look knowing.

"What about camp?" asked C.J.

"I guess camp is over," said Carson. "It's way past the time we should have returned for dinner."

"What are we waiting for?" asked Tank. "Let's go eat! All this excitement has made me hungry."

"Breathing makes you hungry," muttered Sebastian.

"Kirk is probably searching for us," said Cosmo. "When we get back, we're probably kicked out."

"I think I can take care of that," said Dawson. "They don't need to know that my real name isn't Blake Dawson. I'm still the camp director, you know. I'll get to the camp ahead of you and straighten things out."

Dawson, Nakoda, and the chief shook hands with everyone and said their thank-yous and goodbyes. They took Kamia with them and later turned her over to the island's governing authorities.

"Cosmo, how did you do in the Medicine Man competition?" Ollie asked.

The stingrays gathered around as Cosmo explained all the details.

"I would have won easily if not for Ven," he frowned.

"Carson, C.J.," Mr. Crenshaw called.

Mr. Crenshaw talked with the kids and made sure everything was all right before he left to go check on the Baron. The team headed back to camp, replaying the events of the day over and over. Sebastian didn't say a word.

"What's wrong?" asked Carson.

"I didn't get my earrings!" Sebastian exclaimed.

Carson put an arm around her as she began to mumble.

"They would have gone so well with my beige pumps and this little tan shell over the lacy white blouse that my mom got me for my birthday." The two of them swapped fashion ideas all the way back to camp.

"You guys really came through out there today," said Ollie. "I'm glad I'm a Stingray."

"We were following your plans," said C.J. "We may not have known how it was all going to turn out, but still, it was you who decided we should go to Black Reef Island. There's no telling what would have happened if we hadn't found my father. Carson and I can't thank you enough. I wish there was some way we could repay you."

Ollie paused, and a sneaky grin grew across his face.

"Oh, I think I may know how you can do that," he said. "We only have one more day, and we only have one more competition"

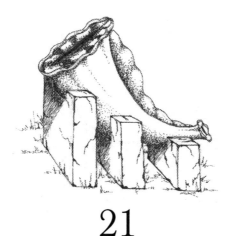

21

Saved by the Slug Searchers

Ollie managed only a few winks during the night. He stayed up late to prepare to win the prize he so coveted. He wrote and erased figures and calculations on a clipboard, devising the solutions and scenarios that could play out and result in a Stingray victory. It was shortly after sunrise when the others woke and stumbled into the meeting room, ready to execute Ollie's game plan.

"It's basically a two-team race to the Domingo Horn," explained Ollie. "The Dolphins are out. They have 82 points and have no mathematical chance of catching us. And barring some ridiculous blunder by the Hermits or ourselves, I don't see how the Dragons or the Scorpions can catch either of us. The way I have it figured, it's us or the Hermits."

"So what's our plan?" Dusty already looked as if he needed a bath, even though he had showered a few minutes before.

"I say we eat first." Tank took his usual position at the doorway to be first down for breakfast. "No use trying to go over this on an empty belly." Tank caressed his belly as if it were his pet.

"This is how it works," explained Ollie. "Kirk went out this morning and set up clues for the teams to track five different animals from camp to the Domingo Horn. He used fur, track impressions, broken twigs, things like that. Each team draws an animal, and three people have to follow the signs. That'll be Sebastian, C.J., and me for our team. Along the way, you must collect three flags that have your animal's face on them. The first team to collect the flags and blow the horn gets 50 points, plus one point for each minute between the time they blow the horn and the time the next team blows the horn. The second place team gets 25 points and the others all get 15 for finishing."

"So if we get there first, we get 50 points?" Carson checked to make sure. "And if we finish ten minutes before the next team blows the horn, we get 10 more points, or fifteen minutes before, we get 15 points, or whatever. Right?"

"That's it," said Ollie. "And that's the tough part. If we come in first and the Hermits come in second, we'll have to beat them by twenty minutes to the horn. If we get there first and they get there third, they get 15 points, so we'll need to beat them there by ten minutes. I've got it all figured out right here."

Ollie handed the board to Carson. Cosmo and Dusty looked at the numbers, graphs, and charts over Carson's shoulders.

"Why don't we just run straight to the horn?" asked C.J.

"Each trail is 3 miles long, and they all lead to the horn's location," said Ollie. "No one knows where that is. It's kept under wraps. But you can't go there until you have the three flags."

"Try not to let your mind wander out there," said Carson to C.J. "It's too small to be out by itself."

"Very funny," said C.J. amid everyone's chuckles. "My mind's just fine. Unlike yours, ever since you hit your head falling off that horse."

"Hey!" Carson looked at C.J. sternly. "Don't you dare!"

Everyone begged to hear the rest of the story.

"You fell off a horse and lived!" said Sebastian astonished.

"Wow!" said Dusty.

"Pretty much," said C.J. "She slipped off the saddle, and her foot got tangled up in the stirrups, so as the horse kept going, her head kept bouncing off the floor."

"You mean bouncing off the ground," said Dusty.

"No," said C.J. "The floor. Dad finally walked around to the back of the horse and unplugged it from the department store wall."

Carson sprang up after C.J., who ran for his life down to the pavilion, with Carson on his tail. He saved himself by sliding in next to Ollie, who sat with

Sebastian going over a book called *Jungle Survival: How to Identify What Is About to Eat You.* After breakfast, the teams went back to their barracks, picked up their backpacks, and reassembled in the center of the camp. The Hermits marched out of their barracks in single file, the entire team chanting *Number One! Number One!* Daegel, along with Kash Jensen and Karletta Bishop, lugged their backpacks.

"No telling what they have in there," said Cosmo to Ollie. "Some things to help them cheat again, probably."

"I haven't seen Dawson or his father yet," said Carson. "Oh—there's Dawson now."

"So how have you enjoyed camp?" asked Dawson through a megaphone. The teams cheered loudly.

"I must say, it has been a most memorable experience for me also," he continued, looking toward the Stingrays with a smile.

"I have to go somewhere shortly, so I may not see any of you again. I thank each and every one of you for coming to Camp Remnant. We love our island and are happy that we could share a little of its history with you. I hope that when you think about some of the things you learned here, you will admire and respect this tribe for their beliefs and for the way they lived a full life. The Wagapi people taught valuable lessons that we should never forget. Remember, we can become wiser by learning from our successes, but greater wisdom and growth result from what we learn from our mistakes."

"Is everyone ready for the Tracker Trail?" asked Dawson.

The teams erupted with a loud *Yeah!*

"Remember, after the race you'll meet under the pavilion for awards, and then home. This island is beautiful, but I'm sure we all want to get back home." Dawson paused for several seconds before he spoke again. "I know you're ready, so follow Kirk to the starting line and off you go."

"I hope you'll be waiting for me when we get back," said Sebastian to Dusty.

"Really?" Dusty grinned behind his thin cloud of dirt.

"No," said Sebastian. "Not really." She gave him a smile back and winked as she headed toward the starting line.

"Don't do anything stupid," said Carson to C.J.

"Don't worry," he replied. "I won't do anything that you would do."

Carson kicked him as he walked away.

"Ollie, I'm sorry about not getting any points for our team," said Cosmo. "I know you were counting on me to put us way ahead."

"It wasn't your fault," said Ollie. "Somehow winning isn't that important to me any more. I think we've already done just fine. Besides, it was Tank's fault."

"What?" Tank took off his cap and swatted at Ollie.

Ollie and C.J. joined Sebastian at the starting line. Kirk Christianson held out his helmet, which had five blue envelopes inside.

"Everyone reach in and pull out an envelope. Open it, and there will be an animal's picture on it."

Daegel stepped up to pick the first envelope. He looked over at his counselor, who held her hand up to her mouth and flashed three fingers. Daegel chose the third envelope and went back to his team while Kirk continued to remind everyone of the rules.

"You'll need to track the animal for three miles through the jungle, or wherever the clues lead, and gather the three flags with that picture on it. If you look around the camp, you'll see colored markers at your starting points. The color corresponds to the color in the top right-hand corner of your photo. That's how you'll know where to start. Then follow the animal to the Domingo Horn. Blow the horn and you're done. I'll be at the finish line waiting on you."

C.J. opened his envelope and screamed.

"What's the matter?" asked Ollie.

"It's a picture of my sister." C.J. held up a picture of a small four-legged animal with a bushy tail. Everyone laughed, except Carson, whose face was redder than a stop sign.

"A Small Eared Zorro," Ollie said. C.J. looked back to make sure Carson wasn't coming to slug him. In the upper right corner of the page was a green dot, and Ollie located the green post near the entrance to the camp. He quickly flipped over the photo and started to draw a picture of the animal's footprints for Sebastian and C.J.

"Is it a bush dog?" asked Sebastian. "Wouldn't you know it?"

"No." Ollie rolled his eyes. "A Small Eared Zorro is like a fox or a small dog. Here, look at its pawprints. This was a good one to pick because it should be easy to track. I was hoping to get the bird picture, though. They always have a bird and it's the easiest ..."

"Yes! We got the bird!" yelled Daegel nearby. "And it's the Quetzal. Man, this is going to be a cakewalk! Its feathers are so bright they almost glow!" Daegel was chest-slamming Kash and started to do the same with Karletta; he paused, and then he decided to do it anyway. The Scorpions drew the Giant Anteater. The Dragons chose the Brazilian Tapir. As fate would have it, the Dolphins pulled the ridiculous Amazon Slug, which was nearly impossible to track, because the slime trails lasted only a short time before they dried up and disappeared.

"I feel like I just went trick or treating and all I got was a bunch of rocks," said Luke Reindorff, the Dolphins' captain.

"A quick reminder, and then you're off," said Kirk. "None of these animals really live on this island, so you don't have to worry about false tracks leading you astray. Is everyone ready? Good. Then you can start … now!"

Sebastian, Ollie, and C.J. took off for the green post. In the mud at the pole's base were pawprints that led down the road away from the camp. They all pointed in the same direction and followed the artificial trail up to the large blocks of rock that lined the entrance. The tracks entered the jungle.

"Here we go." Ollie stepped into a small break in the brush. "Keep a sharp eye."

The tracks weren't as easy to find any more, but the brush thickened and they found traces of reddish brown fur stuck to branches that hung low to the ground. They walked for quite some time before something caught C.J.'s eye.

"There!" C.J. took off ahead of the others. He grabbed a small square cloth that dangled from a vine.

"Here's the first one!" he said proudly, and handed Ollie a flag with a picture of the small fox.

"Is it always this easy?" asked Sebastian.

"It depends on whether we stay on the trail or not," said Ollie. "It's probably not so easy for the Dolphins."

"Which way?" asked C.J.

"We have to find something to follow," said Ollie. "Look around."

They spread out to look for the next sign.

"Oh, major gross!" said Sebastian. "It's definitely not this way."

"What is it?" asked C.J.

"Poop!" she answered, disgusted.

"What does it look like?" asked Ollie.

"Poop," she answered. "What do you mean 'What does it look like?'"

"I mean what kind of animal left it," explained Ollie.

"I didn't stare at it long enough to know that. I'm not the poop police. I don't go around spending all my spare time staring at poop."

Ollie walked over to her and asked her to show him where it was. She pointed to it without looking.

"This is it," said Ollie. "This is Zorro poop."

"You mean to tell me that they actually shipped in animal poop for this competition?" asked Sebastian.

"Of course not," said Ollie. "They molded it from chocolate. See?" Ollie reached down, pinched off a piece and put it in his mouth. He chewed it casually.

"Do you think this tree is tall enough?" Sebastian patted a tree that stretched high into the canopy of the jungle.

"Tall enough for what?" asked C.J.

"That if I climbed it to the top and jumped off from there," she said. "I could be killed instantly so that I wouldn't have to be so totally disgusted by Ollie Einstein any more?"

"This way," said Ollie. "We're wasting time."

The team continued to follow prints and other traces through the thick jungle. Sebastian, leading the way, happened upon more droppings.

She reached down and squeezed off a small bit and was about to place it in her mouth right as Ollie passed her.

"I see you found some bush dog crap." Ollie walked by her without stopping.

"You mean ..." said Sebastian with a quiver in her voice.

"Yep," said Ollie. "That's the real thing."

Sebastian slung the dung off her fingers and frantically wiped them on a large palm leaf.

"We should be getting near the next flag," said Ollie. "I think it's going to be around here somewhere."

"Got it." C.J. pointed up into a tree.

"Oh, no!" said Ollie.

Approximately twenty feet up, a toucan had collected their second flag and used it to build a nest.

"Looks like you're going to get to climb a tree after all," C.J. looked at Sebastian with a let's-see-if-you-really-mean-it look.

"Don't even think I can't." Sebastian slammed her backpack to the ground. She jumped up, grabbed hold of the lowest limb, and started to swing her body back and forth. She did a series of swings and pikes and then dismounted, landing next to the half-built nest. She took the flag, wadded it into a ball and threw it down to Ollie.

"Five years of gymnastics," she said proudly.

"Cool," said Ollie. "Well, thanks." Ollie walked on, looking for pawprints.

"Yeah, thanks," said C.J., right behind him.

"Hey, wait a minute," said Sebastian. "I need help getting down from here. Wait! Come back!"

After about five minutes, Sebastian finally caught up with them.

"Thanks for helping me down from that tree," said Sebastian.

"The only thing I saw up in a tree was a baboon," said C.J.

"You're so funny," said Sebastian. "Why don't you run away and join the circus? On second thought, why don't you just run away?"

"How far do you think we've walked?" C.J. wiped sweat from his forehead.

Ollie stopped, punched a few buttons on his computerized wristwatch, and looked up to find the sun through the jungle's canopy.

"We've been walking for two hours, eleven minutes and forty-two seconds," said Ollie with a serious look on his face. "Give or take two seconds. We need to pick it up."

They trekked on, following clue after clue, until they found themselves looking over a fairly steep rock embankment that had a creek below it.

"Look!" Ollie pointed. "Number three!"

The third flag was on the other side of the stream, and it was evident that if they managed to make it down to the water, the slope on the other side was too steep to climb up.

"It will take a lot of time walking up-or downstream to find a place where we can cross safely," said Ollie.

"There," said C.J. "That tree." C.J. pointed to a dead tree that had fallen across the ravine and made a natural bridge.

"That doesn't look too safe," said Sebastian.

"Sure it is," said C.J. "Watch."

"Wait, C.J.," said Ollie in vain, for C.J. had already stepped onto the tree, holding his arms out to balance himself. He made it look easy as he crossed the bridge quickly.

"Hah! Who needs five years of gymnastics?" he boasted, yelling back across the gorge.

"I can tell you didn't take gymnastics," said Sebastian. "It looks like you did take ballet, though."

She started across the tree with both arms outstretched. She made it to the halfway point before she slipped and then regained her balance.

"Careful!" yelled Ollie.

"I can do this." Sebastian turned to speak to Ollie. In doing so, she threw off her balance and lost her footing completely. She fell straight down from the rotting trunk. Her backpack snagged a large branch and saved her from a perilous fall.

"Don't move!" said Ollie. "Don't move!"

Ollie walked out across the tree slowly, with his arms high and straight. With each step the tree creaked and moaned under him. As he neared the center, it cracked louder and began to bend. Ollie slipped. Sebastian screamed as Ollie regained his balance and caught up to her.

"Take my hand." He leaned down slowly, reaching for her. Sebastian gingerly raised her arm toward his, and Ollie cautiously pulled her up next to him.

"Thanks," said Sebastian.

The tree cracked again and bent down farther in the middle. Two seconds later it did it again; the tree was about to split in half. They turned in opposite directions and ran as the tree broke in half and collapsed into the creek below. Sebastian made it across safely to the far side. Ollie had to dive at the last moment, and he hung from a branch on the near side.

He grabbed hold of a vine to pull himself up, but the vine didn't seem to be attached to anything. Ollie yanked it desperately as he tried to climb the rock face. The vine went taut, and he tugged his way to the top. He looked up and down the bank. No more natural bridges. Four vines hung over the drop-off at intervals, each one closer to the opposite side. He looked at his watch, punched some buttons, and then walked over to the first vine. He spit on his palms and grabbed hold of it.

"Oh, no way!" said C.J. "That's way too dangerous. How do you know those vines are attached to anything up there?"

"Only one way to find out." Ollie stepped back with the vine and then ran forward to swing out over the gorge. He came up short of the second vine and returned to the bank. On his second try, he walked further back and then ran as fast as he could. He swung out again, this time grabbing the vine with his left hand, swinging to the next vine, and grabbing it with his right hand. His momentum carried him to the other side, where he crashed into a thick bush. C.J. and Sebastian ran over and helped him to his feet.

"Did you get it?" He acted like the feat was a walk in the park.

"Got it," said C.J. He handed the third flag to Ollie.

"If you're going to keep getting stuck in trees, we're not going to finish on time." Ollie smiled at Sebastian. She grinned, and the three of them moved down the path, trying to pick up the trail.

"This way!" C.J. pointed at pawprints in the mud. They climbed a hundred yards or so up a wooded slope and came to a clearing just ahead. Ollie threw back several large leaves and stepped out into the open area. There in front of them, sitting on some steps that led to a cobblestone platform, was Kirk Christianson. On top of the lichen-covered rock stage was the Domingo Horn. It gleamed in the brilliant sun, looking as if it produced its own light as the rays reflected off its solid gold shell. The horn was at least twelve feet long from rim to bell, and it rested on three stone supports. Kirk stood and applauded as Ollie and his teammates ran from the jungle toward the platform.

"You barely made it," said Kirk strangely. "Five more minutes and I would have had to blow it myself. They're waiting on Black Reef." Kirk pointed from the plateau down to the small island resting off the north shore.

Ignoring Kirk's remark, Ollie shed his backpack, ran full speed, and bounded up the steps three at a time. He placed both hands around the end of the horn, took a strong deep breath, and blew hard into it. The horn made an eloquent high-pitched sound, loud enough that everyone on the island could hear it, especially the other teams, who sped up their search for their flags and the finish line.

Three solid columns of light shot out from the top of Black Reef Island, blazing up into the sky. One was green, one was blue and the third was a dull white. Sebastian and C.J. joined Ollie on the platform, mouths agape, as they watched three human shapes glide up into the heavens inside the three light rays. Ollie looked over at Kirk, who wore a farewell smile. By the time Ollie looked back, the three figures were gone, along with the lights.

"You knew?" Ollie looked down at Kirk.

"After the eclipse," said Kirk. "There was only a small window of time before they had to go home."

"Home?" said Ollie.

"Home with the great spirits," said Kirk. "He was allowed to come back for his son, but he had to do it near an eclipse in order to get the keys that were sealed in the Hall of King's Souls. There was a limit on the amount of time he had to find Nakoda and return. They didn't plan on someone taking the Book. Without it, they could have been trapped here on earth forever, or at least until the next total eclipse, but that was a sacrifice he was willing to make. Finding his son was most important. You arrived just in time; they placed the necessary items in the Book and were waiting at the altar for the horn to call the spirits to come and take them home."

"How do you fit in?" asked Ollie.

"I am a descendant of the great Wagapi tribe. I will stay here and protect all that is precious to our culture. I own both Crater Island and Black Reef Island."

"And the Book?" asked C.J.

"I know where it is, and I'll take care of it. The Book is safely locked away."

"There it is!" yelled Daegel from the opposite side of the plateau, Kash and Karletta on his heels. The three Hermits pushed and shoved the whole way, tackling each other as each tried to get to the horn first. They wrestled in a pile, trying in vain to get away from one another.

"They may never make it up here," said C.J.

"That's what we want—" Ollie began.

From behind the Stingrays came a long, reverberating sound from the bell of the Domingo Horn. It was Luke Reindorff, the Dolphins' captain, and he waved three flags with pictures of an Amazon Slug high in the air for everyone to see.

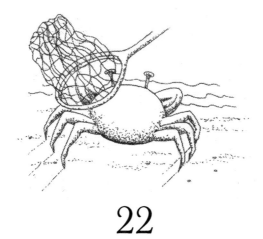

22

Nothing but Net

Kirk Christianson used a two-way radio to contact the camp with the results of the Tracker Trail competition before the contestants returned from the Domingo Horn. Topper posted the results on the leaderboard for everyone to see. When Ollie, C.J., and Sebastian returned, they were met at the edge of the eastern trail by their teammates, anxious to celebrate a remarkable finish to an exciting two weeks. Cosmo and Dusty lifted Ollie on their shoulders and paraded him around the campground. They put him down proudly at the pavilion.

"One more time around," said Ollie. Daegel, Ven, and Bane punched one another, each placing blame on the next. The other teams applauded the Stingrays and their own players for their efforts.

Luke Reindorff reached out his hand to Ollie to offer congratulations.

"I think it's me who should be thanking you," said Ollie. "If you hadn't taken second, we wouldn't have come in first."

Ollie pointed to the scoreboard that listed the Stingrays as the winners of the Adventure Challenge. They received 50 points for the victory and 12 more for the number of minutes that elapsed before Luke made it to the Horn. This gave the Stingrays a score of 203. Daegel and his goons had wrestled for so long that when Daegel finally blew the horn, it was only two minutes before the Scorpions reached the platform. That gave the Hermits a final tally of 202 and second place. The Dragons finished third with 152 and the Scorpions fourth with 136. The Dolphins had a respectable 100 on the nose.

The teams were awarded their medals during a two-hour ceremony under the pavilion, which took a bit longer than expected. When they placed the gold medal around Ollie's neck, he wept for ten minutes, overcome with joy after a solid year of planning. When he finally regained his composure and Kirk was about to ask the next Stingray to come forward, Ollie reached into his back pocket and unfolded a five-page thank-you list in which he acknowledged everyone from his teammates to the producers of his favorite TV show, "Using Mathematics for Everything You Do."

Daegel and his thugs met him at the bottom of the stage when he finished.

"That was the most unfair Challenge I've ever seen," said Daegel spitefully. "You guys cheated every time."

"Shut your piehole," said Cosmo.

"Oh?" said Daegel. "And who's going to make me? You?"

"No, Ollie will," said Cosmo.

"Are you crazy?" said Ven. "You mean this pipsqueak?"

"Maybe not today," said Cosmo, "but one day, and you won't be calling him pipsqueak then."

"Oh, yeah?" said Daegel. "Then what might I be calling him then?"

"Boss," said Cosmo matter-of-factly. Cosmo took hold of Ollie and pulled him away from the bullies toward the Stingray's table.

"I have something for you." Ollie addressed the team. "All of you get a copy. I made them last night." He reached into his pocket and unfolded seven sheets of paper. "It's everyone's addresses, phone numbers, and e-mails. I thought we might want to stay in touch."

"Thanks, Ollie," said Carson. "That's really cool."

"Thanks, dude." Cosmo reached out his hand.

"It's nothing, really." Ollie shook Cosmo's hand.

"Thanks," said Tank. Everyone ducked out of habit, not knowing if anything flew out of his mouth or not.

"This means you can call me anytime," said Dusty to Sebastian.

"Excuse me," said Sebastian. "I wouldn't call you if you and I were the only two people on earth and I had started pulling my hair out because I was lonely and desperately needed someone to talk to."

"Really?" asked Dusty sadly.

"No," said Sebastian smiling. "Not really. I'll call you next Friday night."

The ceremony ended and Kirk dismissed them to their barracks to pack.

"Hey," said Ollie. "It's going to get pretty busy when we walk down there, with everyone packing and our parents helping us and all. How about we shout one good Stingrays, on three?" Ollie placed his hand out with his palm down, and one by one the team slapped their hands on top of his.

"Thanks for being my teammates," said Ollie. "On three. One ... two ..."

"Wait!" said Dusty. "Is it on the three that we yell Stingrays or is it after the three?"

"Would you just put your hand in here and yell?" said Sebastian.

"On the three," said Cosmo.

"Ready," said Ollie. "One ... two ..."

"Wait!" said C.J. "Do we have to yell Stingrays? I mean, can't we yell Camp Remnant, or something else?"

"Stingrays." Carson rolled her eyes.

"On three," said Ollie. "One ... two ..."

"Wait!" said Tank. "I forgot already. Was it on three or after the three?"

"If anyone here feels incapable of participating in this highly sophisticated procedure then do us a favor and don't participate!" said Sebastian. "Otherwise join in and let's get this over with. My arm is about to fall off!"

"On three," said Ollie again. "One ... two ... three ... Stingrays!"

"Stingrays!" yelled Dusty by himself, one count too late.

◆　　　◆　　　◆

"What do you think, Dad?" said Carson, as she slowly shook down the sand to expose her little captive.

"Pretty good," said Mr.Crenshaw. "How do you like those headlamps compared to the flashlights?"

"They work great!" said Carson. "We just keep our eyes on the crab and the light keeps it in view. It's cool. What about my crab?"

"No," he answered. "I'm afraid they get much bigger than that."

"Bigger than the opening of my net?" Carson asked.

"No, not that big, but big enough that you don't want to do this." Mr. Crenshaw reached in with his bare hand and pinched the crab's shell from the rear. He lifted him up, all eight legs trying to wiggle free.

"I wish Daegel was around," said Carson.

C.J. gave up after he sifted sand at least a dozen times and found nothing but net. He returned covered with sand from head to foot and took a close look at Carson's crab.

"All I can find is small ones," said C.J. "just babies."

"You know what I always say?" said Mr. Crenshaw.

"For every baby," said all three of them together, "there's a mother."

"Let's go this way." Mr. Crenshaw pointed down toward the big rocks.

C.J. and Carson took off down the beach. When they reached the boulders, they stopped short and yelled, "Hurry up, Dad! Here's one of the biggest crabs we've ever seen."

"I'll sneak in from the right," said C.J.

"I'll come from the left," said Carson. "Ready?"

"Ready," said C.J. "Look how big it is!"

Mr. Crenshaw caught up and aimed his flashlight at the other side of the rocks.

"Is it the mother?" asked Carson.

"Oh, yeah," said their dad. "It's the mother of all mothers!"

Carson and C.J. both made girly noises, excited and eager to take off.

"On my count of three, you guys take off and go get her. One ... two ... Wait! Do you know if you're supposed to take off after I say three or on—"

"We know, Dad!" they said in unison.

"You better hurry—that monster crab won't be there much longer. Ready? One ... two ... three ... Go!"

978-0-595-42365-1
0-595-42365-5

Printed in the United States
87035LV00003B/1-162/A